I0633050

The Calm in the Storm

The Celtic Sisters | Book 1

Michael Geraghty

Hold Fast Publishing

Chapter 1

The hairbrush moved smoothly through her shoulder-length brown hair over and over as she contemplated what the night might hold. She hated when she had to wear the schoolgirl kit. Chills raced over her at the sight of it in her closet, never mind when she actually put it on. The creepy leers she received from everyone just had her recalling the days when she wore outfits like this to go to school each day. The gray, pleated skirt barely skimmed mid-thigh now, something the nuns would not have put up with in days past, no matter how hard she and her girlfriends tried to get away with it.

The school backpack lay by the front door, making her cringe as she gathered up her purse. She had packed it earlier in the day to ensure she had all her supplies, toys, and tricks. However, forgetting even one item could worsen the evening, especially when dealing with a client unfamiliar to her. She had read over the background sent to her before the date was set to familiarize herself with "John Jones," as the file read, laughing to herself when she saw the name initially. It always amazed her that men thought they could hide easily from the prying eyes of wives, girlfriends, family, friends, or whoever, and then they would make it so easy to be found by booking a hotel room or a service using their credit card with their real name on it.

Pulling her overcoat down from the hook on the back of the front door, she buttoned it up before looking in the mirror one last time.

"Fuck it," she muttered, unbuttoning the coat so anyone gawking would get the whole show.

Thankfully, the short ride in the elevator left her by herself. When she reached the lobby and was greeted by an older gentleman and his companion, she got her first stares. A sly grin crossed her lightly colored pink lips as she blew a quick kiss in the man's direction, startling the couple. Empowerment surged through her when her heels clicked across the marble floor. There was no need to look back—she knew all eyes were on her as she hit the revolving door and left the building.

The walk to the hotel where John waited proved quicker than her initial run-through. Fewer people filled the streets at 11 p.m. on a Tuesday in Manhattan in March. The wind whipped around her, adding a flush to her cheeks that might enhance the schoolgirl look John requested. Unfortunately, her thin, knee-high socks did little to fight the cold as she picked up her pace, her black saddle shoes crunching stray bits of rock salt store owners had sprinkled on the sidewalks.

Upon reaching the marquee of the Radiance Hotel, she marched straight in, nodding to the doorman as he held the door for her. She glanced at the blonde behind the front desk, noting that the young woman readied to say something to her. Instead of letting a confrontation take place, she smiled and placed her index finger to her lips, making the desk clerk her co-conspirator before she pirouetted to the elevator.

The elevator doors closed, and she began her breathing exercises. In, hold, out in four-second increments until the familiar ding sounded and the doors slid open. She noted the cameras positioned in the hallway as she traversed over the stained carpet toward room 413. No lights blinked on them, making her wonder if they were active. Finally, she reached 413 and knocked lightly, shaking her hair so it fell perfectly on her shoulders.

The door chain rattled before it swung open, the lascivious look falling on her immediately.

"Wow," John rasped, licking his lips. "And you are?"

"I'm Rory." She grinned, adjusting the backpack on her shoulders. "Can I come in?"

"Please," John crowed, moving aside so Rory could sidle past him.

Rory scanned the sparse room, noting the half-empty bottle of Johnny Walker Black on the dresser next to the plastic ice bucket. The bed cover was rumpled to match just how John looked.

The guy is willing to drop a grand to book me and pays for this dump, and he looks like this? she thought with a shake of her head.

Rory placed her backpack on the floor at the foot of the bed, sliding it slightly with her saddle shoe to draw John's eyes down her leg.

"Boy, when I said I wanted a schoolgirl that looked like that Gilmore Girl, I never expected—"

"They only call the best for quality customers, John," Rory answered, tossing her overcoat on the lone chair in the corner. She placed her hands on her hips, striking a pose for John. "Do you like it?"

"It's amazing," he said. "You look just like her. And your name—"

"Don't spoil it, John," Rory chided. "You think that's my real name?" she chuckled. Rory moved over in front of John, running her pink fingernails down his stained dress shirt, undoing the buttons as she went. The overwhelming odor of stale alcohol seeped through his skin as she pulled the shirt off his shoulders.

"Did they tell you everything I wanted?" John said softly.

"Of course," Rory purred, stepping away from John to her backpack. She bent at the waist, giving him a clear view of the white cotton panties she'd been sure to wear before she pulled the silk ties out of the bag.

"Get on the bed," she commanded.

John scurried onto the bed while Rory stood at the foot, watching him closely. He propped himself up on the pillows before spreading his arms out. Rory moved quickly, securing the left hand to the headboard before moving to the right side of the bed. When she was done, John tugged but could not budge his hands.

"You're good at this, huh?" he snorted.

"Not my first rodeo, John."

Rory undid John's belt, tossing it aside before tugging his pants off. *Tighty-whities? Really?*

Stifling a snicker, Rory returned to her bag, taking two more silk ties out.

"Spread 'em," she ordered, getting John to open his legs before tying each foot and looping the ties beneath the bed to keep him in place.

"All good?" Rory asked.

John nodded eagerly.

"Excellent."

Rory climbed onto the bed, positioning herself between John's legs. His excitement evident, she traced her nails up his bare legs before reaching over and squeezing his balls.

"Oh my," she feigned awe, "they seem so big and full. It's just my first time, sir. I don't know if I can handle this."

Rory knelt between John's legs and slowly lifted her gray skirt so he could sneak another peek.

John's breathing began to speed up as Rory dropped the hem of her skirt over his crotch. She pulled back her waist deliberately, letting the hem graze over his erection and eliciting an intense moan.

"Fuck, Rory. Enough teasing. Let's get this started."

"Already? I thought I was just getting started. If that's what you want." She shrugged.

Reaching into her bag again, a small foil wrapper glistened between her thumb and index finger.

"Oh, come on," John moaned. "Do I have to wear that?"

"Those are the rules, John," Rory insisted. "I don't know where you've been before me."

"Me? You're the whore," John growled.

"Not nice, John," Rory shot back, gripping the tip of his cock in his briefs and pinching, causing him to howl. "No latex, no fun."

"I'll pay you extra," John said, wincing.

"I guess I'm done here."

Rory climbed off the bed, grabbed the white envelope off the dresser, and counted out the money.

"Geez, John, no tip? Damn. I'm glad I'm leaving."

"No, wait!" John yelled out. "I'll wear the rubber."

"Good boy." Rory smiled. "And the tip?"

"There's extra cash in the top drawer."

Rory pulled the drawer open, noting a change of clothes, another bottle of booze, and a gun, holstered. She paid no mind to the weapon and grabbed the rolled-up wad of cash.

"Thanks," she beamed, sliding the roll into her bag.

"Shit, don't take it all!" John barked. "That's like three grand there."

"Trust me, I'm worth it. You'll see."

Rory reclaimed her position between John's legs, opened the condom, and pulled his briefs down. Although body hygiene was clearly not John's forte, Rory noted internally that she had seen far worse and deftly unrolled the condom down John's mediocre shaft. She gave the tip a gentle squeeze this time, drawing out dribbles of precum.

"Looks like one of us is ready." Rory giggled.

"What about you?" John rushed, breathing hard. "Let's see something."

"Fair enough." Rory shrugged, unbuttoning the crisp white blouse she wore and loosening the tie around her neck. The shirt opened just enough to reveal the delicate white bra beneath.

"Nice," John rumbled. "Keep going."

"I will," Rory answered coyly. "I have a few things to take care of first."

Rory stepped off the bed and looked into her bag.

"What's the fucking deal here? I didn't pay for games. I spent to get fucked."

"Trust me, you're getting fucked, Alexander Joseph Dean," Rory replied.

She glanced up to see John's mouth frozen open.

"What—what did you just say?"

"You heard me," Rory said as she slid on a pair of black nylon gloves. "Or should I call you Alex? That's what your wife calls you. Or Lucky? That's what your pervy thug friends call you."

"How do you know who I am?" John stammered.

Rory watched as he struggled against the ties now.

"Game's over," John said, tugging. "Who put you up to this?"

"You're right. The game is over, Alexander," Rory stated. She removed a small bag and pulled out a syringe. "And I think you know who put me up to this."

"Dullahan," John whispered.

"You can't just take their money without paying it back."

Rory filled the syringe slowly, with John watching, wide-eyed.

"Look, you don't have to do this," John begged. "I'll pay them what I owe. I—I can give you more money."

"Money you took from the Dullahan, the money you earned from the porn you peddle online, or the trafficking you're part of in Singapore? You've been a naughty boy, Alexander. But, I told you, they only call me when they want the best.

"Don't worry," Rory assured. "It's not painful. You'll get drowsy, your breathing will slow, and your heart will stop. No fuss, no mess."

"Wait! Don't, please. My wife—"

Rory chuckled as she held the syringe.

"You're worried about her now? You wanted to fuck a prostitute dressed like a schoolgirl, Alexander. It's difficult to believe you're sincere about that. If anything, she might want to get tested based on how you tried to get me to avoid the condom. Funny how you've managed to stay hard through all this."

Rory's fingernail trailed up the stretched latex, stopping at the sheathed head of Alexander's cock.

"I need an injection point, Alexander," Rory added. "Since you've done penile injections, this should be no big deal for you."

Rory rolled a bit of the condom up to access the lateral side of his penis, where she placed the needle and injected without fanfare. Alexander wriggled furiously on the bed, trying to free himself.

"Wriggling just increases blood flow," Rory added as she sat back. "That works in my favor."

Pulling the condom back down, Rory made slow motions on his cock, keeping it erect.

"You may as well enjoy the moment, Alexander," Rory advised. "It's your last one."

Rory performed slow strokes, rubbing her palm over the head of his cock. Alexander's eyes shut, trying to stall off everything, but Rory's handiwork proved too much for him. He groaned as his body stiffened, and he filled the condom.

Rory got off the bed, looking on as Alexander's breathing began to slow. His eyes bulged slightly as he watched Rory.

"Yeah, your brain and your nerves will stop talking to each other, so you won't be able to speak anymore. Feel free to watch me clean up, though. It usually takes about fifteen minutes, but I'd say ten for you after your performance."

Rory put her items away in her backpack before untying Alexander's feet.

"We don't need these anymore," she remarked before moving up to his tied wrists. Alexander's hands flopped to his sides as each was released. His eyes watched as Rory removed every detail of her presence before she bent to pick up his belt.

She tilted her head, staring at her victim, studying him, before approaching the bed. She looped the belt around Alexander's neck before tying it to the headboard above him.

"Oh, you've done this before, so no one will be shocked," Rory told him. She tightened the belt around his neck before stepping back toward the foot of the bed.

Alexander showed no fight, his face turning purple as his eyes bulged again. Rory glanced at her watch and back up at Alex as a rattle escaped his lips. The telltale sign of his bowels releasing on the bed let her know her work was done.

Rory performed a final check before donning her overcoat and exiting the room. She paced straight to the elevator, following her breathing routine. Finally, she moved to the front door, the genial doorman opening for her again before she was back out into the night of Manhattan.

Rory crossed the street, adjusting the earpiece in her right ear. She pressed once on the piece before speaking.

"Tá sé déanta," she uttered as she walked.

"Maith sibh," the voice replied.

"You took care of everything on your end?" Rory asked as she walked.

"All went perfectly. No issues. I just sent the message to management. The money should be there in about five minutes. Are you off now?"

"I have a few things to take care of first. Then, after that, I'll be in touch."

"Don't go there."

"You know me. I'm a glutton for punishment," Rory stated, stopping at the alley near her hotel. "I'll check in later."

Rory pressed the earpiece to disconnect before an argument broke out. Then, a shadow in the alley caught her eye, and she pivoted quickly in that direction.

Rory walked a few steps down the alley, gripping the folding baton in her right pocket. She came upon a young girl, no more than ten, rummaging through the trash cans. The girl looked frightened at Rory's looming figure.

"I was just looking for something to eat—for my mom and me," the girl said nervously, pointing to a huddled shadow further down the alley.

Rory herded the girl down the alley before facing the older woman. Matted hair and a smudged, exhausted face greeted her. The woman was no older than Rory, perhaps even younger than her. A threadbare sweater covered her shoulders.

Rory reached into her coat pocket and removed the wad of bills she took from Alexander before handing it to the little girl.

"Go take care of your mom," Rory told her. "Go somewhere safe, rest, and eat."

"Thank you," the woman croaked out, tears in her eyes.

"Go gcuire Dia an t-ádh ort," Rory spoke, patting the mother's hand before moving toward the alley entrance and shuffling inside the hotel.

Chapter 2

C hanging and breaking things down after an assignment happened within minutes after years of practice. The costume, clothing, wig, and makeup disappeared into one bag before a recon of the hotel room revealed everything clean and clear to move on. Rory would be left behind, another persona she hoped never to use again.

A shake of her red hair had her natural curls cascading down to her shoulders. She donned a comfortable, casual, nondescript long-sleeved t-shirt and jeans, pulled on her leather jacket, and flung the backpack over her shoulder. Most people would take her for a college student going out for the night before anything else, even if her beauty often caused second and third glances from men around her.

Though just a short walk to the parking garage, she had weapons ready if needed. The collapsible baton sat comfortably in the inner pocket of her jacket on the left while her short shillelagh lay at the ready to the right. The tactical knife strapped to her right ankle was the emergency defense she rarely had to count on. She rarely fully zipped her jacket out of habit, even on nights when the wind whipped through the city. Her training had cured her sensitivities to cold and heat long ago.

A quick glance into the back seat of her white Subaru WRX let her know all was clear before she climbed in and started the vehicle. The seat warmed quickly before she departed the garage, and she was out on the streets and on her way. But, unfortunately, traffic on the FDR never eased, even late at night, making the trip to Forest Hills took nearly an hour even though the mansion was less than eleven miles away from Midtown.

Cranking up the Foo Fighters streaming in her car helped occupy her mind, but her body felt the rush of adrenaline and hormones coursing through. The feelings hit after each job, making her more determined to get to her destination faster as she wove in and out of traffic on the Grand Central Parkway.

Twice she called out for her car to call Danny, but it went straight to voicemail both times. The second time she disconnected, anger bubbling up as she groaned aloud. Then, finally, her car pulled up to the main gate. Lights shone on the black wrought iron across the driveway entrance before two men in suits walked out toward her car. She rolled down the window before the one heavy-set gentleman reached her.

"Hi, Benny." She grinned, squinting as the brightness of his flashlight shone on her face. The brute on the other side used his flashlight to scan the car's rear interior to ensure nothing was there.

"Hello, Cahira," Benny offered politely. "No one said you were coming tonight."

"It's kind of an unplanned visit. Is that okay? Is Danny here?"

"Yeah, of course. I think he's got some friends up at the main house."

Cahira noticed a pull on the passenger side door and swung in that direction. She began to reach inside her jacket after the second tug.

"She's got a bag on the front seat!" the other man yelled to Benny.

"Cool it, Gene!" Benny shouted back. "She's with us. She's practically family."

Benny reached over and patted Cahira's hand to reassure her.

"Sorry. Gene's new. Just following protocol, you know."

"It's all good."

Gene walked to stand next to Benny, pulling his jacket closed to cover his shoulder holster.

"My apologies, Miss," Gene added sincerely.

Gene returned to the guard station to open the gate while Benny gave a casual wave before Cahira shut her window and traversed the long driveway up to the main house. The light posts on the way up glowed brightly, but the dense trees covered and dimmed the area, making it impossible to see if anyone was positioned along the way.

Cahira pulled into one of the empty spots across from the entrance to the house. A few fancy sports cars occupied prime areas, and two limousines sat off to the side, with a couple of young chauffeurs standing around vaping. Both eyed Cahira as she walked from her car and up the marble steps to the front doors. Another pair greeted her in the foyer, but both recognized her immediately and held the entrance open for her to enter.

Loud dance music blared from the rear of the house as she paced along, passing the living room and main dining room. Once she reached the rec room, Cahira noticed the doors vibrating from the din. Swinging the door open, she eyed small groups of people on and around the various couches and chairs. A DJ with full sound gear spun music near the stage set up to the far left, his head facing down at his mix board.

Looking around the room, she saw no sign of Danny. Cahira recognized a few party guests, people she had caught glimpses of over the months and years when Danny went out or partied in. She nodded at a few people as she walked up to the bar at the far right of the room. The long-haired hipster behind the bar, trying to impress women with his pseudo-cocktail knowledge, spotted Cahira and moved over to her.

"Hey there," he started, leaning close to Cahira before she placed her hands on the bar. "What can I get you?"

"You know where Danny is?"

"Danny? Who's that?"

The bartender chuckled, reaching his hand across the bar to place his over Cahira's.

"I promise you, whoever he is, you'll have a much better time with me."

His index finger started to caress her hand, crossing her knuckles.

"Really?" Cahira whispered, leaning closer so her lips were just inches from his right ear.

"He's the guy who let you into this house," she added breathlessly. "And if you don't take your hand off mine, I'm going to bite your ear, drop it in that ice bucket, and then let Danny know you were hitting on me. So, tell me where he is if you want to see the sun come up tomorrow."

A visible shiver moved through the bartender as his head jolted back. Cahira stared him down, her steely blue eyes telling him she was serious about what she said.

"Hey, I'm sorry." The man recoiled, covering his right ear with the palm of his hand. "I don't know a Danny. I just came here with a bunch of friends who said there was a party."

"Tall guy, dark hair, well kept, charming smile, Irish accent. You know him."

"Oh, that guy." The bartender laughed nervously. "Yeah, he's out on the patio by the hot tub. Nice guy. Tell him I said thank you."

"Will do," Cahira added with a smile.

"You aren't going to tell him anything else, right? I mean, I didn't mean anything. I was just trying to—"

Cahira reached quickly toward his right ear, making him flinch before she ran her nails through his hair and laughed.

"It's okay. You were just trying to get laid," she mocked. "Go back to the girls there." She nodded toward the two still seated at the bar.

Cahira strode from the bar up the steps to swing the patio doors open. The extended patio had a fire pit roaring on one end with no one seated around. The telltale giggles emanating from the hot tub area pointed her in the direction she expected to find Danny. Instead, she spotted two blondes perched in the hot tub, facing her direction, with the silhouetted head of a man seated in a lounge chair with his back to Cahira.

"Don't be shy, you two," Danny spoke in his familiar Irish brogue. "You said you were best friends. I'm sure that means you've kissed before. One lingering kiss, and then we can head upstairs to my room."

Cahira stood behind Danny, watching as the blonde in the metallic blue bikini leaned in to kiss her friend in black.

"Quite a vision, there," Cahira said softly in Danny's ear, causing him to spin around.

"Christ, Cat! You scared the shite out of me."

The girls in the hot tub ended their kiss and stared at Cahira.

"Is she joining us?" the girl in black asked, smiling.

Danny spun and looked at Cahira with hope in his eyes.

"Not a chance, boy-o," she said, turning up her brogue now. "I think this is the end of your night with him, ladies."

Cahira tugged Danny out of his lounge chair, past the hot tub, and toward a separate side entrance that led them away from the party. They were halfway up the staircase before Danny pulled his hand from hers.

"What's going on?" he crowed, stopping on the step and leaning against the wall.

Cahira sighed at the sight of him, his white shirt unbuttoned to reveal his chiseled chest and abs. She approached and pinned him to the wall, pressing her body firmly to his. Her lips met his fiercely, her tongue mingling with his, while her hands frantically went to work on his belt.

"Still want to ask questions?" she offered as her right hand slid inside his pants and gripped his hardness through his briefs.

Danny put his hands on Cahira's waist while she lifted her legs up and wrapped herself around him. He struggled with the remaining steps as she kept kissing and his pants slowly slipped. He had barely entered his bedroom before the slacks were at his ankles. Cahira reached behind him to shut the door before releasing him from her python grip.

She tossed her jacket and sneakers rapidly to the side before peeling off her shirt and pushing her jeans down her legs. Cahira sat back on the edge of the bed, spying on Danny watching her as she reached back and unhooked her bra, throwing it to the floor.

"How much more of an invitation are you waiting for?"

Danny tugged off his shirt and stepped out of his pants, pushing his boxer briefs to the floor before he reached the bed. Cahira clawed at him, pulling his body to hers. Danny's lips roamed from her neck to her breasts and back again as she guided his head. Her legs were around him instantly, and she rolled him over so she was on top. She stood on the bed, removing her panties before sitting back between his legs. Her body raged as she slid against him, not letting him inside.

"Where are they?" she huffed, nibbling on his ear.

"What?" Danny asked, lips on her shoulder.

"Condoms, Danny. Jesus. I am so ready right now."

"Feck, Cat, I don't want to go grab one. We're both ready. Let's just—"

"No way. After your little horndog display downstairs, I'm not trusting you. If you want to fuck, wrap it up first."

Cahira sat back, angling her body close to Danny's twitching cock. Her left hand snaked down as she locked her eyes on his. She moaned lightly as she dipped two fingers inside herself before swirling that wetness on the tip of his cock.

"If you want to pass on this, that's fine," she said coyly.

Danny growled before tossing Cahira aside. He stormed out of bed, rifling through his nightstand before grabbing several condoms. Cahira watched with delight as he unrolled the condom and got back into bed, roughly taking hold of her hips before plunging deep inside her. A loud moan escaped her lips as her nails raked down Danny's back, leaving a trail before she cupped his ass and pulled him deeper into her.

"Don't stop," she rushed out, thrusting up to meet his rhythm over and over. Then, knowing she was close, she grinned up at Danny, tightening around him.

"I hope you're there," she gasped. Her brain realized whenever she said this to him, he'd come. Danny shut his eyes tightly within seconds and grunted as he throbbed inside her, giving her just what she needed to climax.

Sweat glistened on Cahira's body as Danny moved off her and went to the bathroom to dispose of the condom. She placed her hand on her chest, feeling satisfaction through her veins before turning to her side to face Danny when he emerged from the bathroom. She slid over as he climbed back in bed with her.

Cahira draped a hand over his smooth chest as her nails reached Danny's nipple. Finally, she pinched one between her claws, causing him to cry out.

"Feck, Cat!" he yelled, pushing her hand away. A small dot of blood trickled from the tip. "What got in you tonight?"

"You did, for a little bit anyway." She laughed.

Cahira climbed from the bed and walked over to the bar cart near the entrance to the balcony outside Danny's room. She helped herself to a pour of Redbreast 27 YO, taking what was left in the bottle into her glass.

"You're out," she said casually before dipping her index finger into the whiskey and sucking a taste off the tip.

"Gee, thanks," Danny groaned. "That's not easy to get stateside, and it's $600 a bottle."

"Stop yer cryin'." Cahira laughed, sipping the whiskey before handing the glass to Danny. "I have some at my place. I'll bring you a bottle to replace it."

A sigh of satisfaction released from her again before Cahira's right hand moved down to Danny's waist and then the tip of his flaccid cock. A few intentional runs had it coming back to life.

"C'mon, Cat. Enough for now," Danny grumbled. "I've got people downstairs."

"Who gives a feck about them? Most of them don't even know you. At least you know I'm not fucking you just for the money."

Danny reached down to the floor and grabbed his boxer briefs, pulling them up to his waist.

"You had a job tonight, didn't you?" Danny asked before grabbing a pair of lounge pants from his dresser.

Cahira propped up on a couple of pillows and crossed her arms beneath her breasts.

"So what if I did?"

"Because you're always horny as hell afterward."

"It's just the rush," she defended. "I tried to call you to let you know I was on the way, but you didn't answer. So now I know why."

"It's just a party, Cat. It's no different from the others. Why don't you come down and socialize?"

"Why? I can have strangers hit on me and watch strip shows at Scores. I don't need to come here for that and then watch you walk off with God knows who for a weak hand job."

"Christ, you're cold," Danny said with a shake of his head. He pulled a green t-shirt on and stood at the foot of the bed.

"You coming down?"

"Not likely," she scoffed, sipping her whiskey. "Have fun with the bimbo twins. Let me know which one has the most silicone."

Cahira peered from the corner of her eye as Danny paused at the door.

"Was it anyone I know?" he asked.

Cahira drained the glass and placed it on the nightstand before tucking the pillow under her head and turning away.

"You didn't order it. So you know I can't tell you anything about it. Go party. I'm going to sleep."

Cahira listened for the door to shut before rolling over. As much as she hoped Danny would change his mind and stay with her, inside, she knew there was little chance of that.

The only light in the room was the soft glow from the moon filtering in the balcony doors, casting odd shadows from trees and furniture on the far walls. Cahira stared at them for a bit, running through the games she used to play with her younger sister when they shared a room back home. Kelly always got afraid when their mother turned the lights off, and they would play games to identify the shadows or make up stories of what they could be. After a while, Kelly always drifted off, leaving Cahira to look and wonder what waited out there for her.

"Not much has changed," she whispered, noting the shadow that looked like a large bird perched on the balcony.

Chapter 3

The rattle of the balcony doors had Cahira bolting up in bed, her hand moving under the pillow to look for a weapon, usually there if she was in her own place. But when her glance gave her a view of the gray sky pelting the doors with light sleet and wind, she eased back onto her pillow. Turning to her right let her know Danny was nowhere to be found, and she saw no signs that he had even been in bed with her.

Cahira rose, stretching and bending before a shiver shot through her. The room was colder than she had anticipated. Not immediately spying her clothes, she reached for the dress shirt that Danny had shed last night and pulled it on. She spotted her panties not far from the balcony doors, realizing she flung them harder than she had thought. She pulled the garment on while examining the clouds and weather out over the back. Surprise always came to her here, with the lush open spaces and property of the mansion betraying their location in Forest Hills, just a few short miles out of Manhattan.

Familiar with the house's layout, she made her way from Danny's suite to the staircase to descend to the main floor. She hopped quickly across the cold marble, goosebumps shooting across her legs as she went, before reaching the secondary dining room the family used when not entertaining. Elegance dripped on the table, with Belleek China adorning the place settings of the smaller, intimate solid white oak table.

Danny's father, Quinn Darcy, had the table brought from the cottage his grandparents owned in Moycullen (though Cahira knew better than to ever spell it this way—Quinn chided anyone that didn't use the proper Gaelic of Maigh Cuilinn).

The door leading to the kitchen swung open as Gilman, Quinn's personal attendant, entered the room with a tray of pastries.

"Miss Cahira, I had no idea you were here." Gilman grinned, placing the tray on the table. "Can I get you tea?"

"You know I don't drink tea, Gilman." Cahira smiled as she sat at the table.

"I know, Miss," Gilman acquiesced. "But I can keep trying. Black coffee, then?"

"Please."

Cahira accepted the fine white porcelain cup filled with fresh brew.

"Thank you." She nodded before taking a sip. "Is Mr. Darcy coming to breakfast this morning?"

"I think it depends on whom you are speaking of, Miss," Gilman said cryptically.

"Either one would be fine."

"The elder Mr. Darcy should be here in a moment," Gilman added, picking up silver tongs and placing an apple turnover on Cahira's plate. "As for Mr. Daniel, I'm not quite sure. I believe it was a late night for him."

"I figured as much." Cahira sighed, picking the corner off the turnover and popping it into her mouth.

As if summoned, Quinn Darcy shuffled into the room, stopping short of the table when he spotted Cahira.

"Ah, a beautiful sight for old, sore eyes." The old man beamed. Quinn used his silver-handled cane as he paced across the marble, his smartly polished shoes shining. Gilman had pulled out the chair at the head of the table, but Quinn made his way past there and straight to Cahira, who stood to embrace him.

"Lovely to see you, dear," Quinn whispered.

"You as well, Seanóir," Cahira replied, kissing him on his smooth cheek.

"You know, you don't need to call me that," Quinn added as he stepped back. "You've earned the right to call me Quinn."

"It's out of respect," Cahira admitted. "My father drilled that into me."

"No doubt he did."

Quinn sat, leaning his cane on the edge of the table as Gilman pushed the chair in for him. Then, without a word passing between them, a cup of tea, a scone, and the latest copy of *The Irish News* appeared in front of Quinn.

"Thank you, Gilman." Quinn nodded. "No scone for you?" he asked as Cahira sipped her coffee. "Evelyn makes them special for me each morning."

"No, that's your treat. So you go ahead," Cahira insisted, knowing she was not a big fan of the pastry.

Quinn whistled softly while he read the newspaper, allowing Cahira time to pick further on her turnover. She split the flaky pastry open and plucked a piece of warm apple from the center before hearing a distant door slam, followed by a litany of curse words as Danny made his way down the hall. Cahira glanced at Quinn, who never looked up from his paper during the commotion.

Danny stormed into the dining room and stood, staring angrily at Cahira.

"What the feck, Cat? Did you come here last night to toss my entire life upside down?"

"What are you talking about?"

"First, you interrupt the party and drag me away from my guests, and then I find out about all the other shite!"

"To start with, no one made you go off with me last night. You have free will and all, and you seemed a willing participant, if I remember correctly. I'm sorry, Seanóir," Cahira added, looking at Quinn. Quinn's eyes never shifted from behind his glasses as he kept reading.

"Never mind him," Danny barked. "Did you do it?"

"Do what?"

"Did you take out Lucky Dean?"

"I don't know what you're talking about," Cahira said casually, returning to her coffee.

"Stop playing with me, damn it!"

Danny slammed his fist on the table, causing the China to jump and his father's tea to rock over onto the saucer.

"I can't answer that, Danny," she replied calmly, noting the rage in his eyes.

"Enough with your feckin' code! Billy just called me and said the cops found him in a hotel room in Midtown this morning with his belt around his neck, hung from the headboard. They say he asphyxiated while jerking off, but we know that isn't true, don't we, Cat?"

"Is all this going somewhere? Do you know how many names I see on any given day? How much research I do all the time? That name means nothing to me."

"Do you know how close I am to jumping across the table at you right now? So don't push me, woman. I want an answer, and I want it now!"

Cahira placed her arms at her side. She knew Danny wouldn't follow through on his threat, especially with his father sitting there. Nonetheless, she decided to push his buttons some more.

"You better make your first move a good one, Danny. You're soft and out of practice, having all these hooligans do your dirty work. You won't get a second shot. I promise you that."

"WHO ORDERED IT?" he screamed.

Danny marched around to where Cahira sat. She had sprung from her seat before he got there, grabbing her fork from the table and putting herself at the ready as she swatted his reaching right hand away.

"I swear, Cat—"

Danny had pulled his fist back, readying to punch, when the blackthorn cane sped through the air and slammed on the table, causing Cat and Danny to jump back. Quinn stood, gripping the handle tightly.

"Enough!" he bellowed. "I'm trying to enjoy my breakfast in peace like I do every day, and you bring this in front of me. I'm not too old to take you, Danny, or I could just let Cahira do it. Sit down!"

Quinn pointed to the empty seat across the table from Cahira as Danny obediently went and slumped into the chair. He snorted as he sat while Cahira calmly retook her spot.

"All I want to know is who hired you to do it, Cat. It's too coincidental not to have been you. So forget whatever weird protocol you think you need to follow. It means shite to me. Give me a name."

Cahira shook her head, infuriating Danny.

"I did it," Quinn said, folding his newspaper and taking off his glasses.

"What?" Danny uttered in disbelief.

"I had Lucky Dean taken care of," Quinn added, sipping his tea.

"Why—why would you do that? He was bringing us a lot of money."

"No, he owed us a lot of money and wanted to get it in ways I don't like the family to be part of. You never should have agreed to deal with him."

"Da, you must be willing to see the big picture here. Money pipelines are not the same as back in your day or Granddad's time. We can make a lot of money quickly by backing guys like Lucky."

"He was trafficking people, Danny," Cahira added with disgust.

"We weren't. Lucky was."

"Right. You just gave him the means to sell women as he wanted."

"You, of all people, have no cause to get self-righteous, Cat," Danny spat back. "This coming from the woman who kills people upon request. That's rich. Keep telling yourself you're doing it for a just or moral cause. It's still killing."

"We don't need the type of business, money, or attention a man like Lucky Dean could bring," Quinn added. "I don't want us to be any part of that. We have plenty of other business avenues that bring money in."

"But Da, the numbers are astounding. People in Morocco are turning millions, and it was coming our way."

"When is it all enough?" Quinn asked, waving his hands around. "I worked hard to ensure you had a good life set up, Danny. We have more than enough money to last ten lifetimes. I think it's time to throttle back a bit, stick to real estate, investments, entertainment."

"Lucky provided access to entertainment," Danny grumbled.

"Not the kind I want to be associated with. I'm sure my great-grandfather—"

"Christ, Da," Danny interrupted. "We're talking 100 years ago during Prohibition. Times have changed since Owen Darcy was around. He would have taken advantage of every opportunity to make cash to support his family."

"It's done, Danny," Quinn insisted, finishing his tea. "Stop arguing over it. If you want to be mad at someone, let it be me. Keep us out of businesses like his, and I won't have to get involved like I did with this one."

A slight cough from the kitchen door from Gilman grasped all attention.

"Mr. Darcy, I'm sorry to interrupt, but you have a meeting at 10 a.m. in Brooklyn. We really need to think about getting ready to go."

Quinn approached Cahira, hugging her again.

"Nice to see you, my lovely," Quinn added, kissing Cahira on the cheek. "You always brighten this place up. I wish he could see that."

"It's okay, Seanóir," she replied quietly.

"Who are you meeting with?" Danny asked.

"Jack Lonergan," Quinn answered, moving away from Cahira and picking up his cane.

"I should probably come with you," Danny insisted. "Give me five minutes, and I'll—"

"I can go myself," Quinn interrupted. "I've been dealing with him for a long time, Danny. Everything is fine."

"Da, Lonergan is a loose cannon. You don't know him the same way I do. I see what he's capable of. You see the ghost of his old man sitting there."

"He wants to talk about some properties we hold over in Williamsburg. It's not anything to be concerned about. Benny and a few others will be with me. I'm going alone."

Quinn turned and winked at Cahira before walking off with Gilman, out of the dining area and toward Quinn's main quarters. Cahira sat back, watching Danny shake his head in disgust.

"He'll be fine," Cahira added to break the silent tension before getting up to pour more coffee for herself.

"He has to learn to listen and trust me more," Danny spoke, looking down at his clenched fists on the table. "And he's not the only one who needs to do that."

Cahira turned back to Danny and saw the stern look on his face.

"Don't start this again, Danny." Cahira sighed. "We live separate lives, remember? That was your idea when whatever this is started between us."

"You could have given me a heads up about Lucky."

"I don't know every relationship you have, especially with people I might have to deal with at some point."

"Bullshit, Cat," Danny answered, thumping his fist on the table. "You get plenty of background info before you do anything. So you think I don't know how things operate with you? Please. You knew what Lucky had for breakfast yesterday, never mind my dealings with him."

"So I'm supposed to let you know who I'm contracted for before I do anything? That's rich. Are you going to call me whenever you go out somewhere before you look to fuck someone, Danny? That would be courteous of you."

"It's not the same thing, Cat, and you know it."

"Right. In my case, it could only get me killed by telling you about it so you can give someone a warning, instead of you having to get tested for God knows what."

"Lucky Dean was a prick, no doubt about it," Danny added, leaning across the table toward Cahira. "He did shitty things, and yes, he owed us money. But he put me in touch with influential people who helped and could assist us and bring us a lot of money and power. If word gets out that the Dullahan were the ones who had him hit, it could create a lot of problems for us. Da never sees the big picture like that."

"I think your father sees a different big picture than you do, Danny—one that has a little bit more insight than yours."

"You're such a feckin' hypocrite sometimes, Cat," Danny barked. "How much did you get paid for your work last night? I'll bet it wasn't a pro bono case. Also, don't pretend that you or Da have some higher morality than me. You've both done plenty of bad things in your past."

"Are you done with the speech now?"

Cahira rose from the table and moved to leave the dining room. Danny gripped her right wrist as she went by him. Instinct had Cahira pull her wrist, forcing Danny to stand up. Unfortunately, she consistently underestimated his strength, and he held his ground. Cahira knew the anger simmering under his skin and behind his dark eyes, but she continued to show no hint of backing down.

"You know, if you weren't so feckin' stubborn, this might all work better," he said through gritted teeth.

"Danny, you need to stop thinking this is something more than it is," Cahira said as she gently placed her fingers over his that held her wrist. Her index finger seductively stroked his before she quickly grasped his wrist, twisted it behind his back, and rushed him toward the wall so he was pinned and had nowhere to go.

"You made it abundantly clear to me three years ago, remember? 'This' is all about sex and nothing else. You had your chance. Yes, I got paid for Lucky. Yes, I knew all about your dealings with him. But don't pretend you know more about me than what I want when we are together. You don't know me at all. You never wanted to."

Cahira leaned in and bit Danny's earlobe, drawing blood before she released him from her stronghold, rattling the picture frames on the wall.

Then she strode out of the room, heading toward the staircase to go back to Danny's room to gather her things.

"Nice shirt, by the way," Danny shouted from the bottom of the staircase. "I want that one back. It's a Tom Ford."

Cahira stopped at the top of the staircase and glared at Danny. She reached down to the hem of the shirt and tugged it over her head, leaving her topless. She balled up the shirt and tossed it down to Danny, watching as it snagged on the top of a tall vase just out of Danny's reach. A sly grin shot across her face as she marched to Danny's room.

A quick move through the room and Cahira was dressed with all her things gathered by the time Danny had retrieved his shirt and paced upstairs. She had her leather jacket on and backpack slung over her shoulder, but Danny blocked her exit from the bedroom as he stood in the doorway.

"Come on. Don't leave mad like that," Danny offered.

Cahira rubbed the palm of her hand over the one-day growth of dark stubble on his cheek and chin. Seeing Danny like this always made her desire grow a bit. She leaned in and kissed him, breaking breathless.

"I need to go," she admitted, placing her head against his chest. "I have to get cleaned up and work."

"You can shower and work from here," Danny replied, planting the top of Cahira's head with soft kisses.

"We both know what will happen if I do that." She sighed, hands on Danny's waist and skidding to his inner thighs.

"I'm counting on it," he answered hungrily.

Cahira's hand dipped further, finding the bulge at the front of Danny's lounge pants.

"The twins weren't enough to satisfy you?" she purred, gripping his hard-on through the cotton.

"Christ, Cat. Just let it go," Danny moaned, closing his eyes.

"I am," she replied, loosening the grip on his cock and pulling away. "That's why I'm leaving."

Cahira ducked past Danny and walked to the staircase, leaving him with his jaw open.

"You're really going to leave me like this?" he yelled.

"I'm sure you can figure out what to do," she answered callously as she trod down the steps and out the front door without looking back.

She entered her Subaru, starting it up quickly and pulling out before she had time to change her mind and go back for a morning with Danny. Once Cahira reached the front gate, she saw Gene standing in the guard house, looking a little more haggard than he had when she arrived yesterday. He dutifully opened the gates and nodded at Cahira before she pulled out and headed toward the Long Island Expressway to return to the city.

With the music turned low, Cahira tapped her earpiece into her right ear.

"You there?" she asked.

"I'm here working," the voice replied. "Where are you?"

"Leaving my latest bad decision. I'll be home in forty minutes if traffic cooperates. Anything I need to know about?"

"Nothing critical. Business as usual on both fronts. The deposit is in."

Cahira let out a big exhale as she settled into the moving line of cars veering toward Manhattan.

"Can you split it the same methods as always?"

"Way ahead of you," the voice answered. Then Cahira heard the light tapping of a few keys on a keyboard. "I already had it up on my screen. I was just waiting to hear from you."

"You're too good."

A quiet moment allowed the music to seep through, revealing "Love Shack" playing over the speakers.

"Seems appropriate," the voice said sarcastically.

"Don't start," Cahira answered, speeding a little to get around a box truck.

"It's better than saying booty call. But was it worth it?"

"We both got what we expected—mostly," Cahira answered, darting back to the right lane to avoid a slow-moving Buick Le Sabre taking up the fast lane.

"Whatever. It's your life. I need to go. Touch base with me later," the voice requested.

"I will. I'm going home to shower and rest. I'll get with you."

Cahira tapped out of the conversation just in time to get to the 35th Street exit to head toward home. But, unfortunately, discussing her 'relationship' with Danny with anyone never proved simple. Their on-again, off-again status grew tiring to Cahira after about a year until they'd settled into whatever they had between them currently. Often, it boggled her mind too, taking up way too much of her time and energy.

Cahira pulled into her usual parking garage, leaving her vehicle in the capable hands of the valets there. She tipped them graciously every time to ensure she had quick access to her car when needed. It took her months after buying her apartment to find a garage she trusted, and now that she had one, she wanted to make it stick.

The private lobby at 35 Hudson Yards allowed Cahira to enter the building without dealing with the many tourists and shoppers coming to the area. She flashed a gentle smile to Duffy, the genial concierge working days, before moving to the elevator vestibule where the private elevator to her apartment awaited her.

Cahira entered the elevator, placing her index finger on the control pad to close the doors and ride up to her apartment. Then, taking the fob from her coat pocket, she pressed the button that undid the bolt lock on the security door to her floor, an added extra she'd gladly paid for when buying the place. It allowed her an extra layer of security in the elevator if anyone could access it. Cameras inside and outside the elevator fed to her computer and smartphone, and the elevator arrival bell could only be silenced through the fob. But, of course, if someone willingly went through the trouble to do all that, Cahira had prepared herself within the apartment to protect herself.

The elevator automatically stopped on the lower level and could go to the upper floor only if prompted again by Cahira's fingerprint. While a staircase leading up from the lower level existed, anyone who got in became tracked by cameras throughout whatever room they ventured in and out of along the way. The audible alarms in the apartment existed purely for show, and that alarm panel didn't do anything other than make noise if Cahira wanted it to. Silent alarms were triggered instead, and the notice didn't go to the police. Before whoever entered knew it, a response team would be on its way, and it wasn't a team they could run from.

Cahira pressed her fingerprint on the keypad again, moving the elevator to the second floor. The door slid open, and she pressed her fob again to turn the alarms off. Lights immediately turned on in the small hallway as she made her way to the master bedroom that occupied the whole right side of the floor. She tossed her backpack on one of the chairs in the room, stripped out of her clothing, and went straight into the spacious bathroom to the walk-in shower. The waterfall faucet flowed hot water from the left side, and she climbed under the cascade to wash off all the previous day and night down the drain, leaving it all behind.

Chapter 4

The calendar moved to spring as the end of March arrived, but the weather continued to hold a steady chill, prompting Cahira to leave her apartment infrequently. Instead, she had groceries delivered, or meals brought up from one of the fine Hudson Yards restaurants, a perk of residency in the building. She spent her time working out in the private gym or pool before turning to her at-home office, occupying one of the extra bedrooms on the top level of the apartment. Anyone walking into that second bedroom might think the place was owned by a James Bond villain. Monitors covered one wall where a desk sat beneath, allowing Cahira to watch the cameras in and around her home and in other locations where her business worked.

Calling it 'her business' always provided Cahira with an internal chuckle and a smile. Triskele Slándáil, or Trinity Security as her American friends wanted her to call it, had established itself as one of the leading firms in the world, providing elite protection for companies, individuals, buildings, and more. The business boasted clients across the globe, but none knew who Cahira was or that she was affiliated with the private company. So before the company began, she took steps to ensure that she was not a face in the company. Only two people within Triskele knew she existed, and she strove to maintain anonymity and let the business's accolades fall to those who deserved it.

Following a late afternoon workout, Cahira returned to her apartment, moving to her computers first to check the status of projects to see if anything required her attention. Then she paced to the small refrigerator she kept in the room to grab a cold bottle of water, pressing it to her warm forehead before twisting it open. She heard the familiar beep of her earpiece, still on her desk, and rushed to pick it up.

"I'm here," she spoke, taking another sip. "Everything okay?"

"We're good," the voice answered. "I was just checking on you. I hadn't heard from you today."

"Sorry," Cahira apologized. "I've been caught in my own head lately. You know how it is after—"

Cahira cut herself short before going further.

"I know," the voice said calmly. "That's why I'm calling. I can swing by tonight if you want. No expectations. We can just bullshit like we used to."

"I don't want you to have to come out," Cahira answered. "It's supposed to be cold tonight, and you don't want to be out in that."

"The hell I don't! I live for the cold. I hate that spring is on the way."

"I forgot who I was talking to," Cahira said with an eye roll. "You were always the nut with the least amount of jackets when we were in the mountains."

"I was just out there with a bunch of prissy girls."

"Very funny, Badb," Cahira replied.

"Seriously, Cat," Badb began. "I don't like the thought of you just stewing around the apartment by yourself all day and night. You spend too much time like that, which doesn't lead to anything good. Let me come over. I promise we won't talk about work. I can get a ride there and be at your place in thirty minutes. We can have a girls' night in or go down to one of the bars in your fancy building."

Cahira sat silent for a few beats.

"Unless you already have company coming over," Badb interjected.

"I haven't seen Danny in weeks," Cahira defended.

"Now, why would you assume I was talking about him?"

"Because of your snide tone in that Irish-lass voice, that's why. It's okay that you don't like him, Badb. There are many times I don't, either."

"It's not even a matter of not liking him," Badb added. "Okay—I don't like him, but he's not good for you on many levels, and you're always off after you see him."

"Let's not do this. These arguments never get either of us anywhere."

Silence held for longer than Cahira's comfort level while she heard Badb typing.

"Are we good?" Cahira asked, hoping for a reply.

"We're always good, Cat. You know that. I'm just trying to look out for you. It's what I do."

"Funny, it used to be the other way around," Cahira smiled.

"That was a long time ago now," Badb answered. "I'm just tying up some loose ends. Let me know if you need anything or want me to come by."

"Got it. Thanks."

Cahira disconnected the call, leaning back in her desk chair as she mindlessly gazed at her computer screen before making rounds on her other monitors. Then, with nothing pressing going on, she went to the shower to soothe herself before heading to her bedroom wrapped only in a towel.

The buzz of the house phone caused Cahira to jump off the bed she lay on while brushing her hair. The house phone only buzzed when it came from the concierge desk, and even then, that was infrequent. Cahira rarely had visitors she planned on, let alone someone unexpected.

Cahira plucked the phone off her nightstand, beginning her breathing routine just in case.

"Hello, Ms. O'Brien," the voice announced on the other end.

Cahira exhaled before answering.

"Hi, Craig," she replied, identifying that evening concierge's tone. "What's up?"

"There's a Mr. Darcy here to see you. You don't have him identified as coming tonight. What would you like me to do?"

Cahira wondered why Quinn would come to see her in the city, something he never did until she heard a voice yelling behind Craig's.

"Feck, Cat, just tell him to let me up!" Danny howled. His voice sounded slightly off, letting her know he had likely come from a party or bar.

Cahira sighed before responding.

"It's fine, Craig. He can come up."

"Yes, ma'am," Craig told her, hanging up.

Cahira dressed quickly, sliding into a pair of black shorts and a white tank top before tying her hair back in a ponytail. She went to the monitors to watch as Danny rode the elevator up. She paced slowly downstairs, arriving at the elevator entrance. She stood outside the steel door, pausing until Danny began to pound on it.

"Come on, Cat! I know you're just standing there. Let me the feck in!"

Shaking her head, she pressed the interior button on the wall to unlock the door, the mechanism sliding so Danny could step out.

"Jesus, it's like riding in a Goddamn coffin to get here," he groused.

"What are you doing here, Danny?" she said stoically.

"I can't come to see my favorite girl when I want?" He smirked, moving his hands to Cahira's hips, leaning in for a kiss.

"No, you can't," she said, giving him a fast peck on the lips. Danny's hands lingered before moving down to cup Cahira's ass.

"I love it when you wear these tight shorts," he growled into her ear.

"You know I don't like unexpected visits," Cahira answered, moving his hands off her body so she could step back. His gray suit was rumpled, and she watched him sway slightly as he smiled at her.

"I was in the city and felt like seeing you."

Cahira turned and walked to the kitchen to the coffee station.

"I'll make coffee." She sighed.

"I don't want any," Danny barked, dropping himself on the sectional couch in the living room before eyeing the bar and moving toward it. "I need something stronger."

"I don't think you do," Cahira spoke from the kitchen as the coffee began to drip. She emerged from the room and saw Danny scanning over the shelving behind the bar.

"It sounds like you've had enough already. Where were you? Sapphire or Scores?"

"Why do you assume I was at a strip club?"

Danny reached for a bottle of Laphroig and poured too much Scotch into a rock glass before lifting it.

"Because you smell like perfume and whiskey, for starters. You only come to the city for two reasons, Danny—women or family business."

Danny drained his glass and turned to pour more. Cahira reached over and took the bottle from his hands.

"What? You're the only one who can show up for a drink and a fuck?"

"Yes, I am," she said forcefully, putting the cork back in the bottle.

"I want my bottle of Redbreast," Danny demanded. "You owe me that."

"I'll bring it to you next time I'm out that way."

Danny's hands were at her waist again, and this time she pulled his cell phone out of his suit jacket pocket. She glanced at his shoulder holster as she removed the phone.

"You're clubbing carrying that? You get arrested again, and they'll hold you this time. Did Benny drive you?"

"They won't do anything to me." He waved her off, staggering toward the couch again. "They never do. Maybe I drove myself here just to see you."

"Yeah, okay," Cahira answered. "I'm calling Benny."

Danny rose from the couch, snatching his phone.

"Christ, Cat, can you give me a little attention, please?"

"I'm tired, Danny. You need to go home."

Cahir crossed her arms, staring down as Danny scrolled on his phone.

"I have business to talk to you about," he told her.

"I have nothing to say about Lucky," she protested. "It's done and over with, and it's not my place to talk about it anymore. That's between you and your father."

Danny scoffed, slapping his knee and smiling.

"It's not about Lucky. And my father doesn't understand all he needs to about how to run things anymore. So that's why I'm here. I need you to take care of Jack Lonergan."

Cahira turned and walked to the kitchen, idly pouring two cups of coffee and going to the fridge to grab milk.

"Here," she said, handing Danny the mug and milk. "I don't have any half and half."

"What? I refuse to drink my coffee with milk," he spouted. "I don't need coffee anyway. I'll just sleep it off here."

"No, you won't. You're not staying tonight, Danny."

"Are you even going to acknowledge what I said about Lonergan?" Danny asked as he poured his coffee down the drain.

"Nope."

Cahira sipped her coffee, leaning against the kitchen counter.

"Why not?"

"Several reasons," Cahira began. "First, you know that's not how I work. I don't deal with any setup directly. You have channels and protocols to follow. Second, I don't take jobs this close together. It raises too many red flags. Third, your father would never give his okay for that."

"Of course Da would never okay it," Danny added. "He still thinks he's dealing with old Jack, not his son. Jack Junior is nothing like his old man. He's trying to soften up Da to take over our businesses and territory."

"How do you know this?"

"I have my sources," Danny boasted.

"Sure you do. Which stripper gave you that tip? Or some reliable source you ran into at McGee's that gave you info over a shot of Jameson's?"

"It doesn't matter where it came from, Cat. I know it's the truth. Da just doesn't want to see it. If I bring it to him directly, he'll say no."

"For a good reason, Danny," Cahira spoke up. "You get rid of Lonergan, and they will know the Dullahan did it. It's going to start a war that will get ugly fast. Your father knows what he's doing."

"Not when it comes to this, he doesn't. This needs to be done, Cat. What do you mean you don't take jobs this close together? What's that all about?"

"People start asking too many questions and looking closely at things, Danny, when people—bad people—start dying within days or weeks of each other. It's not safe, and it's not good for my psyche. I need to decompress and think clearly when I do these things. So I won't do it."

"Not even for a million dollars?"

"Look around, Danny. Do you think that will make a difference at this point in my life? I don't need the money."

"If you don't need the money, why bother?" Danny spat. "Just for the thrill of it? I didn't realize you were that much of a psychopath, Cat."

"You have no idea," Cahira warned. "I don't have to explain myself to you, Danny. If you're done, you can go now."

"If I go through proper channels, will you do it?"

"You have my answer, Danny. You think I take every job that gets offered to me?"

"Cat, come on," Danny complained. He stood and grabbed Cahira again, kissing her neck while his hands began to roam to the hem of her tank top. The familiarity of his touch had her body responding reflexively. She shut her eyes, trying to will the feelings away.

"I need the best. I need you—in more ways than one," Danny offered, his hand sliding under her shirt up to Cahira's right breast.

"Danny, don't," she murmured.

"Do you really want me to stop?" His thumb strummed across her nipple, making Cahira's resolve weaken.

The distant ring of her cell phone snapped Cahira's eyes open and back to reality. The call sounded again before she pushed Danny's hand out from under her shirt.

"I need to answer that, and you need to leave," Cahira told him, stepping away. "Now."

"For feck's sake, Cat. Who cares who is calling right now? If it's important, they'll call back."

The ringing stopped but then immediately began again.

"Go, Danny," Cahira pointed at the elevator. She grasped his arm, dragging him to the elevator door. Then, taking hold of his phone, she pressed the button for Benny.

"He's coming down, Benny. Collect him in the lobby, please."

Cahira hung up and pushed him into the elevator.

"You're really doing this?" he asked in disbelief.

"I really am. See you later," she added, waving as Cahira closed the steel door and sent the elevator down.

Cahira dashed up the stairs, but the phone stopped ringing when she got there. Picking it up, it showed she had two missed calls, both from the same number she did not recognize. Few people had her cell phone number, so getting random calls always alarmed her. Then her phone lit up, letting her know she had a voicemail.

She knew it wasn't Badb—she always used their direct, secure connection. So Cahira pressed play and sat on her bed, putting the phone on speaker to listen.

"Hi, Cat. It's Kelly. I know I'm calling you out of the blue, and normally I wouldn't call you at all and waste both of our time. Anyway, I just wanted to ask—really, I just wanted to let you know—it's Teagan's fourth birthday this weekend, and we're having a party for her. Normally I wouldn't even ask if you might come, but, well, she asked if you were going to show up. Usually, she just gets a gift from you at some random time. She shocked me when she mentioned it. Hey, I don't ask you for much—hell, I don't ask you for anything—I just thought it might be nice if you showed up and made her day. That's it. I don't expect you to call me back or do anything. I told Teagan I would call you, so I am. The party is Saturday at our place, if you remember where that is. Okay. Bye."

Cahira flopped back onto the bed, stretching her arms out and staring at the ceiling. The last person she'd expected to get a call from was her sister. The message rattled her more than she anticipated. She placed the phone on her nightstand and went back downstairs to dump the coffee and clean up before returning to the second floor.

A quick check of the monitors and computer in the office followed before Cahira went to the bedroom and climbed into bed. She stared at the phone on the nightstand, watching the charge light blink in rhythm. Finally, she grabbed the phone, tempted to delete the voicemail and put it out of her head.

Cahira's thumb hovered over the delete button before she pressed the number. The phone asked her if she wanted to return the call, and she paused again. She pressed the off button quickly, turned off the lamp, and rolled away to face the other direction, staring at the wall, the shadows, and anything else that might occupy her mind.

Chapter 5

Getting up before 6 a.m. happened nearly every morning for Cahira, allowing her to get a workout in and jump on anything that needed her attention. However, this morning proved different from others as she lay in bed, listening to Rhiannon Giddens and staring out the window, waiting for the sunrise to crack the horizon.

Cahira continually picked up her phone, gazing at it and putting it down before she would repeatedly play the message from her sister. The edge in Kelly's voice was nothing new to her—it had been there for years any time they spoke to each other, which was infrequent at best. Cahira had left Kelly and her mother when she was seventeen and never looked back. Her first move was back to Ireland to attempt to locate her father again. When that failed, and she had no one to turn to, she joined the military and the ARW. Then her life changed, and she began to fall into the path she found herself currently.

Throughout all the turmoil, Cahira missed Kelly's high school and college graduation, her engagement and wedding, and the birth of her daughter. She kept tabs on her sister and what happened in her life, but she had no actual contact with her other than making sure she sent gifts to Teagan for her birthday, Christmas, or anytime Cahira saw something she thought the child might like or need.

And now, out of the blue, was the call and invitation, even if it was far from heartfelt or sincere. Cahira hardly blamed Kelly for feeling anger and animosity. She had left her younger sister in a lurch to deal with the madness that was their mother, something her sister was woefully unprepared to do. Still, if she hadn't done it, Cahira imagined finding herself in prison for killing her mother, and her sister ending up with Child Services, getting lost in the system somewhere.

Feeling restless, Cahira rose from the bed and went to her walk-in closet. She grabbed her black one-piece swimsuit and stuffed a few items in a gym bag to make her way down to the pool. Swimming allowed her to channel frustration, stress, and energy another way as she did lap after lap. Her ARW and Special Ops training allowed her to become an expert in the water under the worst circumstances imaginable, cutting through the clear pool water as she skimmed with no trouble.

She always got glares from people at the pool. Cahira did little, if any, mingling with the other residents at Hudson Yards. She was okay if people thought of her as 'the rich bitch on the seventh floor' and stayed out of her way. It meant fewer complications in her life. Appearances at the pool meant looks from the wives, girlfriends, or mistresses of the rich men who occupied much of the space. The few men who wandered to swim ogled, but none were bold enough to approach her.

Not even a hundred laps were enough for Cahira, and she left the pool tired and spent but no less preoccupied. She quickly changed in the locker room, stepping into a t-shirt and sweats before heading out. Spurning going back to her apartment, she instead went to the resident lobby for a change of scenery. She spotted Duffy settling in at the concierge desk, adjusting his name tag and straightening his tie.

"Well, fancy seeing you out here like this, Ms. O'Brien." Duffy grinned.

"Good morning, Duffy," Cahira replied cordially.

Bustling residents made their way out of elevators on their way to work, moving past Cahira with little acknowledgment.

"Is there something I can help you with this morning?" Duffy asked.

Cahira snapped from her semi-trance and looked at the older gentleman, his salt-and-pepper hair perfectly cut and combed.

"No, I'm okay," she insisted. She glanced beyond Duffy to the desk area where picture frames sat.

"Are those yours?" she asked, pointing.

"The pictures? Yes, they are," he said proudly. "My kids and grandkids. I like to keep them around me. Craig and I have a deal. I put my pictures up during the day, and he does his in the evenings. That's from Fourth of July in Bethany Beach."

Duffy plucked the gold frame from the desk and passed it to Cahira. She looked at the photo of two men and women in their early thirties, surrounded by five kids of varying sizes and ages. All the kids had face paint of American flags.

"That's a beautiful family," Cahira said, passing the frame back. "You're a lucky man."

"For certain, Miss," he beamed. "I keep at it just for them. I've been able to save enough so we are getting that beach house this year for keeps," he said, pointing to the large home in the background. "We've been renting it for years every summer. I haven't told any of them I bought it, not even the Mrs. It will be a nice surprise when we go down this year."

"Wow, good for you, Duffy. I am sure they will love it."

"Yeah, we've been going there since the wife and I married forty years ago. It will be the perfect place to retire to someday. The years go by fast, you know. Before you know it, the kids are all grown, the grandkids are older, and you wonder where your life has gone. This gives us a place we can all go to and always be home."

Cahira looked on as Duffy placed the photo back on his desk.

"Do you have any brothers or sisters, Duffy?" she asked.

"Ah, sadly, they are gone," he lamented. "I was the baby of the family. My two brothers and my sister have passed on. I have nieces and nephews I see to remind me of them, but I'm all that's left now. It's hard when they are gone."

Cahira nodded, staring off.

"Everything okay, Miss?" Duffy asked with concern.

"I think so," Cahira stated before smiling at Duffy. "Duffy, can you call the garage for my car in about an hour? I'm taking a little trip up north and have to pack up a few things."

"Of course," Duffy spoke. "Another business trip?"

"No, not this time," Cahira answered as she moved toward the elevator entrance.

****

Rapid packing never proved to be a problem for Cahira. She regularly had bags ready to move quickly when needed, but those times were always more for business than pleasure. This time, she was more deliberate in choosing what to pack. Casual wear was not clothing she had a lot of, but Cahira cobbled together some choices and had everything ready just before Duffy buzzed her to let her know her car had arrived.

Cahira grabbed a few things from her hidden spaces around the apartment to be extra prepared if needed. She always had cash, IDs, and weapons in various locations. While looking through the floor safe in her bedroom, she found a small black box. She held it carefully in her palm before lifting the latch to open it. Inside were the items dear to her, things she kept locked away from everyone. Military medals lay stacked, one on the next, until the commendations reached the top lip of the box. Then, a set of keys caught her eye, and she snatched them into her palm to bring along.

The items that caught her eye most were the small brown envelope and black velvet drawstring bag. Cahira plucked the pouch and gently opened it, pulling out two of the necklaces inside. She held them at eye level, gazing at the silver strands that led down to identical charms on the end. The amulets were gold hearts woven into the triple spirals, the symbol of the Celtic Sisters.

Cahira instinctively reached for the necklace she wore daily, matching the ones she kept in her hands. She placed the chains back in the bag and cinched it closed before stuffing it into her jeans pocket. The brown envelope came out next, and she flipped through the photos. The older pictures seemed from another lifetime. Pictures of her with Kelly at their home in Monroe, at the beaches in Delaware with their parents, and Christmas photos by the tree came first. Beneath them were a few of her ARW squad when stationed in the Middle East. The last two were the ones that made Cahira pause.

A seemingly innocent picture of eight young women laughing and smiling around a dinner table caused Cahira's heart to melt. There were no other photos of the Sisters together like that, at least none that she knew of. Their superiors insisted upon that when the unit was first formed. This was done covertly, taken by the waitress at a pub in Dublin on a disposable camera since their cell phones were regularly scanned. Badb developed the pictures herself and then disposed of the negatives to leave no traces other than what was given to each person in the squad.

The other picture was of Cahira and her father, taken before he disappeared. It was right after Cahira had left New York and gone to Ireland specifically to find her father and stay with him. It took some work to track him down to the isolated farm he lived on. They had their arms around each other in front of the barn on the farm, with a few sheep wandering by.

Cahira tucked the photos back into the envelope slowly, putting them away before her emotions got the best of her. She locked everything back into the compartment in the floor, concealing it with the false panel and dropping the carpet back over it. She grabbed her two bags and made her way to the elevator. Once inside, she activated her security system and moved to the lobby to get her car.

When she arrived at the concierge desk, Duffy greeted her with the key fob to her Subaru in his hand.

"Thanks, Duffy." Cahira grinned.

"How long will you be gone for, Miss?" he asked.

"About a week, I think. Honestly, I'm not sure, Duffy. Can you let Craig know I'm gone? No one should be looking for me anyway."

"I will pass it on to Craig. We'll hold any mail or packages for you as well. Have a wonderful trip."

Cahira nodded and headed to her SUV, stowing her bags before getting into the driver's seat. At first, she thought getting back to Monroe would be simple, but she could not recall Kelly's address. So she pulled up Google Maps and popped Monroe on there, choosing the longer route since she was in no rush to get anywhere. She then touched her earpiece to speak with Badb.

"What's up?" Badb chirped.

"I'm on the road," Cahira announced as she made her way out of the city.

"Where are you off to? I didn't think we had anything planned."

"We don't. I just needed to get out of the city for a while. I've been feeling like a caged animal."

"Where are you headed? You're not going to—"

Cahira cut Badb off.

"No, no, no. I had to deal with Danny last night. I don't think I'll hear from him for a bit now. I'm not going to Queens. I need to be further away. Can you—you give me Kelly's address?"

Silence hung in the conversation.

"You still there?" Cahira questioned.

"I am," Badb answered. "I just didn't expect to hear that from you. Don't take me as callous, but did someone die?"

"No one died," Cahira scoffed. "She left me a voicemail last night. It's nothing life-threatening. It was completely out of the blue. It just got me thinking, is all."

"Cat, if she doesn't know you're coming, it might not be the best idea to go there."

"She invited me, Badb—well, she sort of invited me. Teagan invited me. It's her birthday this weekend."

"So you're going just on a voicemail and a four-year-old's invitation? Cat, you've spent years avoiding going back there, and you've had more substantial reasons to go than this. Kelly's wedding, Teagan's birth, your mother's—"

"Please don't," Cahira insisted sternly. "There's something about it right now that makes me want to go there. That should be enough."

"Fine," Badb responded. "I sent Kelly's address to your phone. You can pop it up. Do you have a place to stay up there?"

"I hadn't planned that far ahead just yet. This was very last minute, Badb."

"I can look in the area to see what is available."

Rapid typing filled Cahira's ears while Kelly's home address in Monroe appeared on the screen on the dashboard.

"There are rooms available at the Thayer if you want one," Badb advised.

"No, I'm not dealing with security at West Point. Too risky," Cahira replied.

"How about the Sheraton in Mahwah? They have some suites available for you."

"I don't need anything fancy, Badb. Is there something closer? Monroe never had a hotel other than the James Motel, but there must be something there after all these years."

"There's a Hampton Inn in Harriman if you want that. It looks like it's got some room. Or the Bear Mountain Inn is up there."

When Cahira heard Badb utter Bear Mountain, her eyes lit up.

"The lodge is open?" she asked excitedly.

"It is, or they have stone cottages available to rent. Each cottage has six bedrooms. I can get you one of those."

Memories of walking and hiking through Bear Mountain with her father flooded back to Cahira.

"I want an entire cottage," she blurted out.

"It's pretty pricey to take the entire cottage," Badb answered. "How long were you looking at?"

"Ten days, maybe more."

"That's a long stay, Cat. You're talking thousands of dollars."

"It's still probably less than that place in Dubai I stayed at a few years back. So book it, please."

"You're the boss." Badb sighed.

"I'm not the boss," Cat insisted. "Let's not go through this again. I'm the silent partner. You're the boss as far as everyone is concerned."

"Whatever you want to call it. I have you booked in for two weeks there. You can check in at three, so you have time to kill. Let me know if you need anything else. You know how to reach me."

"Thanks, Badb. You're the best. You always have been."

"Yeah, yeah," Badb brushed it off. "Just be careful, Cat. I don't want you to get hurt if the meeting doesn't work out as you envision it. Going home isn't always what it is cracked up to be."

"I know it all too well," Cahira lamented. "I promise not to get my hopes up too high. I'll stay in touch."

Cahira tapped out of the conversation, turning her focus back to the roads. She headed to 287, passing the Empire Casino and moving toward the Mario Cuomo Bridge. It had been so long since she'd traversed north that it took some thought to realize it used to be called the Tappan Zee Bridge, and the one she recalled looked nothing like the new span across the Hudson River.

The scenery started to get more familiar the further north she went, passing through areas and exits for names of towns she knew well. When she reached the exit for Route 17M, she moved off the highway and took the quieter route. Places like Sloatsburg and Tuxedo had changed little since she last went through them. Memories of days with her family in Harriman State Park came to Cahira as she recalled swimming at Lake Welch and picnics in the park on the days when her parents were together and civil to each other.

Once Cahira arrived in Harriman, she began to drive slower. She still had a few hours before she could check into the hotel. A low grumble in her stomach reminded her that she had eaten little and she began the search for a place to have lunch. Unsure if any of the sites she knew were still open, she drove down Church Street through the heart of Harriman. Remnants of the last big snowstorm still clung tightly to curbs and lawns before she reached River Road and stopped in the parking lot of Millie Malone's.

The signs out front of the bar indicated they had food inside, and the lot appeared half-full of cars for the lunch hour. Cahira climbed out, pulling her leather jacket out of the back seat and donning it to fight the chill in the early spring air. She made her way inside, catching the Irish background music playing as she approached the bar.

A lanky bartender spotted her and raised a hand, indicating he would be there momentarily. Cahira nodded and looked at the senior gentleman nursing a lunchtime Guinness at the bar. His eyes peered out from the corner of his eye before his right hand reached over and grabbed his tweed hat, sliding it toward his body.

"Have a seat, lass," he indicated. "Darren takes every opportunity to stall the ball. I hope you're not in a hurry."

"Nah, I've got time to kill." Cat chuckled. She was always amused at how speaking with an Irish person dragged out her brogue. She grabbed the stool next to the gent and sat, taking her jacket off.

"What's the craic?" the man asked, sipping his Guinness.

"Just in the area after a long time," Cahira noted.

"Ah, a local Irish girl. I knew it!" the man exclaimed, slapping the bar. "No one else would wander here like that at this time of day. What's your name, darlin'?"

Cahira paused before answering. Always reluctant to use her real name, she gazed at the old man and saw the twinkle in his eye, one she always imagined her grandfather likely had.

"Cahira." She smiled. "Cahira O'Brien."

"A beautiful name," he responded. "A fierce one as well, as I'm sure you know. You clearly have some warrior in you. I can tell by your eyes. Are you related to Aiden O'Brien?"

The conversation stopped her dead in her tracks. Cahira hadn't heard her father's name muttered by anyone in years, and the last thing she'd expected was a stranger in a bar to mention him.

"Yes, yes I am," she said quietly. "He was—is—my father."

"Ah, a fine man, Aiden," the older man continued, sitting up straight. "Willing to stand up for what he believed, no matter what. I've great respect for him."

"Did you know him well?" Cahira hurried.

"Paddy knows everyone well," Darren added as he appeared at their end of the bar. "I apologize for the wait. Hopefully Paddy hasn't filled your head with tales about the place. What can I get for you?"

Cahira was still focused on Paddy as he gulped the rest of his stout. Then, finally, she shook off the trance and turned to Darren.

"I'll have a pint," she indicated. "And a lunch menu, please. Can I get you a pint?" she asked Paddy.

"I can't remember the last time I had a beautiful woman offer to buy me a pint," Paddy replied. "I'd hate to turn you down."

"Paddy, you'd take a free pint offered by the Devil himself," Darren mocked.

"Ahh, enough of you! Do your job, you eejit, and get us our drinks!" Paddy shouted.

Darren walked off to pour the drinks as Cahira questioned Paddy again.

"So, did you know my father?"

"I did, socially," Paddy told her. "We had drinks together here or sometimes at the Hibernians' Club if he was there. I'd see him out and about in town or if he was working a job. Twas a sad day when he went back to Ireland."

"How did you know he went there? I didn't think he told anyone where he went."

Paddy chuckled and smiled at Cahira.

"Darlin', when you're an old man, people tend to tell you lots of things, thinking you're deaf, not paying attention, forgetful, or daft. I've heard lots over time. I knew he was going back home. But no one ever asked me about it."

Darren placed the pints on the bar and handed a laminated menu to Cahira.

"Soup today is potato leek," Darren indicated. "The ladies serve up a mean one with soda bread. Perfect for a chilly day like today."

"I'll take a cup," Cahira answered, handing the menu back. "Did you want anything?" she asked, turning to Paddy.

"Oh no, thank you." Paddy grinned. "I've got all I need right here."

He patted his pint glass before raising it to Cahira.

"Sláinte," he offered, clinking glasses.

Cahira nodded and anxiously sipped before peppering Paddy with more questions.

***

An anticipated fast lunch became much longer when Cahira ran into Paddy Walsh. Paddy regaled her with stories of her father, giving her more insight into Aiden O'Brien than she had been able to dig up with the expert help of Badb. While he may not have known of his movements or actions over the last several years, his tales gave Cahira a reason to smile about her family, which often proved elusive to her.

When she arrived at the Bear Mountain Inn, all Cahira could think about was taking a nap. Her head swam with thoughts of her father, sister, Danny, Badb, and jobs. Three pints of Guinness didn't assist her muddled thoughts. The staff at the lodge greeted her warmly, knowing she had booked the entire cottage for two weeks, and promised to take the best care of her possible. She was grateful for their words but just wanted the key so she could collapse and rest.

Entering the cottage, Cahira was greeted by the main room with the stone fireplace as the centerpiece. She worked her way from bedroom to bedroom, doing her due diligence to ensure everything was secure and no cameras were there for prying eyes. Once comfortable in the space, she selected the bedroom closest to the entrance and settled in. A flop on the firm mattress proved all she needed to relax before she drifted off to sleep.

The slightest crack of branches outside rapidly roused Cahira from her nap. Her eyes flew open, staring at the bedroom door as her right hand instinctively went to the blade sheathed down around her right ankle. She peered through the darkness, her eyes adjusting to allow her to notice any movement. Cahira moved from the bed stealthily to the doorframe before she slipped out into the main area.

When the crack reoccurred outside the front window, Cahira lowered her alert level, spying the shadow of tree branches brushing against the eave of the front porch. She flicked the light switch to illuminate the hanging chandelier and brighten the area. Checking the front door, she noted it was locked from the inside still. Cahira also found that she had slept longer than expected when she glanced at her watch and saw it was nearly nine p.m.

Returning to her bedroom to pick up her leather jacket, Cahira exited the cottage, double-checking that the door was locked. Next, she paced the cabin's exterior to examine potential entry areas, checking windows to ensure no weaknesses should a visitor decide to stop by. Once satisfied, she walked to her car and drove off, heading back toward Monroe.

Kelly's address loomed large on the GPS screen, but Cahira hesitated to press it and find her way to that house. Instead, she chose a more familiar route she had driven many times. Weaving over the winding path up Rye Hill Road to get to Berry Road, she was accelerating as she neared the slight rise in the roadway she drove over as a youth. The car became airborne, not nearly as much as she recalled from her teenage years when she and her sister would squeal when her father did the same thing.

When she reached the end of Berry Road, she made the right turn and sped up on the straightaway before she made a quick left turn to School Road. She slowed past the familiar shadows of Rosmarin's Day Camp, recalling times when she and her sister would spy on the day camp kids through the fence and watch all their activities. So it was when she spotted the house on the corner her car crept along. She guided her Subaru into the driveway, letting her headlights illuminate the worn-shut garage door before her.

Cahira killed the car's engine and sat quietly, contemplating whether or not her actions made any sense.

"Feck it," she whispered and hopped out of the vehicle.

Using the flashlight on her smartphone, she found her way to the house's back door. She grabbed the long-unused keys from her jeans pocket, flipping through each one before finding the correct one for the lock. Resistance brought on by age and wear met her when she first attempted to turn the lock, but then she felt the lock disengage, making her glad she wouldn't have to return to her car for her picking kit.

Cahira found herself standing in the kitchen of her parents' old home. She guided the flashlight around the room, taking in the worn wallpaper she recalled from all those years ago when she left home for the last time.

Surprise caught her when there was no smell of must, mold, or anything else. Instead, the kitchen appeared spotless and smelled of lemon cleaner.

Walking through the kitchen, she paced into the open space of the living room. The area looked immense through the flashlight beam, much larger than she recalled when it was filled with furniture and her mother's curio cabinets of knick-knacks she plucked from local garage sales and flea markets.

Eschewing the basement door at the beginning of the small hallway, she made her way down it, the wood floors groaning beneath her feet. The bathroom maintained its pink and white tiling on the floor and walls, her mother's insistence once it was "just the girls" in the house. The door to what had been Kelly's room was shut, cleaned of all the stickers she had pasted on it in her younger years when her love for Disney princesses raged.

A chill raced through Cahira when she paused at the doorway to her parents' bedroom. The door was open, the sliding closet doors off their tracks and leaning against the far wall. The image of the large oak headboard that had occupied the space on the far wall for so long popped into her head as she imagined how the bedroom had looked for years. She remembered when her father's dresser took the area next to the closet. She often would go in to look at the latest items her father had emptied from his pockets after a day's work or from a walk he took to see what treasures he had brought.

Eventually, Cahira turned to face the door at the end of the hall where her bedroom lay. She pushed the door open, entering the room for the first time since the day she'd left, hours after high school graduation. Like all the other rooms, it was stripped of its furniture and trappings. She walked over to the lone window in the room, peering out to the area she often snuck in and out of the house from to meet boyfriends or just to get away from whatever the daily drama her mother went through was.

Cahira blew onto the glass, fogging it lightly, before tracing a shamrock on the area, something she and Kelly did whenever they would get into the cold of their father's old Chevy Cavalier in the winter while he scraped the windshield.

The distinct floorboard creaking in the living room caused Cahira to immediately dim the flashlight lamp of her phone before she moved to the inside wall by the doorframe. The breaths moved in and out rhythmically as she gripped the collapsible baton in her jacket pocket, readying to strike. She listened intently as steps came closer to the hallway. Cahira clicked off the paces, envisioning whoever it was as they opened the basement door and shut it before inching closer to the bedrooms. The illumination of a phone light hit the open door to Cahira's bedroom.

Cahira slyly peered around the door jamb, hoping to catch a glimpse of who might be coming and what she may have to deal with. Instead, the dark frame behind the light gave off a familiar silhouette. The size, shape, and movement rang in her head as she paused.

"Dad?" she said softly, causing the shadow to stop moving forward.

Chapter 6

The word slipped quickly from Cahira's lips before she could catch it. When the figure paused in the hall, she knew she had been heard, and reacted. Cahira rushed down the aisle, leaping after two steps as she bull-rushed and knocked over the intruder with her shoulder, sending the phone and the figure sprawling across the floor. Cahira pounced, pinning their arms beneath her knees as she released her baton, preparing to strike.

Only when the voice cried out, "Stop!" did Cahira realize it was both familiar and female. She grabbed her phone from her pocket, shining the light brightly on her prisoner. The chestnut brown hair partially covered the face before her, but once the head shook to move the strands, Kelly's squint into the light in her eyes made Cahira halt.

Cahira rolled off her sister and continued to shine the light on her. Kelly scrambled to her feet and made her way over to the far wall, flipping the light on the living room ceiling.

"Jesus, Kelly," Cahira said, pushing the button on the baton to retract it. "I was ready to bash your head in."

"For fuck's sake, Cat," Kelly gasped, bending at the knees to catch her breath. Kelly paced over to pick up her phone.

"What are you doing here?" Cahira asked at the same moment her sister asked the same question.

"Mrs. Murphy called me," Kelly said, pointing to the house across the street. "She said someone was in the driveway and thought she saw lights in the house."

"So you came to check it out, unprepared and without anything to protect yourself? Why didn't you call the police? You could have walked into something nasty, Kelly."

"Is my security-crazy sister done ranting now?" Kelly spoke. "There's nothing in the house except the old boxes in the basement of the things you never showed up to collect. If anything, I thought it might be kids breaking in looking for a place to drink or get high. I didn't expect to find you creeping around here. Thanks for returning my call, by the way."

"Don't try to turn this around on me," Cahira shot back. "I have keys to the place. I do own half of it, you know."

"You don't need to remind me, Cat. I've been trying to sell the place for two years now, but you never return calls, emails, messages, or anything that might help me do that. If you let me follow through, neither of us would have to deal with it anymore. So instead, Mickey has to keep coming over here to repair things."

"Who's Mickey?" Cahira asked.

Kelly stared indignantly at Cahira.

"Michael, my husband," Kelly added gruffly. "If you bothered to know anything about me, you would know his name."

Cahira nodded, recalling the lily-white invitation sent years ago asking her to attend the wedding.

"I'm sorry," Cahira apologized. "I guess I forgot."

"Or you never bothered to learn it," Kelly replied. "Why are you here, Cat? Why are you skulking around Mom and Dad's house in the middle of the night? Why are you in Monroe at all?"

"I came up...for Teagan's birthday. You invited me—or, at least, she did."

"Honestly, I never expected you to show up. I did that to appease Teagan. To Teagan, you are just like this magical being that sends her expensive gifts a few times a year. She has you up on this pedestal for some reason. Part of me was glad she wanted me to call you so that—"

Kelly stopped, turning away from Cahira and looking out the living room window.

"So that what, Kelly?"

"So when you didn't reply or show up, she would see who you really are—a selfish woman who sends her presents out of some weird sense of guilt instead of a superhero."

"Look," Cahira said, inching closer to Kelly, "if you don't want me to be here, just say so. I don't have to come to the party or anything else. I'm not sure why I'm here. Something made me want to come to see Teagan...and you."

"I want to believe you, Cat. I really do. I've been down this road too many times, with Dad and then with you. You disappear off the face of the earth for years at a time without a word. You send random packages to my daughter, a girl you've never even bothered to meet, and now I'm supposed to buy that some mystical or spiritual reason has brought you here to reunite and make things all better? You can't possibly expect me to be that naive."

"I know I haven't given you many reasons to trust me—"

"Many?" Kelly scoffed. "How about any? You left me here, Cat. I was fourteen years old, and you left me here with Mom, knowing how unstable she was. You have no idea what I had to live through. But then, once she got physically sick, I also had that burden. You were all I had in the world after Dad left, and out of the blue, I had no one. Not even a letter to say where you were, what you were doing, or even if you were alive."

"I—I sent money to help. I covered Mom's medical bills," Cahira interjected before quickly realizing it was the wrong thing to say.

"Thanks a lot," Kelly snapped. "I didn't care about any of that, and Mom sure as hell didn't. I still had to work all day and then take care of her all night when she would scream, hallucinate, punch, and kick me, calling me ungrateful for all she had done for me while I fed her, changed her, and bathed her. All that time, in the back of my mind, I wondered if you might show up to help. And now, after she's gone and I've finally put my life together and am happy, you decide to waltz in. You know what I have found out, Cat? I don't need you. That time is long gone."

Cahira stood silently and took it all. Kelly's eyes had reddened as her voice raised and she spewed what she'd held in for so long out.

"Nothing I can say now is ever going to change any of what has happened, Kelly," Cahira began. "I left you, and I'm sorry for that. It tore me up inside to do it, but if I didn't, things would have been much worse for both of us, trust me. I needed to escape this place—and her. I didn't come here to cause you any pain. I understand if you hate me. You have every right to feel that way. I don't know what I was thinking, showing up out of nowhere. I won't send anything else to Teagan if that's what you wish."

Kelly stepped deliberately toward Cahira until they were face to face. The anger in her sister's eyes was evident, but Cahira looked on, hoping in some way that her presence helped Kelly.

"If you want to come to the party, that's fine," Kelly added. "Show up and do what you need to do, but don't pretend that you are the sainted aunt that can do no wrong, and don't make promises to her or me that you have no intention of keeping. Tomorrow afternoon at one is the time. It's just a few close friends and some of Mickey's family. Do you know where the house is?"

"I have the address." Cahira nodded. "I'm sure I can find it. Thanks."

Kelly grasped her keys in her hand and moved toward the front door.

"Just make sure you lock up when you leave so Mrs. Murphy doesn't call me again. After Jeopardy, she has nothing to do except stare out her bay window and snoop."

"I guess she hasn't changed that much." Cahira chuckled.

"You're really going to come tomorrow, right, Cat?" Kelly asked as she reached the front door. "If I tell Teagan you'll be there, you will?"

"I guarantee I will be there," Cahira stated firmly. "Can I bring something? Is there something Teagan wants?"

"Just show up," Kelly uttered. "Don't break my daughter's heart."

Kelly exited, leaving Cahira alone in the house. Then, with the overhead light on, she saw the bare white walls covering the years where gaudy wallpaper held the room captive, giving the space a more welcoming look than it ever had when she lived there. Cahira walked to the far wall, turning off the light fixture before she exited through the kitchen door and locked up. Next, she moved to her car, catching a glimpse of Mrs. Murphy across the street, standing at her bay window and spying on her as she climbed into the Subaru.

***

Not wanting to return to Bear Mountain after Kelly had unpacked all the vitriol she had, Cahira drove around Monroe aimlessly. Looking at how much had changed since she ran away thirteen years prior, she spotted many more homes where open space and forest had been, new businesses where there once were none, and some favorite haunts long gone from the spaces they held. Finally, she cruised past the crowded parking lot around the Captain's Table, forgoing that spot in case anyone in some way might recognize her.

Unsure of where to go, she returned to Millie Malone's. A smattering of cars dotted the parking lot, much like when she'd stopped there for lunch earlier in the day. She found a well-lit spot to park and entered the building just as the band finished up their cover of "Statesboro Blues."

Cahira strode to the far end of the bar, bypassing the seat with a 'Reserved' sign positioned on it and standing as she waited for the familiar face of Darren to come down to her after serving up several shots of whiskey to a group of men.

"You're back." He smiled. "I'm always glad to see a returning face."

"I'm looking for a nightcap before heading off," Cahira admitted.

She glanced behind Darren at the selection of bottles.

"I don't suppose you have any Redbreast hiding back there, do you?"

"Are you looking for something particular?" Darren inquired.

"I do like the 27-year." She grinned.

"Well, I don't get much call for good stuff like that around here. I've got 12-year if you are willing to settle for that."

"Fair enough," Cahira agreed as Darren went off to pour.

Cahira scoped the room and watched as the band began to pack up their belongings for the night. Finally, many customers filed out of the bar, leaving two groups seated in booths. She spotted a group of nine, likely college-aged, doing shots at their table. At the other booth, three men sat idly, talking low and enjoying their pints.

Darren arrived with Cahira's whiskey, placing the rocks glass on the bar before her. She plucked the glass up, taking in the sweet smell of malt and caramel before she sipped it.

"Nice," she said, nodding before sliding a twenty-dollar bill onto the bar toward Darren.

"Mind if I go grab a booth?" she asked.

"Help yourself," Darren offered. "The kitchen is closed, so I can't offer you any food, and you got here just as the band ended, but stay as long as you like. There are still a few diehards here."

Cahira claimed a booth in the far corner of the room, far enough away so that she could watch the entrance and close enough where she noticed the hallway that led to the kitchen and likely a back exit door if she needed it. The part of her brain that was always on alert and scanning the area never took a break. She quietly sipped her whiskey, going over her confrontation with Kelly and wishing she had said or done things differently.

The occasional raucous laugh erupted from the table of frat boys to catch her attention while she noticed looks coming from the three men seated off to the right. Two men kept leaning in close to each other in a conspiratorial manner while the third held his pint glass on the table between his hands.

Cahira peeked over the rim of her lifted glass as one of the trio moved up to the bar to speak with Darren. One gent had spoken softly before Darren handed him a glass of whiskey, and the man made his way toward Cahira. She sighed as she knew what was coming next but opted not to pretend she was looking at her phone.

The short, stocky man flipped his dark hair back with his left hand while he presented the glass of whiskey to Cahira.

"Hi there," he said confidently. "I hope you don't mind that I bought you a drink."

Cahira held up the glass she had.

"Thanks, but I've got one."

"No harm in having another one, right?" The man laughed as he placed the glass on the table and slid into the booth next to Cahira. Cahira put up her right hand to stop him from coming too close.

"I really just want the one before I head out," she said, struggling to maintain a semblance of a smile.

"I'm Frank, by the way," he said, not getting the hints Cahira dropped.

"Look, Frank," she said firmly, "let's not make this any more awkward than it needs to be, okay? Why don't you go back to your buddies and finish your Guinness? I'm just looking to have my drink and go. I'm not interested in anything else. So don't make things ugly and embarrassing for yourself."

Frank cocked his head to one side, clearly unaccustomed to getting rejected like that, and was unsure how to process it.

"Hey, I was just trying to be friendly," he said, his voice raised. "I bought you a twenty-dollar drink, for crying out loud. You could be nicer about it."

"I didn't ask you to do that," Cahira answered calmly. "Now, if you won't walk away, I will."

"You're too good to have a drink with me?" he slurred.

"No, you're too drunk and too ignorant for me to have one with you," she replied, sliding out the other side of the booth.

Cahira began to walk across the dance floor when she was greeted by one of Frank's friends. She scanned to see where the third man was, and saw that the redhead had kept his seat in his booth. Cahira breathed and shifted her feet as the man approached, and her hand went into her jacket pocket.

The man nearing her was taller than her, wearing a blue flannel shirt and jeans. He was fitter than Cahira had expected from where she sat and had more of his wits about him than the still-clamoring Frank.

"I'm sorry about my friend there," the man said, running his hand over his stubbled chin. "He's had a bad breakup and drank way too much tonight. He's not a bad guy, really."

"No offense to you or your friend, but if he talks to women like that, he is a bad guy. You might want to get him to a car and get him home before he repeats the wrong thing."

"Don't even talk to her, Eddie," Frank yelled as he closed in on Cahira. "She's just like—"

Cahira pivoted, ready to confront Frank if she had to, before Eddie stepped in and pushed Frank back.

"She's right, Frank," Eddie scolded. "You're too drunk. You need to go home and sleep it off. Red can give you a ride home."

Red joined his friends on the dance floor now, corralling Frank.

"Let's go, Frank," Red ordered, ushering him toward the front door as Cahira looked on.

"No wonder he just had a breakup," Cahira told Eddie. "Whoever she is, she was wise to get away now."

"I know. Frank can be a jackass," Eddie added.

"Then why are you friends with him?"

"We've been friends since high school," Eddie told her. "I guess it's just habit."

"Bad habits need to be broken," she advised.

Cahira glanced beyond Eddie to see the group of frat boys giving a young woman a hard time. Then, she saw her storm out of the bar with the gang trailing closely behind her.

"I appreciate you sticking up for your friend. My advice—find a new friend. Have a good night," Cahira told Eddie as she moved by him and went straight to the parking lot.

She looked around and saw the rowdy boys near a dark SUV, with the girl surrounded by all of them. One man, in particular, had his arms on either side of her head, pinning her against the vehicle.

Cahira marched closer to where they had gathered.

"Everything okay over here?" she questioned loudly, causing the men to turn around.

"We're fine," the man in a dark sport coat in front of the girl answered.

"I wasn't asking you," Cahira shot back. "I'm asking her if she is okay."

One look at the girl's troubled eyes gave Cahira the answer she already knew.

"She doesn't have a problem," the man answered, leering at the girl.

"I want to hear that from her."

Sport coat moved away from the girl and took a few steps toward Cahira.

"Look, lady, I don't know what your problem is, but why don't you run along and mind your fucking business? Unless, of course, you want to join the party too."

Cahira looked beyond Sport Coat and saw the other frat boys were unsure what to do or where this was going.

"Come over here by me," she said to the girl, who began to take thankful steps toward Cahira.

"Don't let her move!" Sport Coat barked. "She doesn't have to listen to you," he spat at Cahira.

The girl took tentative steps toward Cahira until she ran and stood beside her.

"Are you okay?" Cahira said softly.

"Not really," she answered, frightened.

Sport Coat took two steps toward the girl.

"Run inside and tell the bartender to call the police," Cahira spoke quickly, shoving the girl and stepping in front of Sport Coat.

"Now, why did you go and do that?" Sport Coat whined.

"Jimmy, let's go," one of the frat boys shouted. "She's getting the cops!"

"Listen to your friends, Jimmy," Cahira warned. "Leave while you have the chance."

"Everything good?" a man's voice shouted from behind Cahira. Her head spun as she saw Eddie moving toward where she was. The moment she turned, she spotted Jimmy step toward her, readying to make a grab.

Cahira sidestepped as Jimmy missed and stumbled to the ground, skidding against the pavement.

"Do they only let asshole drunks in this place?" Cahira said aloud.

Jimmy scrabbled back to his feet and growled as he raced toward Cahira. Eddie moved to stop him, but it was too late. When Jimmy neared her, Cahira struck Jimmy sharply on his right arm and sent him back down again. He cried out as his left hand moved to his right bicep.

"I think you broke my arm," Jimmy screamed.

"If I wanted to break your arm, I would have," Cahira boasted. "Are we done now?"

Jimmy's friends rushed over to collect him from the ground as Darren appeared carrying a baseball bat from the bar.

The frat boys cleared out, hightailing it to the SUV and pulling out of the parking lot quickly before anything further occurred.

"What the hell was that?" Darren said as he moved next to Cahira.

"Wonder Woman here took out Jimmy Reynolds," Eddie stated.

"You might want to think about some of the clientele you have here," Cahira grumbled to Darren before making her way toward her car.

Cahira stepped to her car until she realized Eddie was following her. She arrived at her vehicle, putting her hand back in her pocket and bracing herself. Eddie immediately raised his hands in surrender.

"Hey, I'm not doing anything, trust me. I've seen what you can do," Eddie confessed. "I just wanted to make sure you were okay."

"I'm fine," she answered, controlling her breaths. "I don't need looking after."

"Obviously," Eddie admitted. "That was pretty amazing what you did there. Where did you learn that?"

"It wasn't amazing, and I shouldn't have to do that if men knew when to take no for an answer," she muttered. "Where I learned it doesn't really matter either. Are we done here?"

"I guess so," Eddie acquiesced, stepping back as Cahira climbed into her car.

She started the engine up, pulled out of the lot, moved down River Road toward Route 6, and headed back to Bear Mountain. She rolled the driver's side window down to allow cold air to beat against her face as she drove.

"So much for a good trip back home," she shouted into the wind.

Chapter 7

C ahira spent much of her morning secluded in the cottage, keeping the curtains drawn and sleeping late. Then, when she pried herself out of bed, she peered around the drapes to see the sun shining brightly outside. Next, she donned her running gear and set out to run around the lake a few times to get a workout in and burn off some excess energy.

Few people dotted the walkways and trails in the morning, with coldness holding on tight and displaying the last bit of winter/early spring weather. Cahira never ran outdoors with earbuds in to keep her aware of her surroundings, instead losing herself in the sights and sounds of the park. Days she spent walking through Bear Mountain, the zoo, and climbing the steps with her father came back to her as she ran along, pushing her as her muscles worked tirelessly through her run.

When she arrived at her cottage, she showered and looked over her clothing options for the party. She opted for a yellow floral dress, something she rarely wore. There were few opportunities for Cahira to don a casual dress, and she certainly could not conceal any weapons with it on. Attending a child's party at her sister's home didn't seem to warrant preparing for a combative situation.

She drove off toward Monroe, looking for a place to go to buy a gift for Teagan. In the past, Cahira had relied heavily on Badb to assist her in selecting just the right present for her niece. This time, Cahira wanted to choose something herself, something that might have meaning to give. Unfortunately, that meant finding a store that would meet her needs.

Cahira's initial thoughts turned to Fran's Hallmark, a mainstay in Monroe for many years. However, when she went to the store's previous location, she found it had gone away. At a loss, she was unsure of what to do next. Her eyes lit up when she recalled Maggie's Celtic Cottage across town.

Cahira rushed across Monroe to Talmadge Court, where she pulled into the parking lot of the florist and Irish gift shop. Her father had often taken Cahira there to buy gifts for Mother's Day, Christmas, birthdays, or anniversaries. When she entered the store, she was met with the sweet smell of fresh flowers and the sounds of traditional Irish music playing over the speakers.

After browsing through all the finery and wares, Cahira settled on an Irish knit cardigan that she guessed the size at and hoped fit Teagan. She also plucked a stuffed bear dressed as a leprechaun before moving toward the front of the store when something caught her eye. A small pair of sterling silver Claddagh earrings sized for children were ideal for her niece.

Luckily for Cahira, the store was happy to wrap the items for her, and she could pick up a small bouquet of daisies and red roses to go along with everything, perfectly decorated for a little girl's birthday. Happy with her selections, Cahira returned to her car with an armful of gifts.

Finding her way to Kelly's home proved easy for Cahira. She pulled into the driveway of the dusty charcoal colonial, balloons festively tied to the mailbox, parking behind several other cars. She sat in her car for a few minutes, tapping on the steering wheel and contemplating how it might go for her to appear at the party.

"Now or never," she muttered softly as she climbed out of the car.

She gathered her gifts and flowers and made her way up the path to the stone front steps, knocking lightly on the door before realizing no one was answering. She pulled open the screen door and let herself in as she awkwardly said, "Hello?"

A bearded man emerged from the kitchen at the top of the wood steps, smiling down at her.

"Hi," he said to her, holding a couple of beer bottles. "Are you one of the moms? I thought all the kids were here."

"Oh, no, I'm not," Cahira stammered. "I'm—"

"That's my sister," Kelly said, coming from behind the man, holding a bowl of potato chips.

Cahira moved up the steps to the top floor, coming face to face with Kelly.

"I didn't believe you would come," Kelly stated.

"I promised you I would," Cahira responded.

"Your promises don't always hold much water, Cat."

The bearded man put the beer bottles on the kitchen counter and stepped between the sisters.

"Are you going to introduce us?" he asked, wiping his damp hand on his jeans.

"Cahira, this is my husband, Michael," Kelly said casually.

"Call me Mickey." He smiled, presenting his hand. "Friends and family all do."

"She would know that if she showed up to our wedding," Kelly jabbed.

Cahira shook Mickey's firm, calloused hand.

"Nice to meet you, Mickey. You can call me Cat."

The three stood silent for several beats before Mickey began the conversation again.

"Well, everyone is outside on the patio since it's such a nice day," Mickey spoke. "Here, Cat, let me take those for you."

Mickey gathered up the gifts, trying to balance them in his hands.

"Wow, Teagan will be thrilled," Mickey added, placing the presents on a table with others.

"Over the top, Cat?" Kelly asked.

"I don't think so," Cahira answered humbly.

"Come on out, Cat," Mickey offered, holding open the door to the patio.

Cahira knew her sister's glare was on her as she moved. Finally, she walked out onto the large wooden deck, where all eyes turned to greet her. Strangers gave her the once over as she was led to an empty table with an umbrella. Kelly placed the bowl of chips in the center of the table and sat across from where Cahira planted herself. Silence reigned once again as the sisters looked at each other.

"Can I get you something to drink?" Mickey offered.

"A bottle of water is fine, please," Cahira asked cordially.

"How about you, Kel?" Mickey asked, placing his hand on her shoulder.

"I'll take a beer," Kelly responded without breaking eye contact with Cahira.

"Gotcha," Mickey said, backing away from the table.

"You don't have to be here," Kelly muttered.

"I'm trying, Kelly, but I'll go if you don't want me to be here."

"Too late." Kelly sighed.

A thundering herd of stomping feet came up the steps to the deck as heads of children appeared, with one rushing over to Kelly and throwing her arms around her waist.

"Mommy!" Teagan squealed. "I went the highest on the swing set! Donovan said he did, but my legs got higher than his, I know it."

"Great job, honey." Kelly smiled, kissing the top of Teagan's head.

Cahira looked at the little girl, her long red hair framing her freckled face and blue eyes. Cahira could swear she looked at a picture of her younger self. The girl looked over at Cahira quizzically.

"Who is she?"

"This—" Kelly hesitated. "This is my sister. Your Aunt Cahira."

"Aunt Cat?" Teagan beamed. She rushed Cahira and gave her an embrace. "I'm so happy you came!"

Cahira put her arms around the girl as Teagan squeezed her. Cahira's eyes caught Kelly's as Teagan held on tightly.

"It's nice to meet you too," Cahira added. "Happy birthday!"

"I knew if I asked Mom, you would come," the girl insisted. "Mom said not to get my hopes up, but I knew you would be here."

"Why don't you go with your cousins and friends, Teagan? I think Aunt Monica was setting up a game in the living room for you all to play."

"Are you going to come in and watch?" Teagan asked Cahira.

"I will," Cahira agreed. "First, I think I'm going to sit and talk to your mom for a bit."

"Don't be too long!" Teagan yelled as she raced inside.

Cahira looked over at Kelly as her sister watched Teagan go. Once the door had closed, Kelly's gaze turned back in Cahira's direction.

"She's beautiful, Kelly," Cahira said.

"Are you just saying that because she looks just like you?" Kelly stated.

"Of course not. Don't be ridiculous. If one of us had a child, you knew there was a chance they would have red hair. It ran in Mom's family, Grandma had it, and so did Dad."

Mickey appeared, holding the water bottle and a cold Corona. He placed each down on the table.

"The kids are having a dance party in there," Mickey added. "You should go and check it out. It's adorable. Donovan is leaping and spinning all over the place."

"I'll be right in," Kelly said, rising from the bench. "Are you coming in?" she asked Cahira.

"You go ahead," Cahira replied. "I'll be there in a minute or two."

Kelly strode to the door and entered the house, leaving Mickey outside with Cahira. Cahira twisted the cap off the water bottle and took a big swig.

"I shouldn't have come," she sighed.

"No, no," Mickey insisted, sitting on the bench. "I know there are some hard feelings between you two. Kelly hardly talks about it, so I don't know all the details, but I know it's been hard for her—probably for both of you. But, on the other hand, you have to start somewhere, right? So stick around for a little bit and give her a chance. Besides, I haven't even started the hamburgers and hot dogs yet, and you don't want to miss out on the cake. Blue Velvet from Carousel Cakes. It's the best around."

Cahira sat back and sighed again.

"Well, how can I pass up hot dogs and cake?"

"Great," Mickey said, slapping his hands together. He looked over to his right over the side of the deck.

"Oh, and it looks like my brother just got here. You'll want to meet him. Up here!" he shouted down. "Let me just run and grab those beers I had."

Cahira sat idly at the table, the umbrella blocking most of the sun from her eyes. She heard footsteps coming up the stairs, but the view of the man's face was obscured by the glare until he made his way over to her table.

"Well, hello, Wonder Woman." He smiled, looking down at Cahira.

"You're kidding me with this, right?" Cahira said with an eye roll.

"Fancy meeting you at my niece's birthday party," Eddie said, sitting across from Cahira.

"Fancy meeting YOU at my niece's birthday party," Cahira retorted.

Eddie sat back and thought for a moment before leaning forward.

"You're Kelly's sister? I thought she was just making you up." Eddie chuckled.

"No, the legends are true," she answered, sipping her water.

"No upscale whiskey today?"

"It's a little early for me," Cahira told him.

Mickey arrived at the table holding a beer and a bottle of Guinness.

"Nice of you to show up, brother," Mickey said, handing the Guinness to Eddie.

"I had to check on that job over in Warwick to make sure everything showed up," Eddie answered, pulling out his church key and popping the bottlecap off. "Looks like we're good to go for Monday."

"Oh, great." Eddie added, "So this is Kelly's sister, Cahira—am I saying that right? This is my brother, Eamon."

"Everyone calls me Eddie." He smiled.

"That's what I hear," Cahira answered. "You can call me Cat."

"I wish I had known that," Eddie said, sipping from his bottle. "It would have made things easier."

"What are you talking about?" Mickey said, confused.

"This is Wonder Woman," Eddie said, pointing the neck of his bottle at Cahira.

"Oh geez," Cahira groaned.

"You mean from last night?" Mickey said in disbelief. "I thought he was telling another drunk-at-Millie's tale. So you really broke Jimmy Reynolds's arm with one hit?"

"I see Monroe is still a small town," Cahira said, shaking her head. "I didn't break his arm. It was just a well-placed blow to make it feel numb. He came at me after I called him out for harassing that girl. He got what he deserved, probably far less."

"I don't know," Eddie interjected. "Harriman PD came after you left Millie's and took statements. They went and busted Jimmy at his parent's house this morning."

"Good," Cahira said smugly.

Kelly's voice could be heard yelling from the kitchen.

"Mickey! I could use a hand in here!"

"Duty calls." Mickey shrugged as he walked into the house.

Cahira looked over at Eddie and studied him. His gray eyes were unlike any she had seen before. Almost steel, looking straight at her, but with a gentleness behind them that she did not commonly experience. He sat confidently, pulling his beer bottle to his lips before placing it down and smiling. His hands indicated manual work, and on this warmer-than-normal day in April, his t-shirt clung to his body, providing Cahira with a hint of his musculature and definition.

"So, how is it that I haven't met you before last night?" Eddie asked.

"Is that what last night was? A meeting? I think you could hardly call it anything like that."

"It's just that Mickey and Kelly have been married for years now, Teagan is four, and I don't recall seeing you at holiday parties, weddings, or anything like that. Seems a little odd to me."

Eddie smiled as Cahira simply stared back at him.

"It's complicated," Cahira said tersely.

"I imagine it is." Eddie nodded. "The few times Kelly has mentioned you, it didn't sound like you two see eye to eye much. It just made me wonder about you."

"Is this how you always talk to people you just met at a party? No wonder you're alone."

"Who says I'm alone?" Eddie remarked, sitting back in his chair.

"No offense, sport, but it's pretty easy to see," Cahira stated. "No wedding ring, or even a sign that you remove the band when you're working a contracting job. Two-day stubble, so you have no one prodding you to shave or dress up for a party, and the way you sat back defensively and crossed your arms just now means I'm hitting too close to home for your liking. Do you want me to go on?"

"Nah, I think you covered it all." Eddie laughed. "Are you a shrink?"

"I'm just someone that has learned how to read people pretty well," Cahira admitted.

"Something tells me you're excellent at almost everything you do," Eddie flirted.

"Guilty as charged," Cahira responded. "I settle for nothing less."

"So then, why is it that you don't have a ring on your finger?"

"Oh, I'm sure there are lots of reasons for that. As you said, I expect excellence in everything. I guess no one has matched me yet."

"It could be you just haven't met the right person."

Eddie leaned forward in his chair, resting his arms on the table closer to Cahira.

"You're probably right," Cahira added, finishing her water. "I haven't."

Cahira smiled and rose from the table, patting Eddie's folded arms after enjoying sparring with him.

"Where are you going?" Eddie asked, turning around.

Cahira kept moving to the deck door.

"I promised Teagan to go inside and watch her play, and I need some more water," she replied without looking back.

"Getting too warm out here for you?"

Cahira stopped as she turned the doorknob and glanced back over her shoulder.

"Why? Does it feel warm to you?" she asked coyly.

"Much more than when I got here," Eddie answered.

Cahira looked back to the door and smiled, entering the house.

Chapter 8

E ddie spent most of the party following Cahira, physically or just
with his eyes. Meeting her at Millie Malone's had been intriguing
enough, but having her turn up at his niece's party—and her niece's
party—seemed more than just dumb luck to him. Her beauty was un-
questioned. Every guy at the party noticed her, whether they were with
a partner or not. She moved with an air of confidence Eddie rarely came
across in anyone, man or woman, these days, and she had no problem
matching him quip for quip when they interacted.

He attempted several more times to sit near Cahira and engage with
her to better understand her body language. As a contractor, he was
accustomed to dealing with people from all walks of life and knew how
to turn people around who might be resistant to his suggestions. Unfortunately, Cahira proved to be a much greater adversary, batting away his
attempts at humor or charm in ways that often left him speechless.

When Kelly and Mickey retreated to the kitchen to set up the candles
on the birthday cake, Eddie followed them. He walked to the cooler on
the floor, retrieved a nitro can of Guinness, and plucked a pint glass from
the nearby cabinet before popping the can open. He noticed Mickey and
Kelly both staring at him as he did so.

"What?" Eddie questioned, continuing his pour.

"Since when do you use a glass?" Mickey replied as he continued to place candles on the cake.

"It's a nitro can," Eddie said defensively. "Why wouldn't I use a glass?"

"Because you've been drinking it out of the can since we used to pilfer Dad's from the garage when you were seventeen," Mickey told him. "I've never seen you use a glass for beer, ever. How about you, Kel?"

Eddie spied Kelly looking over as she gathered paper plates and plastic forks.

"Can't say I have, Eddie, sorry." She shrugged.

"The two of you are nuts," Eddie huffed as he tossed the empty can into the recycling bin.

Kelly moved into the dining room while Mickey approached Eddie.

"You're really into her, aren't you?" Mickey whispered.

"Who?"

"Who? Don't play dumb, little brother. I've seen that look on your face before. I'm talking about Cat, of course."

"What's not to be into?" Eddie whispered back. "She's funny, seems bright, and is friendly to talk to. Not to mention that she is gorgeous."

"Just be careful what you are doing, Eddie," Mickey added. "It's Kelly's sister, for crying out loud."

"What's that supposed to mean?"

"It means I've heard Kelly complaining about her for years. She has a lot of baggage you may not want to be part of. You see her today; she may be gone for months or years. Hell, we may never see her again. This is the first time I have met her. So just don't get your hopes up, is all."

"I'm just talking to her, Mick, that's all," Eddie remarked.

"Mickey, are you bringing the cake?" Kelly interrupted.

"Yeah, yeah," Mickey answered, lifting the cake up and walking to the dining room.

Eddie followed behind, positioning himself behind Cahira off to the right of the table. She was taller than he had thought, nearing him in height. He glanced at the back of her neck, seeing the slender length leading to her shoulder where just the hint of ink from a tattoo peeked out from beneath her dress, which intrigued him more.

"It's not polite to stare," Cahira said without looking back.

"I'm looking at the birthday girl," Eddie answered quickly.

"No, you aren't," Cahira added. "You're looking to see my tattoo, and you've been staring at me all day."

"How did you—" Eddie began before the interruption of the beginning of "Happy Birthday."

Once the song was sung, and Teagan gleefully blew out her candles to applause, Cahira turned to face Eddie. Her body was inches from his, each person in the other's personal space.

"I see a lot of things, Eddie," Cahira said with a sly grin.

She slid past him, her dress lightly brushing against his body as she moved. Eddie gazed at her as she went to the kitchen before he quickly followed her. He found her pouring a cup of coffee from the carafe on the table.

"Can I get a cup of that?" Eddie pointed at the carafe.

"Sure," Cahira said, "but you have a whole pint in your hands too."

"Oh, I guess I forgot," Eddie said sheepishly.

Cahira left the insulated cup on the table and poured herself another, fitting the cap on top, before she wandered out the patio door to sit outside. Eddie snatched the hot cup up in his free hand before moving to the door, working with his knee to pop it open so he could also slip out.

Cahira sat on the far end of the porch, looking out over the dimming landscape as she sipped her coffee. Eddie sat at the picnic table across from her, causing Cahira to turn and look at him before gazing back at the landscape.

"Is it okay that I join you out here?" Eddie questioned.

"You're a big boy. You don't need my permission," Cahira told him without looking back.

"Wow," Eddie answered before drinking his pint.

"Something wrong?" Cahira asked, pivoting to face him.

"Are you always this friendly to people?"

Cahira's eyes widened more than Eddie had expected.

"What do you mean?"

"I've been trying to be nice and friendly since you're the new person here who doesn't know anyone, but every time I say something, you shoot me down with some snarky response."

"Do people still say snarky?" Cahira quipped.

"Geez, I just thought it would be nice to get to know you, is all."

Eddie downed the rest of his pint and slammed the glass on the table, causing the coffee cups to jump. He expected a surprised response from Cahira, but she sat calmly and sipped her coffee.

"Forget it," Eddie spoke, shaking his head. He rose from the table and began to move toward the back door.

"Wait!" Cahira yelled, stopping him in his tracks. "Come back."

Eddie took three steps toward the table and eyed Cahira.

"Sit." She pointed.

Eddie peered, unsure of what to do.

"Please, I'm being sincere now," Cahira added. "I know, it's not always easy to tell."

Eddie slid across the picnic table, watching as Cahira moved her red hair from in front of her face.

"I'm not very good at the party thing or socializing like this," Cahira admitted.

"You're not kidding," Eddie said, annoyed.

"I deserve that." Cahira nodded. "I don't get out much to do things like this."

"Maybe you should so you get some practice."

"That's kind of why I'm here now," Cahira admitted. "I've been a pretty shitty sister, aunt, sister-in-law, and friend for a long time."

"Is it that you just don't want to do that stuff or don't have the time to do it?"

"A little of both," Cahira admitted.

For the first time all day, Eddie noticed Cahira soften a bit.

"What do you do for a living?" Eddie inquired, blowing on his coffee.

"I work long days and travel a lot," Cahira replied.

"That doesn't answer my question. You could work on a fishing boat and do that."

"Would it be so bad if I did that?"

"Not at all," Eddie told her as he stood. He moved to the other side of the table to stand in front of Cahira. "You're clearly quick enough to do it, but you don't have the gnarly hands of the guys I have seen doing that for a living. Those guys toss hundreds of pounds each day."

Cahira looked into the palms of her hands before flipping them back over.

"You don't think I'm strong enough to do it, do you? Your friend Jimmy Reynolds might feel differently."

"He's hardly my friend, but that's beside the point."

Eddie watched as Cahira moved their coffee cups out of the way.

"Come on," she said to Eddie, pointing to the seat next to her while she propped her arm on the table.

"What? You want to arm wrestle me?" Eddie said, laughing. "I'm not going to do that."

"Why not?" Cahira asked. "No one is out here to watch, so if you win, you have no one to gloat to, and when you lose, no one will know—except me."

"That's ridiculous. I do not arm wrestle—"

"Think hard about the words that come out of your mouth next," Cahira warned. "If you say you aren't going to do it because I'm a woman, I'm punching you in the throat. Let's go."

Eddie saw Cahira pat the table with her palm and sighed.

"You know I have nothing to gain by doing this," Eddie said as he rolled up his sleeve slightly. "Perhaps we should up the stakes a bit."

"Sure, whatever you want, tough guy," Cahira said. "What's the bet?"

"If I win, I get to take you out for dinner," Eddie challenged.

"And when I win?" Cahira said, staring Eddie in the eyes.

"What would you like?"

Eddie looked on as Cahira eyed him up and down.

"When I win, you go and get yourself cleaned up."

"That's hardly a big bet," Eddie scoffed. "I do shower every day, you know."

"I'm not talking about showering," Cahira spoke. "You get your hair cut, a good shave, and a manicure to clean up those paws of yours. This way, any woman unfortunate enough to come across you will think you at least take care of yourself nicely."

"I'm not getting a manicure," Eddie answered defensively.

"No one's asking you to get glitter nail polish, Eddie." Cahira laughed. "Plenty of men go for manicures all the time. So crawl into the twenty-first century. Is it a bet or not?"

"Fine," Eddie grumped, putting his arm up. "I hope you brought another dress to wear when I take you out."

"I didn't realize Burger King had a dress code," Cahira mocked. "Are we ready to do this?"

Eddie opened his hand as Cahira wove hers into his. He worked to get a good grip, wrapping his large paw over hers so that it nearly enveloped it.

"I'm not a China doll, trust me," Cahira mocked. "You won't break me by gripping my hand. I don't want you crying when you lose that you were afraid to take my hand correctly."

Eddie grinned as he held her tightly, shifting his weight so his right foot moved closer to Cahira.

"Your body is too far from the table," Cahira advised. "You won't be able to get your shoulder into it."

"What?" Eddie said.

Cahira tugged on his arm as Eddie's body inched closer to her and the table.

"I want a fair fight, so there's no whining and complaining." She smiled.

Cahira opened and closed her hand on Eddie's several times as she positioned herself until they both appeared ready. His face was inches from hers, and he noticed her wrap her long fingers over the nail of her thumb.

"You want to count it off?" she asked.

"Sure," Eddie smiled. "This is your last opportunity to back out and concede."

"Start counting," Cahira stated, narrowing her eyes.

"One... Two... Three," he said.

Her strength immediately took Eddie by surprise. He watched as a determined look shaded over Cahira's face. Her palm turned inward before Eddie could react, forcing his hand near to hitting the table. Only a rapid reaction saved him from a quick defeat as he struggled to regain position, moving his arm back to starting position as he strained.

"Impressive," Cahira grunted as she held her position.

"I'm glad I can impress you," Eddie snorted. "That's one in my favor."

"Don't get...cocky," Cahira replied, moving his arm back downward.

"Oh, you have no idea how I can be," Eddie told her as he fought back again.

Cahira's wrist dropped back when Eddie gained ground. His biceps and forearm strained as he worked on finishing off the match, realizing he was getting close to victory. However, when he looked over at Cahira, she still held that air of confidence.

Muscles straining and teeth gritting, Eddie worked hard to attempt to win, but couldn't bring himself to the conclusion. It was as if she was toying with him, teasing him all the while, knowing she could finish him at any time. Eddie felt Cahira's hand slide up so that her palm gripped the top of his hand. Realizing she had gained leverage over him, Eddie's biceps burned as they attempted to fight back. He swore he felt Cahira's index finger slowly caressing his. His eyes shot to hers and locked on her as a sly grin passed over her lips. Her hand top rolled over his and hooked, curling her wrist inwards. She leaned in, bringing her face so close to Eddie's he could feel her sweet breath on his cheeks.

Cahira dragged Eddie toward her as she pulled his arm down, getting greater leverage and leaning forward to pin him to the table. Cahira sprang back, breathing rapidly, while Eddie collapsed, his head resting with his worn-out arm on the table.

"Was it good for you?" Cahira gasped out.

"It was a little quick for me," Eddie answered, looking over at Cahira and seeing her cheeks lightly flushed.

"That's all on you," Cahira told him. "You need to work on your stamina."

"Thanks for the feedback."

"I hope you know a good barber." She chuckled, standing up and moving next to Eddie. "And I'm sure Kelly can recommend a spa for you for those nails. I can't wait to see it."

"Oh?" Eddie answered, lifting his head off the table eagerly. "You mean you're sticking around for a bit?"

"I thought you were taking me to dinner."

"That was supposed to be if I won," Eddie said, taking a more substantial interest in the conversation.

"What fun would it be for me if you cleaned yourself up and I didn't get something out of it?"

"Well, when, where, and how do I get in touch with you?"

"Boy, you must do this even less often than I do," Cahira said, walking toward the patio door. "You're the local here. You arrange for all that. Kelly knows how to get a hold of me. Work on your leverage. You're strong, but your technique needs some help."

"Is that something you can help me with?" Eddie inquired.

"Maybe." She smiled.

As Cahira walked into the house, Eddie collapsed his head back onto the table over his sore arm.

Chapter 9

Cahira's presence at Teagan's birthday went better than she had anticipated. The confrontation with Kelly didn't hit the high-tension points that caused her worry, and meeting Teagan elated her beyond her expectations. Instead, it was the back-and-forth with Eddie that had caught her off guard.

Arriving back at her cottage at Bear Mountain gave her more time to think about her conversations with a man unlike any she had come across in a long time. Cahira spent so much time amid others like her that she forgot what it was like to be near a 'nice guy' for a change. Eddie put her at ease, disarming her in a manner that rarely occurred, causing her to pause with concern.

Cahira poured herself some Redbreast she had picked up from Star Liquors when she was in Monroe, savoring the flavor with just one ice cube floating nicely in the nectar. She plucked her earpiece from her purse for the first time that day, surprised that her mind hadn't turned to Badb and work before that moment.

She glanced at her watch and noticed it was after nine p.m. and hesitated before tapping the earphone to contact Badb. It wasn't anything critical that she needed to speak about, but she did want to check in. Her head went to her right ear and patted the device, prompting Badb to pick it up in seconds.

"Hey," Cahira spoke, sitting in one of the lounge chairs in front of the fireplace.

"Everything okay?" Badb asked, concerned.

"Yeah, I was just checking in. It's quiet out here in this cottage, which is nice, but it gets..."

"Gets what?"

"I don't know," Cahira added, shifting in her chair. "A little lonely, I guess."

Silence held on the connection long enough that Cahira piped in again.

"You still there?"

"I am," Badb told her. "I'm in shock that you said you feel lonely. You are by yourself 95 percent of the time and don't seem to mind. I try to invite myself over, and you turn me down. I guess your visit is going well, then?"

"Yes, yes it is," Cahira confirmed. "It was nice. Things with Kelly are still a work in progress, but it was great to meet Teagan; her husband is a good guy. Everyone I met there was friendly."

"You actually talked to other people?" Badb added with surprise.

"I'm not a complete recluse, Badb," Cahira said defensively. "I do know how to socialize. It can be important sometimes. I learned that just like you did."

"I know, but I do go out in public, Cat, and practice that. You tend to lean in the other direction. So who did you talk to?"

"Mickey, Kelly's husband, and Kelly, of course."

"Anyone else? I hope you expanded your horizons beyond that," Badb retorted.

"Will you stop?" Cahira added. "Of course I talked to someone else."

Cahira quietly sipped her Irish whiskey without elaborating.

"So, are you going to tell me more?"

"It was Mickey's brother, Eamon—I mean, Eddie. Of course, no one calls him Eamon."

"Wow, I'm impressed," Badb answered. "And how was that?"

"Interesting," Cahira replied. "He's a contractor who works with Mickey and their other brother. We talked on and off all afternoon, and—"

Cahira cut the conversation short.

"And what?"

"Nothing," Cahira told her, finishing her drink.

"What did you do, Cat?" Badb poked.

"It's silly. I shouldn't have even started to tell you."

"Now that you have, you better finish."

"We arm wrestled, okay?" Cahira spat out.

She heard Badb cackling in her ear.

"Did you let him win?" Badb asked.

"Feck no," Cahira said boldly. "You know me better than that. He was pretty good all on his own, though. I have to give him credit for that."

"So, you humiliated him at a party?"

"No one else was around. If Eddie was embarrassed by his loss, he didn't show it."

"Hmmm," Badb hummed.

"What's that tone for?" Cahira asked. "I thought you would be glad for me."

"I am, Cat. I'm just noticing your voice talking about it, is all. You seem to enjoy his company, maybe more than you usually do when you're around guys."

"You're cracked," Cahira rejected.

The buzz and tapping of the cell phone on the coffee table in front of Cahira grabbed her attention and startled her. She picked it up and noticed a text message from a number she did not recognize.

How's Monday at 6 work for you? I got your number from Kelly, BTW. She gave it to me against her better judgment, as she said.

Cahira allowed a smile and laugh to escape her lips.

"What's so funny?" Badb interrupted.

"Oh, just a message from—"

"You gave him your phone number?" Badb sputtered.

"I didn't, not really," Cahira mumbled. "He asked Kelly for it."

"What are you doing, Cat?"

The seriousness of the pitch of Badb's voice caught Cahira's attention.

"There's nothing to worry about, Badb," Cahira assured. "We're talking. What's wrong with that?"

"You know part of what we do, Cat. Anyone that has a way to contact you can be a potential problem. What do you know about this guy? You met once for a couple of hours. He could be anybody, and your sister gives away personal information on you."

"It's her brother-in-law, Badb. So guys can't have my number? Women give out their phone numbers all the time."

"Not women like us. They don't."

"You know, it's a time like this that I think you're just being jealous of me, Badb," Cahira shot back.

"What? Jealous of what?"

"That I might have someone else to talk to besides you. You're the same with Danny every time I see or talk to him."

"Bollox, Cat. You know me better than that. I'm looking out for you, just like I've always done. If you can't see that, you're worse off than I thought."

Silence deafened the conversation again before Cahira's phone buzzed once more.

Are you in, or do I just have to send you a picture of my nicely polished nails that day?

"I have to go," Cahira spoke.

"Uh huh," Badb answered. "Do what you have to do, Cat."

"I'll be fine, Bee," Cahira assured. "Thank you for looking out for me. Love ya."

"Love ya too," Badb replied before disconnecting.

Cahira picked up her phone and began to text her reply.

I'm in. Will I get a paper crown with my dinner?

Cahira stared at the screen until Eddie replied:

Only if you behave.

She chuckled and quickly answered.

I never promise that. Where shall I meet you?

Eddie's subsequent text offered to come and pick up Cahira wherever she was staying. She looked at the text, tempted to provide the information before deciding better about it. It was safer to meet him out—safer for both of them.

All day Sunday Cahira spent outdoors, walking the grounds at Bear Mountain. Memories of the times her father would take her there, sometimes with Kelly and sometimes without, flooded back to her. She walked over to look at the carousel area, climbed the steps for the fantastic view provided over the not-yet budding trees below, and even through the zoo area, where the animals seemed shocked to find a visitor or two during the cool early spring.

The time enjoying the outdoors brought a clearness to Cahira's thinking that had been lost for a while. Most of her work—security or her 'side job'—rarely took her away from New York City anymore. As a result, she missed the outdoors, even craving for days she spent on assignment with the ARW or her other military work, where she traveled the globe and saw exotic locations, albeit often under stressful circumstances.

Once she returned to her cottage for the night, Cahira texted Kelly to thank her for inviting her to the party. She then typed and re-typed a text several times before she got up the nerve to ask Kelly if they could get together for lunch one day while she was in the area. No reply came immediately, causing her to put her phone down and attempt to busy herself. After mindlessly folding and re-folding her clothes and selecting a dress to wear for dinner with Eddie, Cahira poured herself two fingers of whiskey and sat, leaving her phone out of sight and mind.

The ding of the text reply caught Cahira's attention and had her jumping out of the cushioned seat by the fireplace to see the text. Disappointment crossed her face when she saw the text from Danny.

Want to come out to the house tonight? I'd love to see ya.

Danny's 'I'd love to see ya' was his code for he felt horny and had no easy access to anyone or was too tired to go out. Cahira had long ago made sure no one could see when she read her texts, and she tossed the phone aside to ignore what Danny offered.

When the cell phone buzzed again, Cahira groaned and walked back to where the phone was, figuring Danny would keep at her. But, instead, she saw a reply from Kelly.

Sure. Come by on Tuesday. We can have lunch here.

A grin crossed her face as she sat back, picking up her glass and putting her feet up on the leather ottoman, happy that life looked to be falling into place for a change.

***

Cahira went back and forth with Badb most of the day Monday, covering needs for new clients at the security firm, talking about expenses and new hires, training updates, and more. Calls went on until late in the afternoon, longer than Cahira anticipated. Once it reached four p.m., she sighed.

"Have we covered everything today, Bee?" she cut in.

"I have more resumes and background checks to send you if you want to look at them."

"Honestly, no, I don't. You usually take care of this stuff without me. Why the sudden need for my approval?"

"I just thought you might be interested in seeing who we hire for specific projects. You are the expert in most of this stuff, after all."

Cahira recognized the jab as it came in.

"You're just as much the professional as I am, Bee," she retorted. "Probably more so when it comes to this day-to-day stuff. I trust your judgment more than I trust my own."

"Is that so?" Bee chuckled.

"What's so funny?"

"You say you trust my judgment, but when I question you about Danny, your sister, or whatever crush you're feeling right now, you say I'm going too far."

"Christ, Bee. Let's not go down this road again. And, by the way, I'm not crushing on anybody. It was just nice to spend time with someone."

Cahira glanced at her watch again, noting the hour.

"Whatever you say, Cat. Do you want me to send this stuff tonight? I need to make some decisions on things by tomorrow. It would be a big help to me."

Cahira hesitated, considering how best to answer.

"If you really need me to, I can do it," Cahira resigned.

"If you have other plans—" Badb began.

"I do have dinner plans," Cahira rushed out, hoping Badb wouldn't want to deep-dive into details.

"Oh yeah? Anything interesting?"

"Just a place not far from here," Cahira said casually. "I don't want to eat at the inn every night. I want to try different local fares. It gets me out and about."

"Because you're such an out-on-the-town kind of gal?"

"Come on, Bee. You don't have to be that sarcastic with me. Why are you having such a hard time with me getting away? You know I need to do that after a job. I've done it before."

"I don't know, Cat. Something feels different this time. Your head is in a different space. I'm just worried that you may not think straight now."

"I'm fine, Badb," Cahira assured her. "You don't have to worry. I promise you. I'll touch base with you in the morning. Love you."

Cahira took note of Badb's heavy sigh before hanging up and tried not to let it weigh on her as she readied herself for dinner. She picked out one of the few dresses she had packed, a little black dress she routinely brought with her when she traveled since it fit nearly any occasion. Cahira loved how the dress looked and felt, hugging her curves in all the right places. She considered adding a pair of black heels before realizing she would tower over Eddie in them, settling for the black flats she had to keep them on even footing.

Cahira gave herself some extra time to drive over to Chester since she wasn't sure exactly where Christopher's Bistro sat. When she spotted signs for McDonald's and Burger King nearby, a smile crossed her lips, expecting that Eddie chose the location purposely. The sign for the bistro caught her eye just as she drove passed, causing her to curse and turn around before heading back just as the time reached six.

She strode into the restaurant, peering around to try and spot Eddie anywhere. When she didn't see him, she turned to the hostess.

"I'm supposed to meet someone here," Cahira asked, racking her brain to recall Kelly's last name and failing to come up with it.

"Is there a reservation?" the hostess asked politely, smiling.

Pressure built inside Cahira's stomach while attempting to recall the last name.

"I'm sure there is." She chuckled, blushing. "Honestly, I can't remember his last name. I don't suppose there is anything under Eddie on there?"

The woman scanned her list and shook her head.

"I don't see anything. If you want to have a seat at the bar until your friend comes in, you're welcome," the hostess advised.

"Good idea," Cahira added.

She sheepishly made her way over to a barstool, peeling off her cloak and draping it over the back of the chair. The bartender made her way to Cahira, dropping a coaster in front of her.

"Hi there." The young blonde smiled. "What can I get you?"

Cahira looked at the tap options before deciding she needed something more substantial to steel the nerves she suddenly felt. Not spotting any Redbreast on the shelves, she pointed to the bottle of Laphroaig 10-year.

"I'll have the Laphroaig, neat, please," she requested.

"Wow," the bartender said, wide-eyed.

"Something wrong?" Cahira asked.

"Not at all," the bartender replied, reaching for the bottle. "We don't get much call for the Laphroaig, and even fewer women who order it."

The bartender neatly poured out two fingers of the Scotch before adding a splash of water to the beverage and passing the rocks glass to Cahira.

"You clearly know your stuff." The blonde grinned.

"I try," Cahira told her, taking a slow sip. "Thanks."

"Waiting for someone?" the bartender inquired as she ran a bar towel over the space in front of her.

"Yes," Cahira noted. "He's late."

"He," the bartender lamented. "Well, now that's a shame. He clearly doesn't know what he's doing. Be sure to let him know that when he appears."

The front door swung open, and Cahira pivoted to the left to spot Eddie in his leather jacket. He smiled back at Cahira as he walked to her.

"You're late," Cahira said coolly, taking another sip of Scotch.

"Sorry," Eddie added, standing next to her. "The homeowner in Warwick had some questions I had to stay and answer. So I got here as fast as I could."

"Is this him?" the bartender asked as she arrived in front of Cahira and Eddie.

"It is." Cahira nodded.

Cahira watched as the bartender looked Eddie up and down before the blonde turned in her direction.

"You could do better," she said softly, slowly patting Cahira's right hand as it rested on the bar. "If you change your mind, I'm right here."

Cahira smiled, slid a twenty across the counter to pay for her drink, and tipped the bartender before Eddie led her back toward the hostess's podium.

"Was the bartender hitting on you?" Eddie said quietly as they followed the hostess to their table in the far corner.

"Yes," Cahira answered as she moved confidently to the empty chair against the wall, so she faced the entire room. She sat and placed her cloak over the back of the chair.

"Well, if you would rather go back and sit with her..." Eddie chuckled.

"If I get up and go over there at some point, you'll have your answer." Cahira grinned. "I'm willing to give you a shot first."

"Gee, thanks," Eddie answered, shrugging off his leather jacket before he sat facing Cahira. She noted Eddie's eyes scan from her face down, pausing momentarily at her cleavage before moving on.

"You look amazing," he told her. "Much better than I do. What would have happened if I were taking you to Burger King?"

"I might be the best-dressed person there wearing a crown and eating a Whopper Junior."

A waitress appeared, handing Cahira a menu before passing one to Eddie. Cahira scanned the listings but detected Eddie's eyes on her the entire time.

"Don't you know it's not polite to stare? You do that a lot."

"I think only with you," Eddie added.

"I don't know if that's a compliment or creepy," Cahira told him as she put her menu down.

"I was shooting for a compliment. I guess I missed."

"You need to work on your aim."

Cahira picked up her glass, swirling it a bit before sipping.

"I don't know," Eddie responded. "I've never had problems before. I do pretty well when I'm hunting."

"Ah, of course, you hunt," Cahira laughed.

"What's that supposed to mean?"

"Nothing at all," Cahira answered. "I know it's a thing up here for some people."

"My brothers and I have been doing it since we were kids," Eddie said proudly. "Guns and bow hunting. We mainly go for deer, but we've gone out for other animals. Have you ever been hunting or fired a weapon?"

Cahira maintained her cool, taking a sip of her glass of water while uncrossing and recrossing her legs.

"I've hunted before and fired a weapon. So it's not just for he-men like you."

"Not at all," Eddie defended. "I know lots of women hunters. You just don't . . . I don't know. You don't look the part, I guess."

"And what part do I look like, Eddie?"

Cahira leaned slightly across the table, staring into Eddie's gray eyes.

"You look like a city gal—refined, used to the better things in life. You don't seem as if you're the type to trudge through the woods for hours in combat boots and camouflage with a rifle or bow."

"Oh, you don't know me at all," Cahira purred. "You'd be surprised at what I like and what I do."

Cahira spotted Eddie's gulp before he shook it off and grinned.

"It takes a lot to shock me," Eddie answered confidently.

"I'll keep that in mind."

Cahira enjoyed the meal and banter with Eddie as they went through a shared appetizer of Korean barbecue wings and then entrées. Cahira ate a perfectly medium-rare ribeye, potatoes, and broccoli. When she polished off the last morsel on her plate, she spotted Eddie watching her.

"You're staring again," Cahira added, wiping her face with the white linen napkin from her lap.

"I'm sorry, really," Eddie apologized, tossing his napkin on the table next to his plate of half-eaten chicken. "It's not often I sit across from a woman who can clean a plate as well as you did."

"You're pretty easily impressed, Eddie," Cahira answered, sitting back in her chair.

"Oh, I don't know about that. You haven't given me much information about yourself to be impressed with. I've mostly talked about myself all night."

"There's not really much to tell about me," Cahira said. "At least not that I want to say in a public place."

"Really? I didn't peg you as the shy type."

"You haven't pegged me at all. I'm far from shy. I'm particular about who I let in, is all."

"Interesting," Eddie spoke. He took the last sip of his IPA, leaving nothing but stray foam in the glass. "So, does that mean I'm not being let in?"

Cahira crossed her arms under her chest and smiled before leaning forward again, leaving her crossed arms where there were.

"Are you asking me something, Eddie?" she whispered.

The waitress appeared at the table, holding a small placard.

"Would either of you like dessert?" she asked.

Cahira chuckled as Eddie fumbled to regain his composure.

"Um . . . Did you want something?" Eddie inquired.

"I might have room left for dessert," Cahira told him, running her red fingernail over the rim of her empty rocks glass.

"Can we get two pieces of Key Lime pie—to go," Eddie hurried. "And the check?"

Chapter 10

E ddie impatiently waited for the boxed-up desserts and check to arrive at the table. He looked on as Cahira casually sat back in her chair, taking slow sips of the water she had left in her glass. She had toyed with him throughout the meal, and now he couldn't wait to get out of the confines of the restaurant to see how the rest of the evening might play out.

He hurriedly laid cash into the small folder with the check before getting up and putting his jacket on. He watched as Cahira draped her dark cloak over herself, clipping the collar with a Celtic symbol he was unfamiliar with.

"Interesting coat," Eddie commented as they walked toward the front door. "It reminds me of a witch or sorceress."

"Maybe I'm casting a spell on you," Cahira said, smiling as she moved past Eddie when he held the door for her.

"I don't think there is any doubt about that," Eddie replied as he stepped to catch up to Cahira. She waited next to her car as he came up next to her.

"Thank you for dinner," Cahira said calmly. Eddie saw her key fob in her hand already.

"Oh, you're welcome. I mean, you won fair and square, right?"

"I did indeed," Cahira crowed. She pressed the key to unlock the door and climbed into the front seat.

"Do you want your dessert?" Eddie asked, holding up the white plastic bag.

"Of course," Cahira answered, taking the bag from him.

Disappointment enveloped Eddie as he looked to see where he had parked his truck.

"I guess I'll see you around then," he said, dejected.

"Aren't you coming for dessert?" Cahira questioned.

"Oh, I thought maybe you just wanted to—"

"You give up too easily, Eddie. Follow me, and we can go back to where I am staying. See if you can keep up."

"Where are you staying?" he asked. "In case we get separated."

Cahira flashed a Cheshire Cat smile.

"I guess it's on you to stay with me. You've had no problem keeping your eyes on me all night. See if you can do it now—when it counts."

Eddie raced to his truck, throwing himself behind the wheel and starting it up while keeping an eye to see if Cahira had pulled out yet. When he spied her Subaru moving, he took off, working to keep up with her as she made her way onto Route 17.

Thankful for light traffic on the highway, Eddie worked his way steadily so he stayed behind Cahira's vehicle. When she veered off 17 and headed up Route 6, the age of his truck showed as it struggled to keep the pace going uphill. He had fallen back a bit from Cahira but proved capable of seeing her car, even if it was a few positions ahead of him.

When they hit the traffic circle, Eddie wondered if Cahira planned to take him down the Palisades Parkway toward New York City. He prepared to turn there until Cahira continued around the circle and headed toward Bear Mountain. Eddie jolted the position of his truck, cutting off the van behind him that angrily beeped before he turned to follow Cahira.

He watched intently as they neared the Bear Mountain exit, and Eddie sighed, relieved when he saw her get off and drive toward the inn. She pulled in front of one of the cottages just moments before Eddie arrived. The dim bulb glowing from in front of the cabin served to illuminate the cloaked shadow Cahira cast.

"Nice job," she said as he approached her figure.

"I wasn't sure I would make it." Eddie laughed as Cahira opened the cabin door.

"I had faith in you," Cahira said confidently.

Eddie followed her inside, taking in the vast main room as Cahira steered herself toward the kitchen.

"Is there anyone else staying here?" Eddie asked.

"No, I rented the entire place," Cahira answered. "Do you want anything to drink?"

"The whole place? I'm impressed."

"Why?" Cahira answered as she draped her cloak over the back of one of the chairs before handing a can of Guinness to Eddie.

"It's just that I know these places are expensive," Eddie added. "We bid on some renovation work when they were doing them."

"It was worth the expense to have the privacy. Besides, it's only money."

Cahira popped her can of Guinness open and sipped.

"I find that it's easy for people who have a lot of money to say things like that," Eddie countered as he sat.

"There's some truth to that." Cahira nodded. "But I wasn't always in this position. I had to work for it."

"Doing whatever it is that you do?"

"What does that mean?" she asked.

Eddie noticed Cahira had kicked off her shoes and stretched her black nylon-covered legs in front of her before propping them on an ottoman.

"It's just that no one seems to know much about you, including your sister," Eddie added.

"You asked Kelly about me?"

"Of course I did," Eddie told her. "Combine what she told me and what little you have shared with me tonight, and I know that they call you Cat because you were always limber and agile. There's nothing besides that, and that you left home when you graduated from high school."

"My life hasn't been all that interesting," Cahira stated. "It certainly isn't worth rehashing for you. Why can't we just have a nice night and enjoy each other's company?"

"I thought we were doing that," Eddie replied.

"Then why do I have to answer a bunch of questions about myself?"

"It's part of the *enjoying each other's company* thing, Cat," Eddie added. "I told you plenty about myself. Letting someone else in a little bit is part of getting to know you."

Eddie watched as Cahira nodded slightly toward him.

"Okay, that's fair," Cahira agreed. "You can ask me one question, and I'll answer it honestly."

"Wow, don't go crazy or anything, Cat," Eddie mocked.

"Fine, don't ask me anything," she shot back.

"Wait." Eddie put up his hands. "Okay, where did you go after high school? Kelly said you fell off the face of the earth, and she didn't hear from you until years later."

Cahira took a long draw on her Guinness before placing the can on the small table beside her chair.

"I went looking for my father," she answered.

Eddie sat back in his chair, bouncing before he leaned forward.

"Kelly said he was dead."

"He wasn't," Cahira responded. "At least not back then. Maybe not even now, as far as I know. He was in Ireland, right where I expected him to be. But, boy, I'll never forget his face when I showed up at his front door. Surprise, shock, anger, sadness, and happiness all rolled into one."

"How come you never told Kelly that? That he was alive?" Eddie asked.

"He asked me not to tell anyone, so I didn't. I thought it would be great living with him again, and it was, right up until—"

A pall came over Cahira's face when she cut herself off.

"Until what?"

"Until I woke up one morning, and he was gone—again. No note, no indications of where he went or why he left. After three months of living with him, he vanished again without a trace. No one knew where he went. He left me there, eighteen years old, with no money, to fend for myself. So I did. I haven't seen or heard from him since."

"What did you do after that?" Eddie asked.

Cahira smiled at him and rose from her chair.

"I told you one question," she spoke as she stood before Eddie.

"If we don't have a conversation, what will we do?"

Cahira leaned into Eddie as he sat, pressing her body firmly to his, her lips poised and ready.

"Do I have to think of everything?" she whispered before pressing her mouth on Eddie's.

Caught off guard, Eddie's brain hit pause for a moment until his lips and body began to respond to Cahira's. His arms enveloped her, holding her hips as they kissed before their initial break. Eddie peered at Cahira as her eyes opened, and she sighed.

"You're a good kisser," she said quietly. "I wonder what else you are good at."

Cahira stood before Eddie, kicking off her shoes before walking away from him and toward one of the bedrooms. Frozen in his chair, he finally kickstarted himself up and propelled toward the bedroom. He reached the doorframe to see Cahira standing beside the bed, her back to him.

"I was wondering how long it would take you to catch up." She laughed. "Do you think you could help me with this zipper?"

This time, Eddie didn't take the time to consider it.

He marched over behind Cahira as she took her hair and gently moved it aside so Eddie could access the small zipper at the back of her black dress. His fingers gripped it and slowly made their way down the trail, the sound echoing in the room until it reached the small of her back.

Cahira shrugged out of the dress, leaving it in a heap on the floor before she turned to face Eddie. She stood before him and placed her index finger under his chin, beckoning his lips back to hers as she dragged the nail across his cheek. The kiss began as soft and sensual and accelerated quickly to something with greater intent.

"One of us is way overdressed," Cahira noted as her fingers made quick work of the buttons on Eddie's shirt before she pulled it from his body.

"Are you always this aggressive?" Eddie asked, throwing his shirt onto the pile of clothing accumulating on the floor as Cahira went for his belt.

"When I know what I want, I go after it," she purred hungrily. She tugged on Eddie's khakis, dropping them down around his ankles, leaving him in nothing more than his navy-blue boxer briefs.

"I don't see any reason to wait."

Cahira's hand moved over Eddie's abs down to the waistband of his briefs before tracing her fingernail over the rigid bulge.

"Fuck, Cat," Eddie hissed through gritted teeth.

"That's the plan," Cat added, stepping away from Eddie to unhook her bra and shed it before lying on the bed. Eddie kept close watch as she peeled off her black stockings, flicking them away with her toes. She then lay across the bed, putting her head back as she shimmied out of her black panties.

Eddie pushed his briefs off before springing onto the bed atop Cat. Straddling her legs, he leaned into her, kissing the delicate curves of her body, starting at her shoulders before his lips reached her breasts. Cat arched her back, pushing an erect nipple up toward Eddie, and he happily obliged, licking at it before tugging it between his teeth to elicit a low moan from Cat, the first sign of bliss that she showed.

Cat's hands went atop Eddie's head, guiding him to keep moving lower as he kissed his way down from her cleavage, across her flat stomach, to her hips before she gripped his hair lightly and held him in place as his face reached the wisps of red hair. Just one kiss and a long, slow lick from Eddie had Cat's engine racing more as she arched closer to him, letting him bury his face into her.

Eddie's tongue probed lightly at first, relishing in the soft wetness he tasted. Then he swirled closer and closer to Cat's clit, jabbing at her most sensitive area before pulsing against it in rhythm. A quick glance to his left allowed Eddie to spy Cat balling up the blanket in her fist as she moaned. She lifted her hips off the mattress, pressing more against Eddie's mouth as his tongue moved up and down against her before her body tensed, and a loud groan escaped her.

Cat collapsed against the mattress as Eddie resumed soft kisses along her inner thighs. His erection raging; he worked to concentrate on her body more so he could stall the inevitable.

"I need more," Cat panted. "The top." She pointed toward the night-stand as Eddie rose from the bed. He pulled the drawer open and found a box of condoms there.

"Nice to see you planned ahead." Eddie laughed as he opened the box.

"Girl Scouts—be prepared," Cat growled as her hands moved over her body.

"I think that's the Boy Scouts," Eddie added, using his teeth to rip the foil packet open.

"Whoever the feck it is, it's good advice," Cat replied. "Hurry up with that thing."

Eddie climbed back to the bed, but before he reached Cat, she rolled over him and had him on his back. His eyes wide, Cat straddled his waist, raking her nails across his chest and making lines down to his waist. Her index finger toyed under the head of his sheathed cock as he groaned.

Eddie watched Cat's movements closely, from how she flipped her hair back to show her blue eyes locked to his as her hand closed into a fist around him and stroked.

"Cat—oh, fuck," Eddie groaned as she tickled the underside of his cock.

"I think I've tortured you enough." Cat grinned before gliding up and slipping him inside her quickly.

Cat's gasp drowned out Eddie's own as she ground her hips against his. Eddie's hands gripped Cat's waist in a futile attempt to control the pace she moved. Finally, when she found her ideal spot and rhythm, she squeezed against him.

Eddie shut his eyes tight, trying to hang on the best he could.

"Open your eyes, Eddie," Cat huffed out. "I want you staring at me now—especially right now."

Eddie looked up at Cat. Her eyes were wide but controlled.

Cat's hands moved to Eddie's chest, where his heart pounded, as she braced herself against him.

The moment Cat squeezed tightly on him as her second orgasm hit, Eddie went over the edge. A guttural sound unlike one he had made in a long time lept from his mouth as he came.

Cat's body collapsed against his, gasping and covered in sweat. Eddie's arms instinctively wrapped around Cat's back as she clung to him, panting. Both were silent for minutes as they regained control of their bodies before Cat rolled off Eddie.

"You okay?" Cat asked, turning to look at him.

Eddie rolled to his side, facing Cat. Red hair fell across half of her face until he reached over and gently moved it to see her profile and complexion. A rosy glow on her cheeks accompanied a light smile on her lips.

"I'm good," Eddie replied, kissing Cat's shoulder. "That's not how I expected things to play out tonight."

"Expect the unexpected with me, Eamon." Cat laughed.

Eddie recoiled a bit when she called him by his given name.

"No one's called me Eamon in forever," he noted.

"I think it suits you better than Eddie," Cat offered. "It means 'wealthy protector' in Gaelic."

Eddie laughed heartily at Cat's statement.

"I hate to disappoint you, but I think I'm pretty far from both."

"Number one," Cat began as she moved up to lean against the pillows and headboard, "I am feeling far from disappointed right now. But, number two, I think you underestimate yourself."

"My bank account may disagree with you."

Eddie rose from the bed and went to the bathroom to dispose of the condom before re-emerging. He stopped in the doorway to look at Cat curled up on the bed, watching him.

"Wealth doesn't have to be measured in dollars," Cat answered.

"Says the woman with a lot of money."

Eddie got on the bed next to Cat, and she immediately fell into his arms, resting her head on his shoulder as the two lay together.

"All I'm saying is that you have a lot of things that I don't have in my life that make you wealthy," Cat said.

Eddie stroked his hand idly through the locks of Cat's hair.

"I'm not so sure about that."

"You have a closeness with your family that I've never had," Cat spoke. "Hell, you're closer to my sister than I am. I couldn't even remember her last name when I got to the restaurant tonight. You have friends that you go out with and trust. I'll bet you're never alone on holidays or birthdays."

"It doesn't have to be that way for you, Cat. You make conscious choices that create those situations."

"I know," Cat lamented. "I'm working on that. That's a richness you have that I envy."

"Okay, I'll concede a bit on the wealth part of my name," Eddie agreed.

"And I'm sure you are a protector as well," Cat added. "You watch out for your friends. I saw you do that at Millie Malone's. You care deeply enough to sacrifice."

"I'm sure you would do the same thing."

Eddie pulled Cat closer, turning his face to hers.

"For people that mean the most to me, I protect them fiercely," Cat noted. "But my inner circle is pretty damn small. So it's not easy to get there."

"So, where does that leave me?" Eddie inquired.

Eddie waited patiently as he saw Cat consider the question. Then, finally, she rolled onto the pillow beside him, turning away from Eddie.

"I'd say you're hovering on the periphery right now, Eamon."

A soft sigh emanated from Cahira, letting Eddie know she had drifted off.

"I guess I'll take that for now," he added quietly before moving to Cahira, putting his arm around her as her back snuggled into him.

Chapter 11

C at awoke with a start, her eyes scanning the room quickly when she heard the noises. She pivoted to her left and spotted Eddie sound asleep, his bare chest exposed as he snored. The bedroom lights were on, Cahira having left them on when she fell asleep after her adventures with Eddie.

A buzzing sound echoed from the main area again, and Cahira jumped out of bed, grabbing the sleep shorts she had worn previously and slipping them on before she made her way into the other room. She flipped off the bedroom lights before peering into the main area, also brightly lit. It was only when she realized that the sound was coming from her phone that Cahira came off high alert.

She plucked her phone from her purse and saw nine unanswered texts from Danny. Each subsequent text got more vulgar and angry as they went on, indicating Danny was probably out drunk somewhere or horny, and upset he couldn't get in touch with Cat.

Cahira deleted the messages and started walking back to the bedroom, shutting off the lights so that the only glow came from her phone screen and the little moon that still shone through one of the windows at three a.m.

The phone buzzed once more, getting Cahira's attention. She looked down and spotted an incoming call, this time from Danny. When she ignored the call, Danny wasted no time trying her again. Then, realizing he would keep it up until she answered, Cahira pressed accept and moved back to the central dark area.

"Finally!" Danny snarled into the phone.

"What the feck do you want, Danny? It's three in the morning."

"Since when does that stop you from answering calls? You've picked up later than this for work or for my calls. Shite, you've shown up at my house at this time. Where are you?"

"Why does it matter where I am?" Cahira spoke, attempting to keep her voice low and under control.

"I went by your place, and they said you were away. They wouldn't let me up, so I didn't know if you were trying to avoid me."

"They aren't going to let you up if I tell them not to," Cahira explained. "And no, I'm not there. I needed to get out of the city for a bit. Can I go now and get back to sleep?"

"Why are you acting like this?" Danny yelled. "Is this still about the job I wanted you to do?"

"Christ, Danny, just let it go. I told you I needed a break—from everything. So give me some time for me for a change."

"Why don't you tell me where you are?" Danny pleaded. "I can come over, crack open some whiskey, maybe smoke a little so you can relax."

"You know I don't do weed," Cahira added abruptly. "It sounds like you are already drunk or high anyway. So you don't need me to help get you there."

"Maybe I wanted to see you and spend some time together."

"That's usually code for you're horny, and the strip club is closed. So go to bed, Danny."

"Can't we talk this out? Wherever you are, I can get there. Did you fly somewhere or drive? I can get a plane to meet you. Maybe we can swing down to St. Martin's for a few days and lie together at the beach."

"I'm not interested, Danny," Cahira said emphatically. "Please, just let me be. I'm not working or playing with you. I want time alone."

"Everything okay?"

Eddie's voice from behind Cahira had her spinning around to look at him. Eddie wiped his eyes, yawned, and stretched in the doorway before taking a couple of steps in Cahira's direction.

"Are you on the phone right now?" Eddie asked.

"Who the feck is that?" Danny barked into the phone. "Are you ridin' some guy? Who is he, Cat?"

"I can't do this right now," Cahira rushed out before hanging up her phone and returning her attention to Eddie.

"I'm sorry. I didn't mean to wake you," Cahira apologized.

"Is everything okay?"

"Yeah, it's fine," Cahira answered, waving her phone. "Just . . . Well, just an old . . . It was nobody."

"That was a lot of yelling for it being nobody," Eddie stated. "An old boyfriend? Or a current one?"

"No one either of us needs to be concerned about," Cahira brushed off. She marched to the kitchen, going into the fridge to grab a water bottle.

"Cat, if there's something you want to tell me about, it's okay," Eddie told her. "I'm a big boy. I can take it."

"Really, it's nothing," Cahira insisted before she bent over and looked into the fridge again. "Let's have some of that pie."

Cahira pulled the two containers holding the slices of pie from the refrigerator and placed them on the kitchen counter. She grabbed a couple of forks and held them up for Eddie to see. She opened one container and jabbed the fork, lifting bits to her mouth. The creamy pie filling melted in her mouth. She took another forkful and held it out for Eddie.

"Cat, what's going on?" he asked seriously.

"I think a half-naked woman is offering you a taste of pie and more, and you seem to be having trouble deciding to accept. This pie is seriously outrageous."

Cahira placed another bite into her mouth, savoring it as Eddie watched. Finally, he audibly sighed before taking the last few steps toward Cahira as she held out another bite for him, placing it on his tongue.

"Well?" Cahira smiled.

"It is good pie," Eddie admitted. "But—"

Before Eddie could get another word out, Cahira leaned in and kissed him deeply. Then, she gently parted from his lips, keeping her face close to his.

"If you want more pie—or something else—you'll have to follow me," Cahira offered, grabbing up the pie containers as she walked to the bedroom.

***

The sound of the shower running in the bathroom sparked Cahira's eyes open. Unaccustomed to overnight guests, she sat up, draping the top sheet over her bare breasts, and looked at the rumpled blankets next to her. Muffled music came from behind the door, but the voice singing along was unmistakably out of key and Eddie's. Cahira smiled as she propped the pillows up behind her and awaited the crooner to emerge from the bathroom.

The door swung as steam escaped the bathroom, and Eddie emerged with a towel wrapped around his waist.

"I didn't mean to wake you," Eddie spoke as he moved toward the bed. "I hope you don't mind. I used the shower. I have to get over to a new client this morning and . . . "

"And you didn't want to smell like you had sex all night?" Cahira grinned.

"Basically," he answered shyly.

Cahira eyed Eddie as he dressed, getting a closer view of his taut muscles from top to bottom. Finally, Eddie turned to face her as he pulled his t-shirt on.

"Now who's doing the staring?" Eddie said, mockingly covering himself quickly.

"You're right. Sorry, I couldn't help myself." Cahira whistled.

Eddie sat on the bed to put his shoes on. Cahira immediately sat behind him, draping her arms over his shoulder before she began to kiss his neck.

"What do you have planned for the day?" Eddie asked as he struggled to pay attention to his shoes.

"I was going to start by seducing you, but it doesn't seem to be going very well," Cahira stated, nibbling on Eddie's right ear.

"Oh, it's working, believe me." Eddie laughed. "You just can't see it from your angle."

"Maybe I can feel it from back here," she purred. Cahira's left hand slipped below his waist to the front of his khakis.

"Keep that up, and I won't be going anywhere," Eddie growled. He turned his head to kiss Cahira and took hold of her left hand to keep it from unzipping his trousers.

"That's the plan," she added deviously.

"I wish I could, but we can't all lounge around in a cottage. I have to go."

Eddie rose from the bed, looking for his leather jacket.

"There's nothing I can do to convince you differently?"

Cahira knelt on the bed, letting the sheet fall from the front of her body, giving Eddie a clearer view of her.

"Oh, there's plenty you could try to do it," Eddie admitted. "But I need to go. Where did I put my jacket?"

Cahira raced from the bed, dashing into the main area before Eddie could get there. By the time he caught up, she had already donned his leather jacket. The sleeves covered her hands, and the length of the black coat hit her waist, just enough to conceal the panties she wore.

"I guess you knew where it was." Eddie smiled.

"I did. And you can have it if you can get it from me," Cat challenged.

"C'mon, Cat, I really do need to get to work."

"Then come over here and take the jacket off me," she taunted. She reached into the left pocket and pulled out his keys, dangling them in front of him.

Eddie reached for Cat, but her agility quickly moved her away from him. She hopped around the room, from furniture piece to piece, sometimes leaping several feet to reach her mark. Finally, frustrated, Eddie stood in the center of the room, defeated. Cat jumped in front of him, placing her hand under his chin so she looked him in the eyes.

"Don't pout," she said, placing the keys in his hands. Cat added a peck on the lips for good measure.

"Are you always this competitive?" Eddie asked, placing his hands on her hips underneath the leather.

"I am," Cahira admitted. "I hate to lose. It's a character flaw, I guess. Don't take it personally. Kelly used to hate playing Monopoly with me."

"If that's the worst of you, I can live with that," Eddie answered. His hands glided up Cat's sides, resting just beneath her breasts.

"No promises," Cat answered.

"Can I have my jacket now?"

"I suppose so." Cat shrugged. She removed the jacket and handed it gently to Eddie, reluctantly giving it up.

Eddie donned the coat, zipping it halfway before pausing.

"Something wrong?" Cat asked.

"No," Eddie said hesitantly. "It's just that it kind of smells like you."

"That's not a bad thing, is it?"

"Not at all," he added with a smile.

"Can I see you later?" Eddie asked as he walked to the door.

"You'd better," Cat said, pausing as Eddie moved just outside to the front porch.

"I'll text you when I finish working."

Eddie moved to Cat and kissed her slowly before backing away, walking backward as he stumbled a bit off the front porch.

"Careful there," Cahira warned, giggling. "I don't want to break you."

Eddie waved as he got to his truck, driving off while watching Cat wave to him casually from the door.

Cat sighed as she returned inside, locking the door behind her before going back to the bedroom and falling onto the pillows. She curled under the blanket, relishing in the warmth it provided. Physically tired, Cat's mind raced not about what usually gave her concern but about her evening with Eddie. Thoughts of how he felt and made her body respond had her heart pumping before exhaustion got the better of her, and she drifted off.

It was hours later before Cat casually stretched and awoke in a tangle of sheets and blanket. She reached for her phone on the nightstand, ignoring the expected messages from Danny and noting a couple from Badb, checking in with her before she spotted that the time was nearly one in the afternoon.

Cat couldn't recall ever sleeping that soundly and sprang from the bed to quickly dress and get out the door so she could drive to Kelly's place for their lunch date. No sooner had she gotten in the car when a text came from her sister:

Are you coming or blowing me off?

Cat replied 'On my way' quickly and started up the Subaru drive over to Monroe. Tuesday afternoon traffic did little to slow her down, and thanks to her GPS, she remembered how to get to Kelly's in just a few minutes. She pulled into the driveway and raced up the front steps, tying her hair back into a ponytail before Kelly answered the door so she didn't look a complete fright.

Kelly pulled the door open and stared back at Cahira.

"I'm sorry I'm a little late," Cahira apologized as she entered the house.

Kelly said nothing, closing the door behind them and leading Cahira up the stairs toward the kitchen. Teagan sat at the table, munching away on raw baby carrots. She beamed at Cahira when she came in.

"Aunt Cat! You made it!" Teagan squealed.

"I did!" Cat answered, pulling up a chair at the table and grabbing a carrot.

"I already had my sandwich," Teagan told her. "I was too hungry. Sorry."

"It's okay," Cat acknowledged. "I'm sorry I missed it. What did you have?"

"PB and J, of course!" Teagan said proudly, showing her hands with grape remnants between her fingers.

"Go wash up," Kelly added, pointing toward the bathroom.

Teagan jumped off her chair and made her way down the hall, allowing Cahira to turn her attention back to her sister, who was opening the refrigerator to gather lunch items.

"I've got some chicken salad," Kelly spoke, her back to Cat. "I hope that's okay."

"Perfect," Cat said. "You know I love it. Can I help you with something?"

"I've got it," Kelly said, placing a nicely prepared platter on the table. Then, she pivoted toward the kitchen counter to grab some rolls.

"You didn't have to go to all this trouble, Kel," Cahira added. "I would have been okay with peanut butter and jelly too."

"Well, it's not often you come for lunch," Kelly replied. "In fact, I don't think you ever have before."

Cat felt the sting of the barb, even though she knew she deserved it.

"No, I don't think I have," Cat added, attempting to ignore the jab. "I'm hoping to change a lot of that."

Kelly went to the refrigerator again, pulling out a couple of cold bottles of iced tea.

"Unless you wanted something else?" Kelly asked. "I don't think I have any Dom Perignon chilling."

"Stop, Kelly," Cat replied. "I'm not like that."

"Well, how would I know that?" Kelly said. She sat across from Cat, lifting the plastic wrap off the top of the pile of chicken salad.

"I'm trying, Kelly. I really am."

"Is that what this is all about?" Kelly said in a hushed voice. "Or is it just to placate your guilt for all the years, Cat? Tell me now. I expect you to break my heart again, but I won't let it happen to my daughter. She doesn't deserve that."

"I'm not trying to hurt anyone," Cat said sincerely. "I know I've been a shitty sister and absentee for a long time. I can't make up for it in just a day or two. Please, just give me a chance."

Kelly placed the chicken salad on one of the rolls before sliding it toward Cat. Cat grabbed some sliced tomato and put it on the sandwich and a strip of bacon before pressing down on the top of the roll. Next, she grabbed a handful of Fritos from the tray and moved the plate in front of her, staring at the sandwich.

"What's wrong?" Kelly asked.

"Do you have any pickles?"

"Ugh, you're still crazy about pickles?" Kelly remarked, scrunching her face.

"Of course!" Cat said. "If I have a sandwich, there needs to be a pickle. I can't believe you never liked them."

"Probably because Dad made us eat the ones he made himself," Kelly said as she went to the fridge. She pulled out a jar of Grillo's half sours and plopped it onto the table. "I can't even stand the smell of them."

"Dad's weren't so bad," Cat said as she fished a pickle and put it on her plate.

"Well, you two were always two peas in a pod, conspiring something," Kelly said, grabbing some potato chips.

"That's not true," Cat added. "He always tried to include you too. You just didn't want to do a lot of that stuff."

"I'm sorry if I chose to go to dance class over fishing and working on the car. You were always the son he never had, Cat. Once he saw how into the self-defense stuff he was always teaching us, that was it. You were his favorite."

"I don't think he had a favorite."

Cat took a bite of the sandwich, savoring the light mix of chicken, mayo, and celery.

"Besides, you were always Mom's favorite anyway," she remarked.

Cat regretted speaking it as soon as the words came out.

"Yeah, right. Maybe Mom's favorite one to bully, talk down to, and ignore for a lifetime," Kelly added.

Cat placed her sandwich on her plate and rose from the table. She took the wooden chair next to Kelly and sat, looking at her sister.

"I can never say how sorry I am about how all that played out, Kel. Mom had issues she didn't know how to deal with that only got worse after Dad left. I ran out of ideas of how to protect you—us—and I couldn't do it anymore. She was going to throw me out of the house after graduation anyway. She made that perfectly clear to me. So, instead of going to the all-night graduation party, I packed a couple of bags, returned to the house, and left. I wasn't able to face you and tell you I was leaving. Seeing you would have made me stay, and I honestly believe I would have killed her one day. I resolved not to take it anymore that day. It may have been cowardly or wrong, but I had to do it."

Kelly turned to face Cat, tears welling in her eyes.

"You didn't say goodbye to me," she whispered. "It was so bad after you left. The first few weeks were torturous. Then, after a while, I just became numb to it. She treated me more like a servant than a daughter right up until the day she died. I hated you, you know, and then, after a while, I just forgot about you. I figured you didn't exist anymore, just like Dad."

"I never forgot about you," Cat admitted, taking Kelly's hand. "I thought about you all the time, everywhere I went. I wanted to reach out to you many times, but I couldn't. I didn't know what to say or do or if you would even want to talk to me."

"Years, Cat. It was years before I finally heard you were alive and in New York, and you still didn't try to contact me. Do you know how that made me feel? Do you know what it's like to feel like everyone in your family doesn't love or want you? So when I was getting married, and Mickey asked if I had a family I wanted to invite, I said no. He was the one who tracked your address down and sent the invitation to you. It was only on the wedding day he told me about it, in case you happened to show up. I told him not to worry because I knew you wouldn't be there. Then when Teagan was born, you didn't show, and Mom died, and you still didn't come around, but it didn't bother me anymore. Dad was gone, Mom was gone, and so were you."

"I wasn't gone," Cahira admitted. "I always kept tabs on you. So I knew what was going on and where you were at. But I was afraid of what you might think, say, or do if I contacted you. And, you should know . . . Dad wasn't gone either."

Kelly looked back at Cat, stunned.

"What? He's alive?"

"I don't know about now," Cat told her. "But back then, when I first left . . . I found him, Kelly. He was living in Ireland, and I went to him. He was living on Grandpa's farm. It shocked the hell out of him to see me standing there. I spent every cent I had squirreled away to get to him."

"Did he tell you why he left us?"

"No," Cat said, shaking her head. "I got up the nerve to ask him once, but all he would tell me was that it was complicated. I always figured it had something to do with Mom. It wasn't long after that conversation that he disappeared again. That was the last I saw of him."

"How long were you there with him? Just a few days?"

"Three months, give or take," Cat told her.

"You were with him that long and never contacted me about it? You couldn't tell me he was alive or that you were? You couldn't tell me to come and meet you in Ireland? I would have run from here too!"

Kelly slammed her hand on the table, causing the food platter to jump and Cat to sit back.

"Is everything all right, Mommy?" Teagan asked from the doorway. "Look, my hands are clean now."

Teagan held up her two hands, wiggling her fingers. Kelly sniffled and smiled, moving from the table toward her daughter.

"Good job, honey," she said, bending down and hugging Teagan. "Can you play for a bit so Aunt Cat and I can keep talking?"

"But I want to show Aunt Cat my room! She didn't get to see it at the party," Teagan whined.

"I promise I'll come over and look at it in a few minutes," Cat added. "You get started, and I'll be there."

"Okay, but don't forget!" Teagan ordered as she raced off down the hall.

Teagan left the kitchen, and Cat turned her attention back to Kelly.

"Kelly, it was all very complicated," Cat attempted to explain. "When I found him—"

"It wasn't difficult, Cat," Kelly hissed. "You didn't want me there. It was always this secret club that you and Dad had, and I was left out. So you figured you could keep him all to yourself while I was home being Cinderella for Mom, doing laundry, cleaning, and everything else she wanted."

Kelly stood, moving to put items in the refrigerator. She shoved trays and bottles back in before slamming the door shut.

"It wasn't that way," Cat replied softly.

"I'll never know now," Kelly shot back. She slumped into the chair across from Cat and stared at her.

The only sound heard was Teagan lightly singing in her bedroom until the movement of the front door startled the sisters out of their conflict.

"Hey Kelly," Eddie spoke as he climbed the stairs. "Sorry to barge in. Mickey said he left an estimate on his desk. I just need to grab it before I go to see—"

Cat spotted Eddie cross the threshold into the kitchen and he paused when his eyes met hers.

"Hey, you." Eddie grinned. "I didn't realize you were coming here today."

"Yeah, Kelly and I are having lunch," Cat said hesitantly, pointing at the spread.

"Ah, right," Eddie added. "Well, I'll let you two get back to your sister stuff."

Eddie walked down the hall toward Mickey's office, leaving the sisters alone again. The two said nothing to each other until Eddie reappeared in the doorway.

"Got it," he said, holding up the papers. "I guess I'll see you later."

"Yeah," both women said, looking at each other before Eddie uncomfortably moved down the stairs and out the door.

Kelly's glare went from Cat toward where Eddie vacated and then back to Cat.

"Is something going on I should know about?"

Cat sat back, sipping her iced tea, hoping to avoid another uncomfortable topic.

"Cat?"

"We had dinner together last night," Cat blurted out.

Kelly sat in stunned silence.

"Where did you go?" she asked, rising from her chair and moving dirty dishes from the sink to the dishwasher.

"Christoper's Bistro in Chester," Cat replied.

"That's a nice place," Kelly said mindlessly. "We've been there a few times."

Kelly kept placing dishes, picking them up, and repositioning them in the dishwasher so everything fit perfectly.

"He thought I might want some company instead of sitting alone at my cottage," Cat explained.

"Of course you would," Kelly said sarcastically. "It's not like you have any family around here you could call to have dinner with. But, then again, I didn't even know where you were staying or anything, so I guess it makes sense you would talk to someone you barely know instead of me. Oh, I forgot—you barely know me too."

Cat rose from her chair and approached her sister.

"I think it's time for me to go," Cat responded.

Cat gathered up her bag and reached for her jacket on the back of her chair.

"Did you sleep with him?" Kelly asked.

"Jesus, Kelly," Cat tried to brush her off.

"That wasn't a no."

Cat roughly pulled her jacket on, zipping up her leather jacket.

"I'm trying to make things better," Cat told her sister.

"You have a funny way of doing that. You show up out of nowhere, captivate my daughter, tell me you spent months with our father, who I thought was dead, mention next to nothing about yourself or where you have been for the last half of my life, and then let me know you're fucking my brother-in-law. Let me know when the 'better' part is coming."

Cat angrily stepped in front of Kelly, looking down at her smaller sister.

"Don't do this. Not this way. Not with Teagan around the corner. She doesn't need to hear us fighting."

"Now you're giving me parenting advice?" Kelly mocked, wiping a tear from her reddened face. "You're right, Cat. It is time for you to go."

Cat walked down the stairs to the front door before Teagan raced out.

"Where are you going? You promised to come to see my room!"

"I'm sorry, Teagan," Cat apologized. "I have to go. Next time I will, for sure."

"There won't be a next time," Kelly said firmly.

Cat nodded somberly and walked out the door, stepping quickly to her car before rapidly departing. She drove aimlessly around Monroe, unsure where to go or what to do. Finally, her car ended up in the parking lot at Millie Malone's, where she sat behind the steering wheel for twenty minutes, replaying the events of lunch in her mind, before she walked into the sparsely populated pub.

A few late lunch/early dinner people occupied booths and tables as Cat made her way toward the bar. She noticed Paddy Walsh's seat empty but sat beside his empty stool, grabbing the attention of Darren.

"Welcome back," he said with a smile. "Your mate isn't here. He already left for the day."

"I'm sorry I missed him," Cat answered. "Can I get a pint, please?"

"Sure thing," Darren told her.

"The restroom?" Cat asked.

"Straight back on the left. Want me to bring the pint over to the booth there?" Darren asked, pointing to the back corner. "I know you sat there last time. You get a better view of the place from there."

"Sure, thanks."

Cat walked down the hall and pushed the door open to the ladies' room, pausing at the sink to look in the mirror. She steeled herself, putting emotions aside as best as possible while practicing breathing. Calmness crept back into her mind and body as she set aside the rattling confrontation with Kelly.

Cat emerged from the rest room walked down the short hall, and spied Darren at that end of the bar. He smiled at her as she crossed the threshold into the pub.

"Your drink is there, and your friend is there too." Darren smiled, nodding toward the booth.

Cat smiled with anticipation of seeing Eddie, but as she neared the booth, a pall came over her face.

"Fancy meeting you here," Danny spoke, raising his pint as he sat in the corner.

Chapter 12

C at strode to the booth, standing before Danny. The self-satisfied grin on his face proved unmistakable.

"What are you doing here?" Cat huffed.

"What? I can't come to see my special girl? Sit, take a load off."

Cat slid into the booth, keeping her distance from Danny so she was more than an arm's length from him.

"You can get closer, you know. We've been much nearer each other than this."

"I'm fine right here," Cat answered. "Why are you here, Danny? How did you know where I am?"

"You think you're the only person in the world who is good at tracking people down?" Danny laughed. He sipped his pint, placing his glass down. "Ah, you can always tell an experienced Irish bartender. He knows how to pour a pint."

"You didn't answer my question," she said harshly.

"I do know people, Cat. Influential people. I remember you mentioning a sister a couple of times. After that, it was easy to find her and then you. I was watching when you left her place. You looked upset. I thought you could use a friend."

"My sister has nothing to do with anything," Cat retorted. "Leave her and her family alone, or I swear—"

"Will you relax, Cat?" Danny said, raising his hands in surrender. "What kind of monster do you think I am?"

"I know what kind of monster you are. You don't do anything without an ulterior motive to get what you want."

"Ah, you know me too well, Cahira." Danny chuckled. "I do have other reasons for being here. But, first, I want to give you another chance to change your mind about the job we discussed."

"I told you no," Cat answered flatly. "Are you daft talking about these things out in public like this?"

"I really wish you would reconsider. There are a lot of benefits to it for both of us, Cat."

"I don't need the money."

Cat placed her hands on the pint glass, slowly spinning it in her palms.

"Not everything is always about money," Danny told her. "Safety and security are important as well. You, of all people, should know that."

"What the feck does that mean?"

"Nothing at all," Danny answered. "Just something for you to think about."

"Are you stupid enough to threaten me, Danny? Has it gone that far?"

"Why would I threaten you? You're my girl, remember? You are my girl, aren't you, Cat?"

"I haven't been your girl for a long time. Even when I thought I was, I wasn't, you prick."

"So, who is he?" Danny said, draining his pint and waving to get Darren's attention.

"Who?" Cat responded.

"The guy in your room at three in the morning, that's who," Danny told her.

Cat opened her mouth and stopped just as Darren arrived at the table.

"My friend, you are a true bar master," Danny said, turning up his brogue. "Another pint for me, please, and could you bring us a couple of shots of 27 YO Redbreast?"

"He doesn't have any," Cat mumbled.

"You know the place that well already, do you?" Danny laughed. "Do you have Powers then? I'm willing to settle."

"You bet," Darren smiled, taking the empty pint glass with him.

"Is it him behind the bar?" Danny said softly. "The voice doesn't seem right to what I heard."

"Stop it, Danny," Cat said coldly.

A din came from the front of the pub as Cat's view immediately moved from Danny to the entrance. Four prominent men in overcoats entered the room, surrounding a dark-haired man not much smaller than Danny.

"What the feck is Lonergan doing here?" Cat said softly to Danny.

"Oh, that's right," Danny snorted. "I got so caught up in everything I forgot to mention that to you. Da and Lonergan are meeting up here. Funny coincidence. Lonergan has a house by the water at Greenwood Lake. He came up here and arranged to meet Da and me to discuss things. They'll be here for a few days. I'd be happy to pass along the itinerary to you."

"You can't do this right here," Cat answered. "Too many witnesses, no easy exits, and there are cameras in the front of the pub."

"It's nice to see your new boyfriend hasn't dulled your instincts. I'm not doing anything. I'm sitting here having a drink."

Darren arrived at the table with a fresh pint for Danny and two shot glasses filled with whiskey.

"Here you go." Darren smiled, placing the drinks down.

"Thank you kindly, sir," Danny replied. "Say, barkeep, I'd like to buy a round for the gents that just sat across the way there if I can. They come from good Irish stock."

"Of course," Darren agreed, walking back to the bar.

Cat scanned the room, looking for potential trouble at all angles. Then, realizing she had no weapons, she scouted for weapons of opportunity if needed. Perhaps Eddie had dulled her instincts.

"Who's coming, Danny?"

Danny moved a shot glass in front of Cahira and smiled.

"Look at you, your senses all tingling. Do you feel the rush yet? Or does that come only after you do it? You're usually wet by the time you get to me."

Danny moved closer to Cahira, placing his hand on her thigh and inching further between her legs. His roaming fingers reached the zipper of Cat's jeans before her right hand moved down to stop him.

"Danny, don't," she insisted, gripping his wrist.

"Are you imagining it right now? How would you do it, Cat?" he whispered, his lips next to her ear.

Cat's hand shook as it held Danny's wrist tightly. Her mind raced with fragmented thoughts of how she would take out Lonergan and his men. She hadn't performed a public execution like that since her days just after the ARW, and even then, it had been planned out weeks ahead of time with everything in place in Morocco, where it was easier for her to disappear into a crowd.

"I can't do this," she murmured. Danny's lips were on her neck as she closed her eyes and saw the scene vividly, Lonergan's chest exploding open as she fired into it after taking out the four henchmen with rapid fire.

"I think you can," he said seductively.

"I said no," Cat shouted with more resolve, her eyes flying open as she shoved Danny away. Her raised voice garnered the attention of others in the pub, including Jack Lonergan.

"Relax, Cat." Danny's attempt to soothe Cat did little to ease her. He tugged at her sleeve to pull her back down next to him in the booth.

"I wasn't expecting you to do anything right now. I just wanted to see how revved up I could get you thinking about it. It didn't take much, I have to say. I have the paperwork in my car if you want it."

A loud clearing of a throat snapped Cat's attention toward Jack Lonergan. He lifted his rocks glass toward Danny, who politely nodded back.

"I can't wait for you to get rid of him," Danny muttered. "The cheeky, smug bastard."

"I have to get out of here," Cat rushed out, forcefully rising from her seat and moving away from Danny.

"Everything good?" Darren asked as Cat sped past the bar.

"I just need some air," Cat gasped, glancing at Lonergan and his men as she went by them, each ogling her differently.

Cat burst through the door into the parking lot, breathing heavily as she bent at the knees to avoid hyperventilating. Light wisps filled the air as she worked to control her breathing, closing her eyes tightly. Then she felt a hand on her shoulder and prepared to react, pulling away expecting to see Danny. But instead, she spotted his father with Benny next to him.

"Are you okay, darlin'?" the old man asked. "What are you doing here?"

"Seanóir," Cat responded. "I'm okay. I—I'm up here visiting family. I didn't know you would be here. Danny is—"

"Right here, Da," Danny interrupted as he walked toward Cat. His swagger angered Cat, and she lightly pounded her balled-up fist on her thigh as he approached.

"Jack Lonergan is here already," Danny advised. "I bought him a drink, so he should be in a good mood."

"Excellent," Quinn spoke, patting his son on the shoulder. "We won't talk specifics tonight. Not out in the open like this. He has us meeting at his place on Friday."

"I don't feel good about that, Da. Meeting him trapped at his place sets us up. We're at his mercy there with no easy escape. Suppose he tries something?"

"He's not going to do anything, Danny. We're working out details to put the nonsense behind us. Not everything is a plot against us."

"Still, I would feel better if we had extra protection. No offense, Benny, but he'll have a compound full of people against just you," Danny cautioned. "I think Cat should come with us."

Cat stood shocked, unable to respond immediately. Quinn glanced over to gauge her reaction.

"She's not here working, Danny," Quinn told him. "I don't want to force her into anything."

"Forced?" Danny guffawed. "She loves this stuff, and it's not like we wouldn't pay her well for her time."

All eyes turned to Cat, waiting for her to reply.

"It's up to you," Quinn said softly, placing his hand on hers. "You are never under any obligation to work for us. You know that."

Cahira nodded slowly toward Quinn, avoiding eye contact with Danny.

"You know I'd do anything for you, Seanóir. Just tell me when and where."

"Thank you, Cahira." Quinn smiled. "I'll have Danny get you the details. We're staying at a place nearby. You can meet us there, and we'll drive over together."

"Of course," Cat said solemnly.

"Do you want to join us now?" Quinn asked. "Drinks and dinner. Strictly social."

"No, thank you, Seanóir," Cat replied. "I . . . I already have plans. I'll wait to hear from you."

Quinn opened his arms, and Cat stepped in to hug him. She looked over his shoulder at Danny, who beamed, knowing he had gotten what he had hoped for all along.

Cat stepped back from the embrace, smiled at Benny, then scowled at Danny before making her way toward her car. No sooner had she gone the few yards to her Subaru when the familiar pickup truck pulled into the parking lot next to her.

"This just keeps getting better," Cat grumbled under her breath.

Eddie paced over to Cat, putting his hands on her waist and bending to kiss her before she could react. The kiss overwhelmed her, and she didn't want it to stop as she wrapped her hands around his neck.

"I didn't think I would run into you here," Eddie said with surprise. "I was meeting the guys here for a drink before I came to see you."

Cahira looked to her left, toward the entrance to Millie Malone's. She spied Quinn and Benny going inside, but Danny held the door open for them, looking at Cat and Eddie while he did so.

Cat calmed her nerves, putting out of her mind what Danny might be considering while watching Eddie kiss her.

"You okay?" Eddie asked. "You look a little on edge."

"Just worn out, I guess," Cat admitted as Danny slowly moved out of her sight, and she could turn her attention back to Eddie.

"It wasn't a great lunch with Kelly," Cat spoke. "There are a lot of hard feelings that still need to be worked out."

"I'm sorry," Eddie told her, taking her in his arms. "Why don't you come in and hang out with us? Then we can drive back to your cottage together."

"Why don't you come with me now?" Cat offered. "We could pick up some Chinese takeout and stay in the cabin all night."

"I promised my brothers I would have a drink with them," Eddie answered. "It's kind of our thing on Wednesday after work. We could have a quick one and then go?"

"No," Cat said firmly, then realized her tone may have been over the line.

"Are you sure you're all right? Did I do something wrong?"

"I'm tired, have a headache, and feel stressed. I'll go back to the cottage. See you later."

Cat climbed into her car and started it up, spotting Eddie staring at her.

"I'll come up as soon as I'm done, okay?" Eddie said, muffled through the glass.

Cat nodded slowly before pulling out. Her mind played out different scenarios for her ride to Bear Mountain as she went over how she would work out the mess before her.

***

Eddie sat at one of the empty tables at Millie Malone's, holding the Guinness just poured as he awaited his brothers' arrival. Cat's behavior in the parking lot worried him. She appeared rattled and on edge, far from the calm and in-control personality she'd displayed in the few days he had known her. He scanned the room, noticing the large party of men gathered at the two booths toward the back of the pub. The men were out of place in Harriman, with most of them dressed to the nines in dark suits, while three others—two younger men and one older—sat alone at the next booth talking.

"Snap out of it, brother," Mickey said, slapping Eddie on the back before sliding into the wooden chair next to him. Red joined them at the table, sitting across from his two older brothers.

"Huh?" Eddie said as he recognized the arrival of Mickey and Red.

"You're gawking at those guys over there," Mickey said quietly. "They don't look like the type that appreciates getting stared at."

"Yeah, the last thing we need is another bar fight while we're in here," Red joked. "Darren will never let us come back."

"Those aren't the guys who fight you in a pub, little brother," Mickey said, leaning over the table to speak surreptitiously.

"What are you talking about?" Red said, spinning around to look at the men.

"Jesus, Red," Eddie spoke, slapping his hand on the table to get his brother's attention. "Could you be more obvious?"

"I have no idea what you two mean." Red shrugged before sipping his stout.

"They look like particular businessmen." Mickey nodded to the trio in the one booth. "And the other group is their muscle."

"Mob guys? In Harriman?" Red said, turning to look again.

"Red, knock it the fuck off," Eddie scolded.

"They don't look like mobsters," Red added.

"They're an Irish mob," Eddie spoke. "I've heard bits and pieces when they get loud. They all have brogues, at least the three there."

"I thought that was just movie shit," Red stated.

"Do you get out at all?" Mickey said, shoving his brother's shoulder and rocking the pint in Red's hand, spilling some. "They're involved in all kinds of stuff in the city, up here, all over the East Coast. I'm surprised we don't see any of the Cosantoir here too."

"The bikers are legit," Eddie interjected. "They aren't in with the mob. They're all Sandhogs."

"Yeah, and who do you think is involved in all that union stuff?" Mickey snapped back. "I worked contracting jobs in the city, Eddie. It's all tied together, believe me."

"Ah, you're full of it," Eddie waved off. "But I do wonder what they are doing here."

Darren appeared at the table, holding three fresh pints for the group.

"We didn't order another round, Darren," Mickey stated. "I'm not paying for this one."

"It's all taken care of," Darren replied. "The gent at the table over there saw Red spill his drink, so he offered to buy you guys a round. Be grateful."

Darren pushed the fresh pours in front of them. Eddie looked down at the full pint in front of his half-finished glass and then glanced over at the table. He spotted one of the younger men, dressed smartly in a suit jacket that likely cost as much as Eddie made on a job, raise his glass toward Eddie and smile.

Eddie nodded thanks, a bit wary of why they rated free drinks.

"I guess they like us," Red added. "They probably saw my red hair and knew we were Irish too. Should we thank them?"

"Sit and drink," Eddie advised. "I wouldn't say anything to them. Just be cool, Red."

"Are you guys ordering food tonight or just taking one of my tables?" a young woman asked.

All eyes looked to the waitress next to the table, who smiled at them, holding her pad in her hands.

"We do have extra drinks to finish," Mickey stated. "Let's get some food tonight. Any specials, Olivia?"

"Lobster bisque soup, a French dip sandwich, and we have chorizo tacos tonight," she replied. "Other than that, it's the regular menu."

"I can't stay," Eddie said, drinking more of his Guinness.

"What?" Mickey replied. "Where are you running off to? It's Wednesday."

"I know, but I really need to go see—"

Eddie stopped short before saying her name, but his brothers already knew where the conversation was going.

"You're going to see Cat, aren't you?" Mickey asked bluntly.

"So what if I am?"

"Eddie, what are you doing? What good can come out of this?"

"Christ, Mickey, I can't believe you. What good? How about I like being around her? Is that enough?"

"You've known her for a couple of days. How much do you know about her? Once she's done with whatever she's doing around here, she's going back to the city or flying off to some other place, and you'll never see or hear from her. You heard when Kelly called me earlier in tears over their lunch today."

"That's sister shit," Eddie brushed off. "They have a lot between them. It's not the same thing."

"Right," Mickey scoffed. "She doesn't tell the truth or the whole story when it suits her. She would never do that to you. Man, don't get blinded by—"

Mickey raised his hand and stopped, shaking his head, before picking up his drink.

"Don't get blinded by what?" Eddie snarled. "Finish what you were going to say, Mick."

"Don't get blinded by some woman who has slept with you a few times that you know nothing about. I'm sorry, but it's true."

"Guys, come on," Red intervened, trying to keep the peace. "Let's not do this. It's Wednesday. We leave shit aside when we hang out after work, remember?"

"I'm just trying to give you some advice, Eddie," Mickey added. "No one really knows her, and her track record is piss poor at best. I don't want to see you moping around if things go south for you. You remember what happened with Britney, don't you?"

"That was years ago and a completely different situation," Eddie defended. "I like Cat. We connect for whatever reason. So you guys should be happy for me."

"I'm good with it," Red added. "It means I get another pint for free once you leave," Red said as he pulled Eddie's extra glass from in front of Eddie toward him.

"Can you be serious for two feckin' seconds?" Mickey said to his younger brother. "I can't tell you what to do, Eddie, but—"

"Just leave it there, Mick," Eddie stated, rising from the table. "You can't tell me what to do. I'll talk to you guys tomorrow."

"Eddie, don't leave pissed off," Mickey added. He got up from his chair and stood in front of Eddie.

"We're all good, brother," Eddie told him. "I'm not pissed off. I know you're looking out for me."

Eddie walked out of the pub, waving to Darren as he went, before getting to his truck. He sat behind the wheel for a few minutes, texting Cahira to make sure she was okay, but he did not get a response.

He maneuvered his truck to Tin Tin's, a local Chinese takeout place, and ordered food for himself and Cat before wandering outside to kill time before his order was ready. Business in the shopping plaza was light, with few cars parked since many shops had closed for the night. He paced over to Cyrus Jewelers, glancing at the sparkling displays of necklaces, rings, and bracelets bouncing off the lights and windows.

Eddie turned from the window just as a dark Cadillac Escalade slowly made its way past him and eased down the lot toward Stop and Shop. Usually, the appearance would not have caught his eye, but he had seen similar vehicles parked at Millie Malone's when he arrived. He watched as the luxury vehicle moved through the fire lane in front of the supermarket before turning and coming to a stop, facing his direction and idling in a parking spot.

Not thinking more of it, Eddie returned to Tin Tin's, sitting at one of the small tables as he awaited his food and watching his phone to see if Cat would return his messages. Once his order was ready, Eddie grabbed the plastic bag filled to the brim with cartons and returned to his truck. Looking both ways before crossing the lot, he spied the headlights of the Cadillac pointing in his direction from their spot.

Eddie pulled the truck out of the lot and began the trek toward Route 6 to drive to Bear Mountain. He turned up the music, cranking out Foo Fighters loudly and singing along as he went. He traversed the road to the traffic circle, driving toward Bear Mountain. One look at his rearview mirror let him know the vehicle behind him. Still a fair distance away, it had its high beams on and didn't dim them when Eddie's truck came into view.

"Dude, turn your brights off!" he muttered as the vehicle got closer.

Luckily, Eddie turned off to the right at the next exit, following the road to where the lodge sat. The car behind him followed suit, pulling back a bit as he went and entered the lot for the hotel and drove toward the cottage where Cat's place was.

Eddie hopped out of the truck, walking to the passenger side to remove the bag of Chinese food before slamming the door shut. He paced in the darkness toward the front door of Cat's cottage, catching a hint of headlight beams off in the distance. The lights crested the slight rise in the dirt road before reaching Cat's cabin, illuminating part of the front porch enough to get Eddie's attention.

He pivoted as he got to the front door, pausing before he knocked. While he couldn't identify the vehicle's details, the shape and size closely matched what he knew would be an SUV like the Cadillac he spotted. He rapped on the door loudly before Cat appeared.

"I brought Chinese," Eddie said, staring off in the direction of the headlights.

"You didn't have to do that," Cat replied. "You should have hung out with your brothers."

"No, I wanted to see you," Eddie answered, looking back as Cat's red hair, tied into a ponytail, hung over her left shoulder.

"Is something wrong?" Cat inquired.

"No, it's all good," Eddie added as he stepped inside, shutting the door behind them.

He paced toward the central area, putting the food bag on the table.

"I wasn't sure what you liked, so I picked up a bunch of the classics—egg rolls, lo mein, beef and broccoli, General Tso's chicken, stuff like that."

"There's enough food here for a party," Cat commented. "You may have gone overboard a little."

"Chinese leftovers are always great anyway," Eddie spoke.

"True," Cat responded. "And I do tend to work up an appetite after . . . " She smiled as she wrapped her arms around Eddie's midsection, pressing her body close to his. With her head on his chest, Eddie ran his hand down Cat's back before he turned his head, looking toward the front door. He noticed a glow behind the front window curtains and broke off the embrace to investigate.

"What are you doing?" Cat asked.

"I think someone was following me," Eddie spoke as he reached the small drapes covering the window.

"What?" Cat said with concern.

"I noticed this car when I was picking up the food. It wasn't a big deal, but it drove by me slowly and hung in the parking lot, watching me. Then, on my ride here, I could swear someone was tailing me—not closely, but enough for me to notice it. When I got out of my truck, I could see headlights in the distance by the hill, and just now, I saw lights outside, like they were pulling up near my truck to see it."

Eddie peeked out and saw the unmistakable shadow of the Escalade just a few feet behind his truck.

"It's the same car. The Cadillac I saw," Eddie said, turning toward Cat before moving to the front door.

"Eddie, don't go out there!" Cat warned, moving quickly to stop him from exiting to the porch.

Eddie was out the door, standing on the porch, watching as the car idled.

"There something I can help you with?" he shouted.

No windows rolled down or doors opened as the Cadillac kept its motor running.

Cat appeared next to Eddie, draped in her cloak to cover up. Eddie noticed she caught her breath when she spotted the SUV.

Eddie took steps to move toward the car before discovering Cat's grip on his arm, holding him back.

"Eddie, don't," Cat warned.

"It's probably some asshole rich kids with nothing better to do," Eddie said.

He attempted to move again, but Cat held a tight grasp on him.

A dim light shone inside the vehicle, and the passenger side window slid down. A bright light lit up inside, flashing toward Eddie.

"Get down!" Cat shouted, pushing Eddie to the side, so he tumbled on the porch while Cat moved to the other side.

Eddie watched as the car quickly backed out of the space and tore out of the area, heading back toward the entrance.

"Are you okay?" Eddie asked, sitting up and moving toward Cat, crouched and peering over the porch's stone fence, her arms under her cloak.

"I'm fine," she answered stoically.

"I think they just took pictures," Eddie said, calming himself. "Damn kids. It was probably some prank or hazing thing. They wanted to see how much they could scare me."

"Maybe," Cat spoke. Eddie looked on as she surveyed the area, moving out to where the car had been parked. He then watched as she moved to his truck and pulled a small flashlight from inside her cloak. She began running the light along the truck's base and the wheel wells.

"What the hell are you doing?" Eddie asked. "Let's just go inside. It's over."

Cat paused at one of the tires, reaching up into the well before she got up and approached Eddie. When she arrived next to him, she opened her palm and showed him the small button with a magnet on the back.

"It's an air tag," Cat told him. "They wanted to track you."

"What for? So they could keep messing with me?"

"You need to come inside," Cat said seriously. "There are a few things we need to talk about."

Chapter 13

C at guided Eddie toward the sitting area. She sat in one of the chairs as Eddie sat across from her, still unsure of what had occurred.

"I don't get why a bunch of kids would want to track me and mess with me," Eddie spoke, reaching for one of the egg rolls sitting in the small bag.

"It wasn't a bunch of kids," Cat said.

"Then who was it?"

"Eddie, I have to tell you something about me. It's something I tell very few people, but I think you need to know about it now."

Cat shifted in her chair before lifting her head and looking into Eddie's eyes.

"I don't know how much Kelly has ever told you about me."

"Not much, honestly," Eddie said. "Usually, the only time your name would come up was in a bad or snarky way. Sorry."

"That's okay," Cat nodded. "It's pretty much what I would expect. I work in security."

"I think she had mentioned that at one time," Eddie agreed. "So, is it like warehouses, hospitals, and stuff? You're a guard, an office worker, what?"

"Not exactly. Yes, we do some stuff like warehouses and whatnot, but it's also a lot of private stuff. High-tech protection for the rich, famous, and powerful, among other things. I'm not a guard or a salesperson. I own the company. An old friend started it with me after I left the military."

The confused look on Eddie's face let Cat know he wasn't wholly getting where she was going.

"You were in the military? What, like the Army or Navy? Kelly never mentioned that."

"Kelly doesn't know about it," Cat said solemnly. "It was while we were . . . estranged, I guess. I was in the ARW."

"I don't know what that is," Eddie shrugged.

"It's the Army Ranger Wing," Cat explained. "It's a Special Ops force part of the Irish Defense."

"So, sort of like the Navy SEALs?" Eddie asked.

"Yes. We did some training exercises with them."

"Wow," Eddie stated, crunching the egg roll. "You are a real badass then, aren't you? So what does that have to do with kids' pranks?"

Cat took a deep breath, trying to decide how far to go with this conversation.

"Even though I'm not the face of the company, there are people who know who I am, what my past is, and what I do. Some are people you don't want to know or mess with. They may have seen you with me and wanted to find out more."

"People are out there that want to hurt you?"

"Yes," she stated plainly. "I'm sure plenty of bad people would like to see me dead."

"You're not pulling my leg with all this, are you?" Eddie asked seriously.

"No, I'm not. Hanging around with me is a risk, and it's not something I want to subject people I care about to. That's one of the reasons I'm so distant from Kelly. She doesn't need to know about any of that."

"But if she did know, she might understand more about why you've kept away, Cat. It could help smooth things over."

"She can't know about any of this, Eddie," Cat said. "You have to promise me you won't tell her anything about what I just told you. I don't want there to be any connections between the two of us that people could use to hurt her or her family."

Cat paced the room as Eddie sat quietly. She hoped this explanation would be as far as she would have to go about her life, past and present.

"If you want to leave, I get it," Cat told him, finally sitting back down. "Someone knows you were with me, which puts you in danger."

Cat knew exactly who that someone was. The Escalades regularly had parking spots at the compound in Forest Hills, and she'd spotted Danny watching her with Eddie. So it only made sense that he would want to learn more about him and do God knows what.

Eddie rose from his seat and squatted in front of Cat, looking directly into her eyes.

"Hey, I'm not easy to scare off," Eddie said softly.

He placed his index finger under Cat's chin, tilting her head up before kissing her lightly. The kiss grew in intensity as Cat placed her hands on Eddie's cheeks, steadily rising from her seat until both were standing.

"Eddie, are you sure—" Cat began before he placed his hands on her hips, leaning in to kiss her again.

"I'm sure. Don't worry about me."

Eddie's hands had dipped to the hem of Cat's oversized shirt, lifting it slightly so he could touch her bare flesh. Cat sighed as his fingertips grazed across her belly.

"I think the Chinese food can wait a bit," Eddie offered before taking Cat's hand and leading her toward the bedroom.

Cat stopped short, tugging Eddie's hand and pulling him to her as she collapsed onto the couch with Eddie atop her.

"It's too far of a walk to the bedroom," she smirked, undoing his belt buckle as he lay on her.

***

Cat snuggled close to Eddie, her head resting on his shoulder while he slept soundly. The couch proved larger and a better play space than Cat anticipated, leaving both of them too tired to move to the bedroom. Eddie had pulled the blanket off the back of the sofa to drape themselves in, but the heat they had generated kept Cat mostly uncovered even while they slept.

A slow rumble in her stomach had Cat deftly prying herself away from Eddie's arms to move toward the table where most of the Chinese food remained. After two steps, a chill raced over her body now that she was apart from the warmth and comfort of the sofa, causing Cat to bend over and slip the oversized shirt back onto her body. She fished out a small container of pork fried rice before moving to the kitchen to retrieve a fork, scooping a glob of cold rice into her mouth.

Cat leaned against the sink, eating silently, gazing at Eddie as he slept. Worry consumed her now that Danny knew who he was. Badb had been right—she'd let her guard down and made mistakes, giving too much away by trying to come home. Added to the expectations of going with Quinn to Jack Lonergan's on Friday, Cat didn't like what she saw on the horizon.

A slow creak out on the porch snapped Cat to attention. She quietly slid her food onto the counter and made her way stealthily to the hook where her cloak resided. She reached to one of the inner pockets, grabbed her shillelagh, and gripped it in her left hand. A large shadow appeared behind one of the shades of the front windows as the creaking continued.

Cat moved to her bedroom and slid the side window open, pushing the screen to the ground. She climbed out the window, hopping onto the cold, rocky turf below her. She ignored the sharpness of the stones at her bare feet as she crept close to the cottage wall until she reached the front. Peering around the corner, she spotted a hulking figure attempting to peek inside without luck.

Cat calmly crouched, positioning the cudgel in her hand, her breathing steady and focused. Her vision adjusted to the darkness as the figure turned his back to her and moved to try the next window.

Cat sprang into action, leaping across the porch in just three moves while barely making a sound. The head of her shillelagh struck the left shoulder, left forearm, and then the left thigh of the intruder in rapid succession before he had a chance to react. A loud grunt filled the air as Cat stood over her victim, stomping on the left hand beneath her with her heel. The crack of bone heard and felt pushed her adrenaline further as the attacker let out a muffled cry.

Headlights flashed across the front porch in Cat's direction, and the moment they glimpsed her body, she leaped to her right into the darkness, laying down with her head next to the prone assailant's ear. She reached over, grabbing him by the throat and steadily applying more and more pressure.

"The only reason I'm letting you live is so you can tell Danny that if he tries to do anything to Eamon or my family, I will make his life a living nightmare until he takes his last breath. Got it?"

The assailant let out a slow gurgle, rapidly nodding his head in agree-ment until Cat released her vise on his throat. A loud gasp escaped his lips as his chest heaved, and he cried out in pain.

"Bobby, you okay?" a voice echoed from the car.

"Fuck no!" Bobby yelled. "She broke my fucking hand!"

"Get in the car!" The voice barked back.

Cat listened closely, identifying the growl from the car as Gene.

"Listen to Gene, Bobby," Cat hissed into his ear. "Get out of here and deliver the message to Danny. If I see you again, I will take your fingers as a souvenir."

Cat shoved Bobby forward and watched as he limped to his feet, grasping his shattered left hand as he shuffled toward the headlights. Bobby ducked into the back of the car as it peeled away down the gravel road.

Cat crouched, looking over the stone as the car disappeared from view. Her heart rate remained steady before she stood, quietly making her way across the porch toward the front door.

When the cottage door swung open, Cat stepped back. The reac-tion had her planting a kick to the midsection as Eddie tumbled to the ground, gasping for breath. Cat was on top of him, holding her cudgel and ready to strike until she looked into Eddie's face. His wide eyes had her halting her actions before she did something she would regret.

"Eddie, I didn't mean to— There were people out here," she rushed out, placing her right hand on Eddie. "Don't panic. Take deep breaths. Try to relax. I just knocked the wind out of you. I'm so sorry."

Cat kept her hand on Eddie's solar plexus, trying to guide him through the spasm as quickly as possible. She looked around to make sure no one else was nearby or watching. While scanning the porch, her eyes settled on a manila envelope near the doorway. Danny had them leave the dossier on Jack Lonergan.

"Jesus, Cat," Eddie rasped as he coughed a few times and attempted to sit up.

"Go slow," Cat insisted, helping him to a sitting position.

Eddie put his head between his knees while Cat rubbed the back of his neck slowly. When he lifted his head, Cat rested her forehead against his. Eddie's sweat was evident, and Cat lifted her head back to see the color slowly returning to Eddie's face.

"I think I'm okay now," Eddie huffed out.

"Give yourself another minute to recover," Cat insisted.

"What the hell is that thing?" Eddie asked, pointing to the shillelagh lying next to Cat.

"It's a shillelagh," she said sheepishly. "I didn't mean to brandish it like that at you. I was caught up in the moment. But, Christ, I could have killed you."

Eddie reached for the weapon, but Cat snatched it up before he could get it.

"I thought shillelaghs were those walking sticks old men in Ireland used," Eddie added, still working to regain normal breaths.

"They can be," Cat added. "Traditionally, they were used as weapons."

"The better question is, why do you have one with you?"

"Let's get you inside," Cat said, helping Eddie. She skirted passed the manila envelope, kicking it with her foot so it was out of view underneath the bench on the front porch.

Cat assisted Eddie back to the couch. He closed his eyes and worked at his breathing more while Cat held his hand.

"You didn't answer me," Eddie said as he rested his head on the back of the sofa. "Why do you have that thing?"

"Do we need to get into this right now?" Cat answered. "Just relax."

"You were ready to bash my head in, Cat. That look in your eyes—it was scary. Then, you were a whole other person. I think I deserve an answer."

"I always carry it with me," Cat said, resigned. "It's for protection. I made it myself when I was with the ARW."

Cat tentatively held it out so that Eddie could take the weapon. She looked on as he contemplated the cudgel, feeling the weight of it and examining the wood.

"You carved it yourself?"

"Yes," she answered plainly.

"It's better work than most carpenters I work with," Eddie replied, trying to crack a smile. "How did you learn how to do that?"

"My father taught me when I was a kid," Cat told him as she reached for the shillelagh. Eddie flopped it to his left hand, out of her reach.

"Why is it heavy like that?"

Cat hesitated before answering.

"There's—there's lead in the murlan."

"The what?"

"Murlan. It's the knob at the top. There's a solid ball of lead in it."

"Jesus," Eddie muttered before passing it back to Cat. "So you really could kill someone with it."

"Yes," Cat said bluntly. "But you can kill someone with nearly anything, Eddie, if you know what you're doing, or sometimes even if you don't. Accidents happen. People get lucky."

"Get lucky? Is that what you call it? Seems pretty callous, Cat."

"It's not callous at all," Cat replied. "Just a fact that you have to be aware of. Everyone is a potential killer in the right circumstances."

"I don't think I could live thinking that way," Eddie spoke. Cat saw the seriousness in his look. "That means you never trust anyone."

"It doesn't have to be that way," Cat told him as she rose from the sofa and paced the room, "but yes, trusting another person is not easy to do when you live the kind of life I do. I told you, my inner circle is tiny."

"Does that mean you don't trust me?" Eddie asked.

Cat stopped in front of Eddie, looking down at him.

"It's not that I don't," Cat spoke. "I've told you more in a few days than I have shared with nearly anyone, including my sister. But there's a lot about me you don't know or understand—a lot you wouldn't understand."

"How do you know that unless you trust me enough to tell me, to let me in? Clearly, there's more to this than you owning a security firm, Cat. People are chasing after you. I want to help you."

"You are helping me, believe me," Cat answered.

Cat climbed onto Eddie's lap, placing her knees on either side before leaning in and kissing him. His warm hands gripped her thighs as she shifted on his lap.

"Are you trying to distract me?" Eddie asked as he moved his hands around her thighs to her backside.

"That depends," Cat said, nibbling on his ear. "Is it working? It feels like it is," she added as she ground against his lap.

"We're not done with this," Eddie added, attempting to sound authoritative as his voice quavered each time Cat gyrated her hips.

"Oh, I know we're not," Cat moaned lightly.

Chapter 14

Morning arrived too quickly for Cat as she lay in a tangle of sheets, her legs entwined with what she thought were Eddie's until she realized he was not in bed with her. The muffled sound of the shower running got her attention, and she saw the door to the bathroom cracked open. As she stretched, she felt soreness in her feet and calves. Glancing down, Cat noticed a scratch trailing up from her left heel to the middle of her leg, along with some dirt and gravel on the bed and the bottom of her feet.

Cat shuffled her way to the bathroom, opening the door to a blast of steam from the shower stall. She peeled back the mauve curtain to see Eddie, eyes closed, with lather on his face, turned toward the water.

"Mind if I join you, Eamon?" she cooed as she climbed into the shower and pulled the curtain closed.

"Geez, I didn't hear you come in," Eddie jumped, rinsing soap from his face.

"It's one of my many talents," Cat added, grabbing the soap bar and gliding it over Eddie's back.

Cat's lathered hands moved down to Eddie's waist before snaking forward, moving to his inner thighs before reaching for his quickly rising cock. Her hands slickly stroked up and down and over the head, inducing a groan from Eddie.

"Another of my talents," Cat said into Eddie's ear.

She pressed her body tightly to his, her breasts against his back as she stroked him slowly.

"Am I doing it right, Eamon?" she asked innocently.

The heat from the steam and hot water added to the intensity of the action as Cat's body warmed quickly. Her body involuntarily rubbed on Eddie's, her sensitive, erect nipples brushing on his back and sending waves of pleasure to her core.

"Cat—fuck," Eddie groaned again as he moved to spin around and face Cat.

Water pelted Cat's body, heightening her sensitivity as she restored her grip on Eddie's erection. She toyed with the engorged head, swirling her fingernail over the tip and making Eddie jump.

"What do you want, Eamon?" Cat asked as she worked him with her right hand as her left went behind Eddie's head, running through his dark hair.

"Seems pretty obvious to me," he growled hungrily.

Eddie grazed his thumbs over Cat's nipples, causing her to close her eyes and relish the feeling. Before she knew it, his hands took hold of Cat's face as he kissed her deeply. He walked her back against the shower stall wall, the water barely reaching her now, as his hands explored her damp body. She moaned as the first finger slid inside her, and her left hand raised up automatically as a second entered.

"What do you want, Cahira?" Eddie said, his fingers touching her deeply as his mouth closed around her left nipple.

"You—I want you," she gasped, feeling the pressure building.

"I want the same thing," he growled, moving his lips from her breast to her neck. "I don't have a—"

"It's okay," Cat panted. "It's okay."

Cat wrapped her legs around Eddie as he slid into her. He held her as she moved up and down, water pouring down on him until he swiveled around, letting the water pummel her body as she moved.

Cat shut her eyes, putting her head on his shoulder as she tightened her legs around him. Eddie pinned her to the wall underneath the shower head, groaning deeply as his body went rigid, and he came. Cat's own orgasm was moments behind as he filled her, placing her mouth roughly on his shoulder as she moaned into him.

Eddie held her tightly, keeping Cat in place as she rode wave after wave of pleasure. Then, with her eyes shut, she rested her head on Eddie's shoulder until he placed her down and stepped back. The hot water hit both of them again, and Cat felt it relaxing her tense and taut muscles as she panted.

Eddie's left hand moved the wet hair from in front of Cat's eyes. Her left hand pressed against his chest, allowing her to feel the rapid beat of his heart. She looked on as Eddie picked up the shampoo, and Cat voluntarily spun around so Eddie could lather her hair.

His fingers gently massaged her red tresses before he moved her hair over her left shoulder. She felt his hands stop for a moment as Cat looked straight ahead at the shower wall.

"Everything okay?" she asked, knowing what was coming next.

"Yeah," he answered. "I was looking at your tattoos, and—"

"The tattoos are a Celtic raven, and the knot is the Celtic Sisters Knot," Cat added stoically. "The other thing," Cat moved her right hand behind her, touching the spot on her back just below her left shoulder, "is a scar from where I got shot and stabbed."

Eddie's finger traced over the lightly faded scar, about two inches long, and the mark indicated where she had been shot.

"I didn't think women were in combat like that," Eddie said softly.

Cat spun around, facing Eddie, so the water hit her back.

"I wasn't regular military," Cat told him. "What we did was different. We went places—places no one wanted to go to do things only a few people were willing to do."

"I'm sorry that happened to you," Eddie consoled.

"I'm not," she answered boldly. "It made me a better person, stronger mentally and physically, and it created a bond with my teammates that made us closer than any family could ever be."

Cat stepped out of the shower and grabbed one of the fluffy white towels hanging on the rack, drying herself off before wrapping it around her body. Eddie followed suit, trailing her from the shower stall and into the bedroom. Cat sat on the edge of the bed, using a separate towel to dry her red hair.

"It must have been tough going through that with all men," Eddie added, reaching for his boxer briefs. "Hazing and all that."

"That was only when I first started training," Cat replied. "After that, my unit was all women."

Eddie stopped and looked at Cat with shock.

"Really? How is it that I have never heard of that before? Something like that would be a big deal worldwide—an all-female special-ops squad."

Cat paused, realizing she had said more than she'd meant to.

"I really shouldn't be talking about any of this."

"Why not?" Eddie exclaimed as he donned his shirt. "This is some badass James Bond, Jack Reacher stuff. People would love to know about it."

"Because we aren't supposed to talk about it, Eddie," Cat reasoned. "It's not glamorous like you see in movies. It's scary, real, nasty shit where people get hurt and die on purpose. The sounds, the smells, the impact—that doesn't just disappear thirty seconds after the fact."

"So . . . you've killed someone before?"

Cat paced over to the dresser and idly grabbed clothes.

"Cat?"

"Yes, I've killed people. In combat and on purpose. Can we let this go now?"

Cat silently dressed, knowing Eddie's eyes were on her the whole time, and not for the usual reasons.

"What?" she said, exasperated, as she pulled her jeans on.

"I don't know," Eddie added, shaking his head. "You were so casual about your answer. I don't understand how it wouldn't get to you more."

"I never said it doesn't get to me, Eddie," she added, slipping her boots on. "This is why I don't talk about it."

Cat stormed out of the bedroom to the kitchen, grabbed the coffee pot, and filled it, tapping her foot impatiently while she waited for the water to reach the top.

"What's the matter?" Eddie stated, appearing in the kitchen.

"Nothing at all," Cat said tersely as she poured water into the coffeemaker.

"All I said was I'm surprised how you answered."

"It was how you said it, like I'm some kind of automaton that just did what I was ordered to do. Watching people die, whether they are your enemy or . . . or people close to you . . . is not an easy thing—ever. You don't forget any of them. Being callous about it is how I try to detach myself from it. I'm sorry if that offends you."

Cat tapped her left foot rapidly as she stared at the coffeemaker.

"Why does this thing take so feckin' long?" she yelled.

Eddie wrapped his arms around Cat as she faced away from him.

"Hey, I'm sorry," he comforted. "I didn't understand. I'm not trying to upset you. I would never do that to someone that I—"

Cat spun around and faced Eddie, placing her index finger on his lips.

"Please don't say what I think you're about to say," Cat rushed out. "We've only known each other a few days, Eddie. You can't feel that way about me."

Eddie kissed Cat's finger before moving her hand down, holding it.

"Why can't I? It doesn't matter how long it has been, Cat. You know when you fall for someone, and I'm falling hard."

"You can't," she said softly. "Don't do this—to either of us. I'm not loveable, and I've let enough people down in my lifetime. Don't add yourself to the list. I don't want to hurt you too."

"I'm not giving up on you that easily," Eddie whispered back before kissing Cat's lips.

Emotions churned inside Cat as she fought to maintain control through the kiss and embrace.

"I have to get to a job," Eddie spoke. "I'll come by after work. Think up something fun that you want to do later."

"You mean what we've been doing hasn't been fun?" Cat added as she walked Eddie to the door.

"Oh, believe me, it has been," Eddie told her as he opened the door. "That was the best shower I ever had. I've never felt so clean and dirty at the same time."

Cat, unable to stifle a laugh, broke into a smile.

"That's what I wanted to see," Eddie replied, grinning.

Cat watched him from the porch as he walked to his truck and got in, honking the horn to her as he pulled away. As soon as the truck was gone from view, Cat reached down under the wooden bench and retrieved the manila envelope before going back inside and locking the door.

She poured herself a cup of the coffee she'd made before sitting at the table, staring at the envelope. Cat released a deep sigh before cracking the seal on the package and removing the contents. She laid out the contents, including a schematic of Jack Lonergan's place in Greenwood Lake, a complete background, and his protection around him.

Cat pushed the documents away from her and recalled the air tag she had removed from Eddie's car. She went to the bedroom to retrieve it and angrily picked up her phone, pressing redial on Danny's number before she had time to think about it.

The moment she heard someone pick up, Cat started ranting.

"What the feck do you think you're doing?" Cat shouted. "Coming to my place with your goons skulking around, taking pictures, and tagging his truck?"

"Well, good morning to you too, sunshine," Danny laughed.

"You think this is a joke, Danny? Is your ego that big that you think I can't get to you?"

"Oh, I know you can," Danny answered. "I just love hearing you get all fired up like this. By the way, you did a real number on Bobby. His hand is broken in three places, and you dislocated his shoulder with your club."

"He's lucky I let him go back to the car," Cat growled. "Trying to break into my cottage? I would have killed both of them."

"Now, I never told them to do that," Danny defended. "They were just supposed to leave the dossier there and go. But, instead, they went rogue on me there, thinking they would impress me if they roughed up your boy toy a bit. I think they learned their lesson, or at least Bobby did."

"Leave him alone, Danny. I'm warning you."

"You mean Eamon Brennan of Three Brothers Construction, LLC? I've got to tell you, Cat, I think you could do better. From my glimpse of him at the pub and this picture, he's nothing special. He's got a pretty unremarkable background too, and not much in the way of financials. You must be paying every time you go out."

Cat sat silently, seething, her foot tapping away.

"Have you told him all about yourself yet, Cat? About your little side hustle? I'll bet that makes for some hot bedroom talk while you're fucking him. It probably really gets your motor running. Or have you held back that little tidbit of information? I'm sure he would find it fascinating. I have his cell phone number here if you want me to give him a call."

"Why are you doing this?" Cat hissed into the phone.

"Because I want you to remember who you are and what you are, Cat, especially to me," Danny said bluntly. "Have you looked at Lonergan's intel? I bet you couldn't resist as soon as good old Eddie left you."

Cat's stomach boiled with hatred for Danny as he poked at her.

"You know I can't do this in one day," Cat answered. "Even with the information, it takes a lot of planning. I can't walk in there and do it without an exit strategy and study. It doesn't work that way."

"Oh, I know," Danny replied. "I don't expect you to go in there and put a bullet between his eyes tomorrow, as much as I would love it. But I'm sure you could whip up one of your little concoctions to slip him if you wanted to."

"I don't have access to any of that stuff right now, and they will never let me get that close to him. So I'm only going because your father asked me to be there, Danny. It's for his protection and peace of mind and nothing else."

"Sure, sure," Danny said sarcastically. "It's a good opportunity for you to do some recon too. And then, maybe next week, you can finish the job and put him out of his misery. It will be fun to see you in action tomorrow, though. I don't think I've ever been with you when you're on the job. I always just get the after-party."

"Enough of this," Cat snapped. "This is the last warning you get, Danny. Back off with the following, the background checks, everything. I mean it. It ends now."

"Fine," Danny said abruptly. "We'll pick you up tomorrow at eleven. Will your boyfriend be gone by then, or will we get to meet formally?"

"Go to hell," Cat added, and hung up.

Cat spent the next few hours reviewing the information, familiarizing herself with all the ins and outs of Lonergan's mansion on the lake. There were many potential exit points, but the info indicated guards were positioned at all of them around the clock, including on the boat dock with water access. Cat realized the most straightforward way in and out is to be invited and leave without suspicion. It meant getting to know Lonergan more, which also meant trying to make sure she was noticed by him.

The constant texts throughout the afternoon from Danny, prodding and teasing her relentlessly, agitated Cat to her last nerve. So when her phone finally rang, she picked it up violently.

"If you don't leave me the feck alone today, I swear—" Cat spat.

"Jaysus, Cat, hello to you too," Badb said in shock.

"I'm sorry, Bee," Cat rushed out. "It's been . . . Well, it's just been. I've been meaning to talk with you. But, unfortunately, I've just been caught up in research."

"Research for what? Isn't that usually my job?"

"Yeah, it is. Quinn Darcy is here, where I am. He and Danny are meeting with Jack Lonergan at Lonergan's compound, and they want me to come along strictly in a security capacity."

"When are you doing that?" Badb asked.

"Tomorrow morning."

"That's not enough time, Cat," Badb answered. "You can't get every-thing put together that fast."

"It's not a job, Bee. It's just protection," Cat insisted.

"Still, it's not safe to do that. You could be walking into God knows what."

"I know," Cat agreed. "Do you think you could look at everything for me and pull a report together?"

"I'll have to put everything else aside if you want anything reliable before tomorrow," Badb admitted.

"Please," Cat asked. "It's kind of important."

"Sure. No problem."

Cat sighed with relief.

"Everything else going okay?" Cat questioned.

"Not really," Badb said, her tone getting somber. "We have a prob-lem."

"What is it? I thought I took care of all the business stuff already."

"It's not the business that's the problem, Cat."

"Now what?"

"I got a notice this morning—an alert, actually. Someone tried to access your personnel files."

"At the office? You said it's not a business problem."

"Not your office files, Cat," Badb explained. "Your ARW files. They didn't want to take no for an answer. When the computer denied them access a few times, they tried to call about them."

"What?" Cat said, astonished.

"The calls get routed to me when that happens. So I just said they were classified and denied them. They didn't get anything."

"Who was it?" Cat asked.

"Cat, it's probably the end of it right there. I just wanted you to know about it."

"Who was it, Bee?" Cat insisted.

Badb sighed deeply before she began.

"It had initiated from the state trooper barracks in Central Valley, NY. When they couldn't get anywhere, they called the FBI field office in Goshen. So that's who called me."

Cat's mind raced, putting the pieces together.

"Cat, don't jump to conclusions," Badb insisted. Maybe Danny was—"

"Danny would have no reason to look into my background. He knows enough of the dirt already. It was someone else."

"Care to enlighten me?"

"No," Cat spoke sharply. "I'll take care of it. Let me know as soon as you have the stuff on Lonergan. Thanks, Bee."

Cat hung up the phone, grabbed her jacket and keys, and left the cottage, intent on driving to Monroe.

Chapter 15

Frustration with slow-moving traffic on Route 6 had Cat seething more and more as she considered what happened. Even though Badb had not come out and said it, Cat knew the undertones of the phone call. She was making mistakes she would never usually make because emotions were getting in the way.

When she finally arrived at her sister's home, she raced from the driveway up the front steps and knocked rapidly on the door. When no one answered, Cat began pounding on the door.

"Kelly!" she yelled, trying the locked front door. "Let me in!"

"Cat?" a scratchy voice spoke out.

Cat looked around before noticing the doorbell camera with the speaker posted to the left of the door.

"Kelly, I need to talk to you," Cat insisted. "Open the door."

"I'm not home," Kelly answered. "The camera let me know someone was at the door. Teagan had a doctor's appointment today. What do you want?"

"I need to know something," Cat spoke, looking into the camera.

"Are you going to let me know what that is, or do I have to guess?"

Cat stepped back, realizing her error. There was no conceivable way Kelly would have initiated an investigation into her background.

"Where are Eddie and Mickey working today?"

"What? Why do you need to know that?"

"Please, Kelly. It's important."

"Hold on," Kelly said, trying to hide the anger in her voice.

Cat waited, shuffling her feet back and forth as she looked around before Kelly spoke again.

"They are working over in Warwick again, but they are going for lunch right now," Kelly replied.

"Where are they going?"

"Christ, Cat, I don't know. Probably Eddie's Roadhouse, if I had to guess. That's where they usually go over there. Look, I have to go. The doctor is here."

Kelly cut off the conversation before Cat added anything else, leaving Cat to return to her car and get directions to the restaurant.

Finding her way through to Warwick and Eddie's Roadhouse, Cat parked and abruptly entered the café, scouring the room until she spotted the table where Mickey and Eddie were seated.

"Can I get you a table?" a waitress asked politely.

"I see where I'm going," Cat spoke as she marched over to where the two men sat. She stood next to them, getting surprised looks from both.

"Cat? What are you doing here?" Eddie asked. "Have a seat."

"No," she barked. "We need to talk. Now."

"What's wrong?" he asked innocently.

"We're not getting into this in here," Cat insisted. "Come with me."

Cat strode across the restaurant, eyes on her, as Eddie trailed behind, attempting to keep up. When she hit the sidewalk out front, Cat spun around to face him.

"What's going on?" Eddie asked.

"Why did you do it?" Cat hissed.

"Do what?"

"You checked my background, or at least you tried to. Did you think I wouldn't find out?"

Eddie took Cat's arm and walked a few steps to the left, away from the front of the building, before Cat shrugged her arm away from him.

"I didn't . . . Well, I mean, I did, but I didn't think—"

"You didn't think you would get caught so quickly," Cat interrupted.

"No, that's not what I was going to say," Eddie answered. "Look, I worried about you after our conversation this morning. It weighed on me. Mickey saw that and asked what was wrong, so I told him. He said he knew someone at the trooper barracks, the same person who helped him find you before he and Kelly got married, and that maybe he could fill me in on what you went through so I could understand better."

"Do you have any idea what you've done?" Cat shouted. "How much trouble you can cause for me? Christ, now Kelly is going to know all that too!"

"Know all what? Mickey didn't even say he had heard back from the guy yet. So how do you know all this already?"

"Because that stuff is classified, Eddie," Cat explained. "They aren't giving that information to anyone, not even the FBI. What I did was covert. I explained to you that no one is supposed to know it."

"The FBI?" Eddie said with confusion. "How are they involved?"

"Because Mickey's friend was denied access to my records and must know someone at the office over there. They tried instead and got turned down, but that doesn't mean they will stop digging."

"Cat, I'm sorry," Eddie said sincerely, attempting to take her hand. Cat snatched her hand back quickly. "I didn't know any of that would happen. He's my brother. He was trying to help me because he knows I care about you."

"You have a funny way of showing it," Cat spat. "You talk about trust, Eddie, but how am I supposed to trust you when you do something like this? This is why I don't let people in. Just forget it."

Cat turned at paced off toward her car as Eddie ran to catch up.

"Cat, wait," Eddie pled. "Let's talk about this."

"There's nothing left to talk about," Cat said soberly as she sat in her car, slamming the door shut. She pressed the starter button as Eddie banged on the window. She pulled away from the curb without looking back, focusing, steel-eyed, on the road ahead of her.

***

Cat ignored messages and phone calls all day from Eddie until she finally replied to his last text, begging her to speak with him.

Do not come here tonight.

That lone line said all she had to say regarding the situation.

Badb emailed Cat a short time later, giving her the more-detailed report she wanted on Jack Lonergan, his henchmen, and his home on the lake. Always amazed about how much Badb gathered through her resources, Cat had more than she had expected at her fingertips. She spent most of the night going over facts, layouts, and backgrounds so she knew what to expect in nearly any possible situation.

When she finally went to bed, exhaustion overtook her, but she had trouble falling asleep. She had expected, and perhaps even hoped, that Eddie would show up at the cottage tonight to explain himself. As angry as she was, a part of her yearned for his comfort and caring.

The first sign of daybreak had Cat out of bed and focused. She went for a run, something she hadn't done in days, to help clear her head and get her body and mind back on track. She did miles throughout the

Bear Mountain area, tackling various terrain to push herself and get her muscles burning and active.

Cat arrived at the cottage, showered, and readied herself for what lay ahead. She let her hair cascade past her shoulders before donning the black jumpsuit she kept in her car at all times. It was form-fitting and sleek, allowing Cat to move freely as needed while still looking appealing enough to catch Jack Lonergan's eyes.

Knowing she would likely be searched for weapons when they arrived at Lonergan's home, Cat grabbed her cloak and opened the inside. One pocket, hidden and padded on the interior, was large enough for her to slide her shillelagh into without it being detected. She stashed the weapon securely, using an inner Velcro strap. It would be the only weapon she carried with her, leaving her more vulnerable, but she had little choice.

The crunch of gravel outside caught Cat's attention as she moved to the front window and spied a lone Cadillac Escalade idling outside. Cat put on her cloak and fit the small earpiece into her right ear, security that allowed her to communicate with Badb in an emergency if needed. Benny appeared on the passenger side, holding the door open for Cat as she emerged from the cottage.

"Thank you, Benny." Cat nodded as she climbed into the vehicle.

"Of course." He smiled.

Cat sat in the back with Quinn Darcy in the seat next to her. She was behind Danny, who spun around in the front and grinned at Cat.

"Good morning," Danny added.

Cat greeted his salutations with a scowl before turning to Quinn.

"Good morning, Seanóir," she said softly.

"Ahh, it 'tis." He beamed. "I woke up, so that always makes it pleasant." He chuckled. "Let's hope it stays that way."

The ride from Bear Mountain to Greenwood Lake passed in near silence, with nothing more than Danny whistling "Danny Boy" as they neared Lonergan's place on the lake. Benny pulled the vehicle up to the large front gate, cameras positioned to look at the car as he rolled down the window. He waved up to the lens, and the gates slowly opened. Cat began breathing exercises, readying herself as they worked down the driveway toward the home.

The image of the palace before Cat's view had become familiar to her with all the recent pictures and details Cat had gone over. She spotted two snipers positioned on the roof, unexpected but good to be aware of.

"They have shooters on the roof," Cat noted as they pulled up.

"I'm sure it's precautionary," Quinn assured the others as he toyed with his cane.

"Good to know, though," Danny added. "Nice pickup, Cat."

Cat acknowledged nothing as Benny stopped the car by the front steps. As soon as the engine cut, two of Lonergan's men, dressed in dark suits, appeared to open the passenger side doors to allow Danny and Cat out. Cat immediately pulled her hood up to conceal much of her face, letting her hair hide her expression and eyes. Any cameras in her direction would pick up little more than the cloak.

Benny had opened the door for Quinn and assisted the older man out of the car and around to where Danny and Cat stood. The quartet followed Lonergan's men up the steps and through the large front doors into the foyer, where four more men stood waiting.

"Quite the welcoming party," Danny added snidely.

Cat scanned the room, checking the corners where she thought cameras might be stationed, but she found none. A flight of stairs lay off to the right, partially obscured. She suspected at least two more men positioned themselves there if needed.

"I need to check for weapons," one large man in glasses said as he stood in front of Danny.

"Have at it," Danny offered, spreading his arms as the man patted him down. He then slid over to Cat, nodding to get her to open her cloak. Reluctantly, Cat pulled down the hood and held the covering to the sides while the man's hands roamed her body.

"She's good," the man nodded.

"You don't know the half of it," Danny quipped, laughing.

"Don't be crude, boy," Quinn snapped, rapping his cane on the marble floor.

The henchman turned to Benny, and Benny just opened his coat to show his holster and gun.

"You're not getting it," Benny said sternly.

"Oh, is that so?" The man grinned, taking off his glasses and placing them in his suit jacket pocket.

"Leave him be, Jackson," a voice echoed as footsteps entered the room.

Cat glanced over to see Jack Lonergan approaching quickly, adjusting his tie as he moved ahead of the two extra bodyguards with him.

"It's not like we don't have enough guns in the room already, right?" Lonergan laughed. "Seanóir, welcome to my humble home," Lonergan said as he offered his hand to Quinn.

"Thank you, Jack." Quinn smiled, shaking his hand. "I don't think I have ever been out here before."

"Yes, my father never liked it much," Lonergan lamented. "He didn't want to leave the city for anything. It offers me a place to get away and relax."

Lonergan moved over to shake Danny's hand firmly.

"Always nice to see you, Danny," Lonergan said cordially.

"Jack," Danny answered tersely.

"And who is this you brought with you?" Lonergan asked, his gaze moving up and down Cat's body in her jumpsuit. She had made sure to leave just enough unzipped to tantalize the imagination.

"Cahira," she said, her face softening with a smile.

"What a lovely name," Lonergan replied, smiling broadly. "You certainly brighten up this testosterone-filled room."

Lonergan led the way across the foyer, leading the group to a large sitting room with a fireplace roaring. Quinn sat in a plush, highback chair, with Benny positioned next to him. Danny landed on the sofa, looking at Cahira to hopefully join him. Instead, she opted for another highback chair that placed her squarely in Lonergan's view in his leather seat.

Cat scanned the area, noting the two men waiting at the doorway and the one who stood behind Lonergan. No obvious cameras stood out other than the one positioned over the glass doors that led outside to a darkened patio. More comfortable with their safety, Cat removed her cloak, leaving it behind her so she could access it if needed. The shedding of the coat all but guaranteed she would garner Lonergan's attention more than the conversation.

Jack's henchman distributed drinks for all, glasses of Midleton Whiskey he kept for the occasion.

"I purchased this at an auction last year," Jack stated, holding up his crystal rocks glass. "It's a 47-year-old bottle of rare whiskey. Once I heard about it, I knew I had to have it to save for a special occasion like this. It cost a pretty penny, so I sure hope it's worth it. Nothing but the best for you, Quinn."

Cat glanced at Quinn as he swirled the liquid in his glass, eyeing its motion before he held the glass under his nose.

"I appreciate it, Jack," Quinn smiled, raising his glass. "Sláinte mhaith."

All in the room hoisted their glasses before taking a sip.

"Oh, that's good stuff, Jack," Danny added.

"It better be for fifty grand," Jack scoffed, sipping his glass more.

"So, gents, I know you didn't come out here just to share my whiskey and make me jealous that you have this beautiful lass with you," Jack said, placing his glass on the small table beside him. "Are we ready to talk some business?"

"What would you like to talk about?" Quinn asked, folding his hands on the knob of his cane before him.

"Well, Quinn, you know I've had my eyes on some of that land of yours over in Forest Hills for quite some time. But luckily, our business growth has been off the charts the last year or so, and I need more space for warehousing, distribution, housing, you name it. So, if we can work something out, I would be glad to cut you in on some of the profits. But, of course, I would give you more than a fair price for the land."

"Exactly what is the business you are planning for that area?" Quinn asked solemnly.

"Well, Quinn, I have many interests, as you understand," Jack spoke. "There might be a little of this and that around there. It's a little early for me to get into specifics. I want a large parcel, so it's likely to be in several places. But, like I said, I am more than happy to give you a stake since it is the Dullahan area—say 20 percent?"

"That's a good deal, Da," Danny said. "We make money on the sale of the land and monthly profits. It will give us a chance to expand things as well."

"I'm not as concerned about expansion any more, Danny," Quinn chimed in. "I'm trying to scale back and just work with what we have."

"This is perfect for you, then," Jack added. "Passive income and lots of it, and you don't have to do a thing unless you want to do it."

"But what about that neighborhood you're looking at?" Quinn said, leaning forward. "There are houses of families that have been in the area for generations. Will they just be displaced? And the surrounding areas? Once your businesses are established, how safe will they be? I'm not too naive to understand the types of things you are involved in, Jack. Many of those 'interests' of yours may not be the best for the community around there."

"Quinn, I understand your concerns, but you have to know I will offer every homeowner a fair price for their place and give them time to relocate. You have my word on that. As for the community, I'm sure that bringing businesses to the area will mean jobs for those willing to work."

"I'm not sure very many people will want to be involved in the type of jobs you offer, Jack," Quinn said stoically.

"Hold on now, Quinn," Jack interrupted. "I'm no Lucky Dean, God rest his soul. I'm not peddling down into the depths he would go. Are some of my interests on the edge? Perhaps, but back when you and my father were running things, all those businesses were far from legit. Without some of the local politicians and police in your pockets, we wouldn't be sitting here today."

Cat looked on, spying the furrowing brow of Quinn Darcy as he rolled the knob of his cane in his palm. The conversation continued in a heated fashion, with Lonergan and Danny pleading with Quinn to reconsider his staunch approach. Eventually, voices became raised, and Cat saw an opening.

"I'm sorry, Seanóir," Cat said, bowing and rising from her chair. "Mr. Lonergan, would you mind directing me toward the restroom?"

"Oh, no problem, dear." Quinn smiled.

"Of course, Cahira." Jack grinned, standing next to her and leading her toward the open doorway where two of his men held posts.

"Just down the hall on the right." Jack pointed.

Cahira smiled back, her eyes hidden slightly behind her hair.

She strode toward the bathroom, knowing that Lonergan and his men were watching her as she moved. When she arrived at the right door, she turned to face it and spotted Lonergan still looking at her before she went inside.

The powder room was ornate with gold fixtures, fittings, and a large, gaudy mirror over the sink. Cat checked the room carefully for cameras and microphones to ensure she wasn't watched before she tapped her earpiece.

"Everything good?" Badb answered quickly.

"I just wanted to ensure you were there if I needed you," Cat answered. "They're talking business, and Quinn is making it difficult for Lonergan and Danny. I don't think much will come out of tonight. Things look pretty lax once you're in the house. Security is soft, and his men don't look like they would be much trouble."

"Are you going to do something now?"

"No, it would be difficult with Quinn here," Cat replied. "I would worry for his safety. If I went for Lonergan, someone would go after Quinn. I don't know if I could move fast enough to do the job and care for him. I have to be here alone with Lonergan."

"Good luck with that," Badb spoke. "He's hardly ever by himself. I have only picked up cameras outside and on the boat dock. None are in the house. He's so cocky that no one will try to get to him; if they do, he thinks his guys can take care of it."

"I'm pretty confident I can get him alone," Cat added.

"No doubt. Just be aware, okay? There's a space upstairs on the floor plans that is not defined. I don't know if that's his office, his bedroom, or what. You could be walking into anything if I can't see it somehow."

"I'm always on things, Bee. You know that."

The silence on the line was evident to Cat.

"I know I haven't been myself lately, Bee, but this is work. It's different, and you know it. I'll let you know if and when."

"Okay. Love you," Badb added before signing off.

Cat exited the bathroom, moving back toward the sitting room where voices echoed louder than when she had first left. She sidled past the two guards, both watching her as she reentered the room. As Quinn looked on, Danny and Jack were both yelling from their respective locations.

"This doesn't have to be settled tonight," Danny insisted, placing his glass on the coffee table.

"No, it doesn't, but it doesn't seem like your father will budge his stance. I can't hold out forever, Danny."

"You two eejits shouldn't talk about me like I'm not here or in the grave," Quinn barked, rapping the tip of his cane on the hardwood floor. "I still get to call the shots for the Dullahan, and I don't see how it will benefit the community or us."

"Da, the money alone is a benefit," Danny pled.

"How often do I tell you it's not about money? We have enough money to live on for generations, boy. No doubt Jack's family is the same. Don't get to the point where you find yourselves knee-deep in shite you can't get out of for a few more pennies. My apologies for the language, Cahira," Quinn said, nodding to her.

All eyes swung in Cat's direction as she stood inside the doorframe.

"Not necessary, Seanóir," Cat replied.

"I think I've said all I need to say today, Jack," Quinn added as he rose from his chair.

"But, Da," Danny intervened, "we haven't had the chance—"

"Tomorrow is another day," Quinn stated. "You're welcome to stay if Jack will have you. I can send the car back here for you. Are you coming, my dear?"

"Of course, Seanóir," Cat told him, watching Quinn walk toward her. Benny had snatched her cloak off the chair she occupied and handed it to her so she could put it on.

As Cat turned to follow Quinn and Benny out the door, Danny drained his whiskey glass and slammed it down.

"I'm sorry, Jack," Danny mumbled.

"No worries." Jack grinned. "We'll get it done, right?"

Cat walked a few paces behind Quinn as they moved toward the front door. Danny caught up and passed her, immediately attempting to get Quinn's attention to keep him from leaving. However, before Cat crossed the threshold to descend the steps outside, an arm took hold of her. She spun around to see Jack looking at her.

"I'm sorry we didn't get more chances to speak," Jack told her.

"Me as well," Cat said plainly. She moved her left arm from Jack's grip before reaching to shake his hand. "Perhaps we can meet another time."

"Not to be forward, but are you free for dinner tonight?" Jack asked, keeping hold of Cat's hand. "My chef has some fantastic lamb chops for tonight, and now that the whiskey is opened, I need someone to share it with."

"I'd like that." Cat smiled, letting Jack think he was controlling the situation.

"How's seven tonight? I can send a car for you."

"Not necessary," Cat waved off. "I like to drive and be in control."

"I think I like the way that sounds," Jack spoke.

"Oh, you should."

"Do you think Danny will mind?" Jack said quietly.

Cat spotted Danny climbing into the front of the Escalade while Benny awaited Cat's arrival by the rear passenger door.

"Why should he mind? He doesn't own me. I'm my own woman, Jack. I do what I want. I look forward to tonight."

Cat maneuvered the steps, sliding into the Escalade while giving a look and wave in Jack's direction before Benny shut the door.

Benny followed the circular driveway toward the exit, leaving another gate on the far side of the compound. The passengers sat quietly, with Cat gazing out the window as the sun poked through the gray clouds that moved in.

"Well, that was a feckin' waste of time," Danny grumbled. "We're pissing away an incredible opportunity, Da. We can make millions and do next to nothing."

"I'm not ready to displace all those people—families that have worked with the Darcys and the Dullahan for decades—for nothing that benefits them. Someday you'll see the importance of all that, Danny."

"Whatever, Da," Danny said in disgust.

"So what were you and Jackie boy whispering about?" Danny said, turning around to look at Cat.

"We would have been louder if we wanted you to hear," Cat replied, garnering a chuckle from Quinn. Quinn reached over and patted Cat's hand.

"You must have caught his attention if he took the extra time to walk out with you."

"I guess I did," Cat added bluntly.

Cat's thoughts turned toward preparation for the evening and how it might or might not play out. Finally, when the car reached Cat's cottage, her plans had gelled to where she had rested comfortably in the back seat.

"Thank you for coming along today," Quinn rasped to Cat as she went to get out of the car. She leaned over and kissed Quinn on the cheek.

"Anything for you, Seanóir," Cat acknowledged.

Cat emerged from the Escalade, and Danny immediately confronted her.

"Can I come and see you tonight so we can talk about . . . things?"

"No, you can't," she added sternly. "I have plans."

"Mr. Wonderful gets first dibs, I guess?"

"Don't be an ass, Danny."

"What? I just wanted to know where I stood in line." Danny smirked.

"You're not even in the building."

"You don't want to even talk about the Lonergan stuff? I have some ideas that—"

"I don't need your ideas," Cat cut him off. "It's not a team effort, Danny. I do things on my own schedule, time, and way. I'll let you know when I'm ready."

"Cat, we may not get another chance to—"

"Go home," she insisted as she moved to the cottage's front porch and away from Danny.

Once inside, Cat went to her bedroom, unzipping the jumpsuit she wore and peeling it off before sitting on her bed. She grabbed her phone to check for messages and calls and saw nothing, not even a simple text from Eddie confirming he had listened to her.

She tossed her phone onto the bed, going to her clothing to see what she might wear to dinner with Lonergan.

"I guess that's that," she resigned as she flipped through her choices hanging in the small closet.

***

Not finding anything suitable in what she brought, Cat hopped in her car and headed toward Woodbury Commons to shop for a new dress. The crowds surprised her as tourists and shoppers alike made their way along the pathways to the different stores. The offerings reminded Cat of shopping in Manhattan, with storefronts for Prada, Ferragamo, Gucci, and other high-end shops.

Cat made her way to Neiman Marcus, garnering looks from the salespeople as soon as she entered. Cat never carried herself as someone with money, and her leather jacket and jeans did little to diminish that impression. She spotted a sleeveless emerald-green dress with a strappy back, and knew immediately it was ideal for catching Jack's vision. The gown sported a deep V-neck and a slit on the left that would leave little to the imagination.

Cat plucked the dress from the rack and moved toward the dressing room. The moment she had it on, she knew it was right, and had no problem investing in it and a matching pair of shoes. She toted the items back to her cottage and began preparing herself for the evening.

Even though she had told Danny she didn't have any poisons, she knew that was a lie. She never traveled without something, and her experience and study had made her expert enough that she could concoct something using ingredients from the shelves of the local drug store if needed. The issue would be getting the opportunity to slip anything into a drink or onto food that Lonergan might have.

Cat went to her jewelry bag, picking up a pair of earrings and noticing an emerald ring ideal for the situation. She held the ring in her hand, recalling when it was given to her as part of the Celtic Sisters. On the surface, it appeared as nothing more than a family heirloom with silver insignia on each side. Cat touched the Celtic Sisters Knot on the left so that the emerald popped up, revealing a small space underneath where a poison could be stored. Shutting the top, she pressed the ring's left, and a small pin emerged from the bottom. Properly dipped, a simple poke with the pin could inject more than enough to paralyze or kill someone.

Cat returned to the bathroom, opening her toiletries bag and grabbing a small vial. Anyone looking at it might think it was a simple perfume sample. Cat, however, knew what it really was. She had held this vial of VX in her kit for years, never having cause to use it since she always prepared something else. However, the last-minute nature of this job left her with little else to work with. It would take just one drop on the sharpened point of the ring to deliver a fatal dose of the nerve agent, with activation occurring within minutes.

The vial went directly to the small clutch purse Cat planned to use for the evening along with a few other items. She checked herself one final time in the mirror before donning her cloak, ensuring the shillelagh remained hidden. She stepped out to the front porch, feeling the chill on her stocking legs as she moved toward her car. Before she reached the driver's side, headlights flashed in her eyes. The truck came to a stop, and Eddie leaped out, keys in hand.

Cat placed her purse on the passenger's seat before pivoting in Eddie's direction.

"Cat, I know you didn't want to see me, but—"

"Eddie, please, I don't want to get into this. Just let it go."

"Can you at least give me that chance to explain myself? I think I deserve that much. So let's go inside and talk."

"Eddie, I can't right now. I have to go."

Cat steeled her nerves, stepping into her car. She watched Eddie move closer to the driver's side window. His gaze scanned her body as he noticed how her hair, makeup, and dress appeared.

"You going out somewhere?" he questioned.

"Yes, I'm meeting someone, and I don't want to be late," Cat added curtly.

"I see," Eddie said, resigned.

"No, you don't, Eddie," Cat interrupted, deciding now was the time to pull the band-aid off. "You don't want to see what my real life is like. The image you have of me in your head, or what you want me to be, that woman doesn't exist. You can't fix me or change me, Eddie. This is who I am. You're better off knowing that now."

"I never said I was trying to change you, Cat," Eddie argued. "I thought I could understand you more if I knew more about you. Since you didn't want to let me in, it seemed like an opportunity. I didn't think it would—"

"That's right, Eddie, right there," Cat spoke, slamming the driver's side door closed and opening the window. "You didn't think about how it would affect me. You weren't considering me at all. You did it for yourself. I can't talk about this anymore. I need to go."

"Can we talk later? After you get back? I want to fix this."

"I'll be late," Cat added tersely, staring straight ahead.

"I don't care about that. I planned to go to my campsite for the weekend, but I can postpone it."

"Go to your camp, Eddie. You'll be better off."

"Cat, come on. Don't do this."

"I can't do any of this right now," Cat answered, refusing to turn and look Eddie in the eyes.

Cat backed the car around and sped out of the parking area, kicking up loose gravel as she attempted to switch her emotions off. A quick glance in the rearview mirror showed Eddie's shadow standing there, watching her car disappear from view.

Chapter 16

The dark drive to Greenwood Lake passed slowly. She recalled the directions from earlier in the day and refused to put music on during her trip, concentrating solely on her breathing and the mission. Usually, she had weeks to prepare herself for a job so that every move was planned and any hiccups were anticipated. Walking into a job without deep background and recon left too many openings for errors or unplanned interactions.

Cat arrived at the compound, slowly pulling up to the gate with the cameras. She rolled the window down, looking into the lens as lights on the closed fence lit up the area.

"Yes?" a gravelly voice scratched over the intercom.

"Cahira O'Brien," she spoke. "I'm here to meet with Mr. Lonergan."

Cat sat quietly awaiting a reply as she looked around at the gate, spotting cameras on both posts.

"Come up to the house," the voice spoke as the steel fence slowly swung open.

Cat drove slowly, peering along the driveway to see if she spotted anything that hadn't been there during her initial visit. When she arrived at the front of the house, she pulled to a darkened spot near the front steps, figuring the cameras might not get a good look at her with her hood up. Then, grabbing her clutch, she stepped quickly from the car and up the steps to the front door, where she was greeted by a large gentleman in a dark suit.

"You'll need to open the cloak," the man huffed.

Cat undid the silver hook and pulled her hood back, letting her red hair fall around her. She stretched out her arms like raven's wings so the man could check the coat and her.

His hands roughly gripped the cloak as he looked for pockets, not finding any of the hidden locations Cat had custom-sewn into the garment. He then stood before Cat, readying to put his hands on her.

"Do you really have to do that?" she asked. "Where am I hiding anything in this?"

A slight blush passed over the burly man's face before he stepped back.

"Can I see your bag?" he asked, holding out his hands.

"Of course," Cat answered, passing over the small clutch.

The man sorted through the few items he found inside, passing over the vial and lipstick before removing several small foil packets and holding them up.

"You never know how things may go." Cat smirked. "A girl has to protect herself."

Embarrassed again, the man shoved the items back into the purse, handing it back to Cat.

"You can follow me, Miss," an older man, neatly dressed, indicated.

Cat paced alongside the gentleman, getting a better look at some of the artwork and decor Lonergan had placed in the home. Cat had trained her eyes to look for the unusual, and Jack certainly had some odd tastes regarding the paintings and sculptures.

When they arrived in the dining room, Cat was directed to a smaller table away from the central dining spot.

"May I take your cloak and bag, Miss?" the man asked.

"Cloak, yes. Bag, no. I like to keep that with me if that's okay," Cat said, holding her clutch.

"Certainly, Miss," the man answered, taking the cloak from Cat. She eyed him as he hung the item on a coat rack inside the dining room entryway.

"May I get you a cocktail? Mr. Lonergan will be joining you in a moment."

"A vodka martini, please. Belvedere, if possible." Cat smiled.

"Certainly," the gentleman agreed as he marched over to the large brass bar cart on the far side of the room.

Cat paid little attention to him while he mixed the drink for her. Instead, she scoped out the room, looking at access and exit points. There was one swinging door to the far right near the bar cart, likely leading to the kitchen. The other door, to her left, remained closed, with the entryway behind her. The small table she sat at was nicely set with fine China, silverware, and crystal. The linen napkins had delicate green embroidery of the Lonergan family crest, proudly featuring a knight's helmet.

"From County Tipperary," Jack's voice echoed from behind Cat, having her spinning around in her chair.

"What's that?" she asked.

"The family crest," Jack indicated, pointing to the napkin. "The family line is from there. We originally settled in Pennsylvania before my great-great-grandfather came to New York. What about your family?"

"County Clare," Cat answered, rising from her seat. "My parents were born and raised there before coming to New York. I still have family there, I'm sure."

"Wow," Jack said, ignoring whatever Cat said to him as his eyes scanned her body. "You certainly know how to dress for an occasion. Gorgeous," he added as he kissed Cat's right hand, spotting her ring.

"I see even your jewelry matches you perfectly. Green all over with red hair. What a fine Irish lass. Your eyes, though," he added, gazing into them. "The blue is . . . unusual. Are they contacts?"

"No, everything you see is all me." Cat smiled. "Red hair and blue eyes are quite the genetic anomalies."

"It's one of the things that makes you special, I'm sure," Jack told her.

"That's right, but just one of the things." Cat smirked.

The gentleman's clearing throat ended the pseudo-flirting Cat undertook as attention turned to him, holding a silver tray with a martini glass.

"Your drink, Miss," he said with a nod.

"Why thank you," she replied, taking the drink from the tray.

"Anything for you, Sir?" he asked Lonergan.

"I'll have some of the Midleton we opened today, Franklin, please," Jack replied, while never taking his eyes off Cat.

"Please, sit." Jack gestured toward Cat's seat.

Cat delicately sat across from Jack, placing her drink on the table.

"I'm so glad you decided to join me tonight," Jack began. "As much as I love Greenwood Lake, it can get quiet and lonely here in the winter and early spring. Most people only want to come here in the summer. So it's nice to have some . . . companionship."

"I appreciate the invitation, Mr. Lonergan," Cat acknowledged.

"Oh, please don't start that." Lonergan waved her off. "Call me Jack. I don't need the honorifics like Quinn Darcy."

"I call him Seanóir not out of duty but respect," Cat explained. "He's earned that."

"Understood," Jack answered. "My Da was the same way—rest his soul. I just never bought into it, I guess. Let's keep this as informal as possible, Cahira."

"Fair enough," Cat told him. "You can call me Cat, by the way."

Franklin arrived with Jack's whiskey, placing the glass on the table.

"I'll go check on dinner." Franklin smiled before backing out of the room via the far swinging door.

"Well, Cat, here's to a pleasant evening then," Jack added, raising his glass. "Sláinte."

"Sláinte," Cat replied, tipping her glass before sipping the martini.

Franklin appeared with salad plates, deftly placing one in front of Cat before moving toward Jack.

"Caesar salad," Franklin noted before stepping back.

Cat took a small forkful of the dressed lettuce, getting a piece of salt Parmesan with the bite.

"So, Cat, how long have you worked for the Dullahan?" Jack asked.

"I don't work for them," she said casually. "Occasionally, I work with them, especially when Seanóir asks me to."

"Okay," Jack answered. "And what is it you do for them besides looking beautiful?"

"Isn't that enough?" Cat smiled.

"It would be for me." Jack laughed. "But something tells me that isn't why Quinn asks for you."

"I act as an adviser," Cat told him cryptically, poking at another piece of Romaine.

"What do you advise him on?"

"Whatever he asks me about."

"So why is it that he had you come with him today?" Jack questioned. "He didn't ask you anything while you were here. In fact, it seemed he had made up his mind before he walked through the door."

"I was just here to observe and listen, Jack. If that's what he wants me to do, that's what I do. He still decides things on his own. He's the one in charge, no matter what I say."

"Danny doesn't seem to see it that way." Jack laughed. "He made it sound like this was a done deal to me. That's why the meeting took place."

"Danny doesn't always see things clearly," Cat said abruptly, reaching for her martini.

"And you two aren't . . . together?" Jack asked, pushing his half-eaten salad to the side.

"I told you, Danny doesn't own me. No one does. I make my own decisions regarding everything I do and get involved in. Danny doesn't like strong-willed women."

"Well, his loss is my gain."

Jack sat back in his chair and sipped more of his whiskey.

"Maybe," Cat told him, leaving her salad aside.

"I'm sure I could find a place for you in my organization if you feel unwanted. I'll bet you give great advice."

"I work for myself," Cat said, tasting more of her drink. "As for the advice, I haven't had any complaints from anyone."

Cat sat back in her chair, crossing her legs so that her left leg bared itself mid-thigh.

"Is it getting warmer in here?" Jack noted, polishing off his drink.

"I'm fine," Cat told him. "But if it's too warm for you, we can cool it down."

"I don't think that's necessary," Jack spoke, loosening one button of his shirt collar.

"Well, I wouldn't want you to overheat so early in the evening."

Franklin appeared at the side of the table, clearing the salad plates.

"Are you ready for the next course?" Franklin asked.

Cat leaned forward, resting her chin on her left palm, giving Jack a more explicit view down her dress.

"Do you think the chef can hold off a bit, Franklin? We're going to head upstairs for a bit."

"Of course, sir. I'll let him know," Franklin agreed.

"Aren't you hungry?" Cat purred.

"Famished," Jack said, standing from the table and taking Cat by the hand. "But I might prefer to dine upstairs, where we have more privacy."

"But all the food is down here," Cat spoke, playing innocently as she grabbed her purse.

"I don't think that's what I'm hungry for."

Cat followed along as Jack moved them across the floor to the door on the left. Jack opened the door, leading them down a small, darkened hallway to a steel door with a push-button panel.

"Where are we going?" Cat asked, watching Jack intently as he punched in the four-digit code to open what was an elevator door.

"I don't let just anybody upstairs," Jack spoke, peering at Cat greedily.

Jack led her into the dimly lit, confined box before pressing the singular button on the wall to get the elevator moving.

"I could have taken the stairs," Cat noted as the elevator crept upward.

"This goes right to my special room," Jack indicated. "We won't be disturbed in there."

"What's so special about it?"

"You'll see," Jack added cryptically.

The elevator stopped, and Jack pressed the button again to open the door. Cat waited for him to step out first before tentatively following him. Motion lights activated as he moved, allowing Cat to see what the room held. A large four-poster bed occupied the left side of the room, while three closed armoires sat on the wall opposite. The St. Andrew's Cross on the far wall was unmistakable.

Jack sauntered to the first dark oak armoire and flung the door open, displaying various BDSM toys neatly in place.

"This one is my favorite cabinet," Jack offered, mesmerized by the various devices before him.

Cat took a closer look at the room. No cameras were visible, but Cat didn't discount for a moment that Jack recorded everything that went on in this space to play back for his personal enjoyment. No windows were visible, and as far as Cat could tell, the elevator was the only way in and out. An unease slipped over her, one she rarely felt.

"You're not afraid of a little pain, are you?" Jack grinned.

"Not at all," Cat retorted as she walked to the cabinet, grasping a leather crop and feeling its weight. "I do relish dishing it out."

"Oh really?" Jack said, taking off his tie. "I'm the top here."

"Trust me, you want to be the bottom with me," Cat said, waltzing toward Jack as she tapped the crop in her hand. "I'll take you places you never knew you wanted to go." Cat used the leather tongue of the crop, dragging it down over his shirt and belt before reaching his crotch and giving him a playful tap.

"I don't know," Jack added skeptically, moving toward Cat. "I'm not one to give up control—ever."

Jack pulled Cat to his body, pressing himself to her as his hands roamed her back, looking to untie the strings of her dress before giving up and moving down to her buttocks.

Cat gave him a little leeway, letting him get a quick feel before his hands moved to her waist and toward her breasts.

"Give yourself over to me, and it will be a night you never forget," Cat hissed into his ear, grabbing the apparent bulge at the front of his trousers.

"You have my attention," Jack grunted as Cat's fingers toyed with his zipper.

"I'll have that and more before I'm done, Jack. Have you used that before?"

Cat pointed the crop toward the St. Andrew's Cross.

"I've had people on it before," Jack huffed with excitement.

"You are in for a treat, then. Strip."

Cat stepped back, tapping the crop lightly against her leg as she watched Jack disrobe. She looked over to the cabinet as he took off his pants, spotting an item on the shelf. She moved over, grabbed the leather shorts folded there, and tossed them at Jack's feet.

"Put those on," she commanded.

Jack nodded rapidly, grasping the shorts and working them up his legs. Once he had them zippered and buttoned, the tightness accentuated his erection even more.

Cat strode back in front of Jack, running her hands over the leather. She circled, examining each inch of him, before standing behind him. In her heels, she was equal to his height. Her hands moved over his backside before gliding around as she took his left nipple between her fingernails and pinched it.

"Are you ready for this?" Cat spoke.

"Yes," Jack answered quickly, grunting as his nipple became more sensitive.

"That's 'Yes, Miss' to you tonight," Cat added, swatting his backside with the crop.

"Yes, Miss," Jack howled, clearly surprised at the force of the sting.

Cat stood in front of him again, putting her hand in the waistband of his shorts and leading him to the cross.

"Front or back?" Cat asked. "I'll be kind and let you choose."

"Front," Jack rushed out.

Cat spun Jack around before forcing his back against the cross. She leaned in close as she shackled each of his hands, pressing her breasts in her satin dress against his chest. She made sure he could see down to her cleavage when she knelt to do his ankles.

"Hmmm, you have no idea what having you like this does to me, Jack," Cat said proudly.

Cat turned and surveyed the room, spotting the door to the bathroom on the right slightly ajar.

"I'm going to freshen up for a minute. You think of the possibilities of what happens next, Jack. Be prepared to tell me what you think I should do, and I'll decide if it fits my plans."

Jack tugged on the shackles lightly as Cat strode to the bathroom, her heels echoing on the floor.

Cat turned the light on in the bathroom and shut the door quickly, Exhaling loudly. She fished her earpiece out of her purse, placing it in her ear and tapping it.

"I hope you're there," she whispered.

"What's up?" Badb answered quickly.

"Bee, I'm at Lonergan's. I'm doing it tonight," Cat spoke. "I just wanted to ensure you knew where I was in case—well, in case."

"Cat, it's too fast. I haven't had a chance to figure out that room."

"No need. I'm there right now. It's Jack's little play dungeon. No doubt there are good reasons he doesn't want people to know about it."

"Cat, you need to tread carefully. What if—"

"I have him shackled up right now. He's expecting the experience of a lifetime. I guess that's what he's getting."

"How?"

Cat paused as she took the ring off, pressing the insignia to pop out the needle.

"VX," Cat answered bluntly.

"Wait—how do you still have that? That's not something you just handle."

"It's fine, Bee. I've got it covered. Just a dot. That's all I need, and then I am out of here."

"If you don't do it right, it can kill you too, Cat."

"I know what I'm doing, Bee. I've used it before," Cat added as she pulled the vial from her purse.

"Years ago, and under controlled circumstances," Bee warned. "Not from the bathroom of some mob boss."

"I've got this. I need to get moving, Bee. He's tied up but won't be patient forever, and I want this done and over with. I'll get in touch afterward."

Cat clicked out of the conversation and looked down at the vanity where her vial and ring sat. She reached back into her purse, pulled out the foil condom wrapper, and opened it. She unfolded the latex gloves in the packet instead of the condom, putting the protection on before carefully plucking the vial and twisting off the top. She tilted it carefully, just enough so the tip of the pin soaked lightly in the concoction, before pulling it back and closing it. She pressed the ring closed, put the gloves and vial back in her purse, and placed the band securely on her finger.

One last controlled breath escaped her before she opened the bathroom door confidently. In the dim lighting, she saw Jack where she had left him, prone and vulnerable, his head straight back on the cross.

"Are you ready for all this, John Francis Lonergan, Junior?" she asked as she strode toward him.

Cat received no verbal response from him as she paced forward, setting off an alarm in her head. Then, when she moved within a couple of feet of Jack, she saw the problem.

An ornate dagger handle protruded from Jack's throat, pinning his head to the cross. A trail of blood trickled down his chest and stomach before dripping onto his leather shorts. His wide eyes showed no signs of life at all.

Cat spun around, surveying the room quickly to see if she could spot anyone else with her. Her eyes reflexively adjusted to the lighting as she crept away from Jack's body and toward the only exit from the room. Pausing in front of the open armoire, Cat grabbed one of the leather paddles, gripping it so she had a weapon.

She pressed the elevator button, moving back as she expected it to open and find an attacker inside. Instead, she heard the elevator move up from the bottom floor. Whoever had come in and killed Jack had already left and could be waiting in the elevator or downstairs.

Cat listened intently for any sound—creaking, moving, footsteps, a breeze—but the only sound was the cable of the elevator groaning its way upward. When it came to a stop, Cat moved to the side, crouching down and readying to attack as the door swooshed open. But, instead, she leaped inside, spotting no one.

She quickly pressed the button to close the door, keeping anyone in the room. Cat spied around the room, seeing no indication of blood, dust, footprints, or anything else. Finally, she spotted the hatch at the top of the elevator, locked and latched from the inside.

Cat's brain kicked into survival mode. Get out of the elevator, grab her cloak, and get out as calmly and quickly as possible. Expect the unexpected, and be prepared for guns.

The elevator came to rest, and she pressed the button to open the door to the darkened corridor. She used the small compact mirror in her purse to look into the hall for anyone or anything before safely exiting and going the four steps to the door to the dining room.

She slid into the dining room, leaving the door open slightly. The room had been cleared of signs that a meal had been there not long ago. The crystal chandelier that hung over the main table was off, leaving just a couple of tea lamps on low on the buffet as the only light shining.

Cat moved to the coat rack, grabbed her cloak, and quickly donned it, putting the hood up. Then, leaving the dining room, she scurried down the hallway toward the foyer, where two guards were stationed. Both men rose from their seats as she approached.

"Leaving already?" the one on the left asked as he moved to open the door for her.

"Yes, I'm not feeling well. Thank you," Cat rushed out as she darted out the door and down the stone steps.

She arrived at her car, pulling the keys from her purse and scanning around. Then, finally, the stillness of the evening allowed her to hear it—footsteps moving away from her and toward the tree line ahead.

Cat climbed in and started her car, pulling out without causing an alarm. She moved the vehicle down the driveway toward the exit, keeping close watch as she went and put her brights on. When she arrived at the closed gate, it slowly opened for her to leave as she pulled onto the main road to the left.

A cleansing sigh released from her lips until she spotted it, standing near the extended stone wall of the compound. A cloaked figure peeled its hood back just enough for her to catch a glimpse of the red hair and pale complexion.

Cat slammed the brakes on and pulled to the gravel shoulder. She put the car in park, grabbed her pen light, and pulled her cudgel from her cloak in one motion before getting out of the vehicle. Then, shining the flashlight to the incline area by the wall where she saw the figure, she saw nothing. Her heels made motion more treacherous and safety vulnerable, but she reached the spot, looking around in the nearby culvert, in the trees, and across the road where more wooded areas lay.

The cawing behind her startled her as she shone the light and spotted the singular crow perched on the stone wall. The ebony bird's eyes glowed before the bird lifted off and went across to the woods.

Cat raced back to her car and took off. She pressed her earpiece, and Badb responded right away.

"Done?" Badb spoke.

"Yes, but not by me," Cat answered as she drove cautiously.

"What? How is that possible?"

Cat struggled to focus on the road ahead as she went around the lake area.

"Bee, I saw Ana."

Chapter 17

"That's not possible, Cat, and you know it," Bee answered.

"I know what I saw, Bee. It was her. There's no mistaking it. Red hair, pale skin, the cloak—it was all there."

"Your mind is playing tricks on you," Badb reasoned. "With everything going on around you, it's not a surprise. You've been dealing with a lot of turmoil. This is why we don't do jobs so close—"

"Bee, you're not listening to me!" Cat yelled. "Ana killed Lonergan. Someone is trying to pin it on me. I saw Carog, too. Ana never goes anywhere without that feckin' crow."

"It doesn't make any sense, Cat," Badb reasoned. "They disappeared right after . . . after all the nastiness. I would have heard something if Ana or anyone else was still around. And why would she kill Lonergan?"

"I need to get back to Bear Mountain and gather my stuff," Cat said solemnly. "I don't know how long it will be until someone discovers Lonergan's body, but once they do, his crew will be out looking for me."

"They'll come after the Dullahan too," Badb countered. "They know you're associated with them. So Quinn might be in danger, and Danny as well. It's going to start a war."

"It's no accident it happened this way, Bee. Ana knew I would be there. She knew how I would be dressed. I guarantee her image shows up somewhere on Lonergan's cameras."

"Hold on," Bee added, going silent.

Cat drove along, working hard to obey traffic laws as she moved closer to Route 6 and Bear Mountain.

"I was able to get into the cameras at his compound," Bee spoke. "There are three obvious shots of a cloaked figure leaving the house and crossing to where it looks like your car is parked. It sure looks like you."

"Did they come down the front steps?"

Cat heard the keyboard clacking in the background.

"No, you just appear by the bottom steps as if you came from the side."

"I exited the front door," Cat insisted. "Two guards were there and saw me."

"I doubt anyone will care about that," Bee told her. "All they will remember is that you went in to have dinner with Lonergan and went upstairs with him. It doesn't matter who saw you leave when. So they will put his death and you in the same boat."

Cat pulled into the Bear Mountain property, and while she wanted to rush toward the cottage, instinct told her to slow down and pay attention. If Ana knew Cat would be at Lonergan's house, then whoever else was involved knew where she was staying. She could be easy prey and leave Lonergan's murder wrapped in a tidy bow for police with her dead body.

"I'm going inside the cottage," Cat said quietly to Badb. "Listen for me."

Cat unlocked and entered the cottage, finding everything just as she had left it when she went to meet Jack Lonergan. She stealthily moved around, kicking off her heels and moving in stocking feet toward her bedroom. Once inside, she grabbed her bag, stuffing her belongings inside it before turning to her computer and putting it away. She quickly peeled out of her dress and stockings, sliding into a t-shirt and black leggings, before putting sneakers on and moving out the door.

"All good?" Badb broke in.

"I'm out." Cat sighed. "I need to drop off the keys inside and figure out where I am going from here."

Cat checked out at the front desk, dealing with staff asking her over and over what was wrong until she gave them a story about needing to take a work trip. Then she returned to her vehicle and sat for a moment, trying to decide where to go.

"You can go home," Badb told her.

"Sure, and just lock myself in and hope no one comes looking for me? No thanks," Cat answered.

"I hate to say it, but what about going to Danny's? At least there, you would have a backup, and then you could keep an eye on Quinn."

Cat placed her hands on the steering wheel, tapping them lightly.

"I need you to do something for me, Bee."

"Sure."

"Eddie told me he has a campsite. Can you find it for me?"

"Seriously? A campsite? There are a thousand different places he could be. It could take me days to track it down."

"He was going there this weekend," Cat explained. "He made it sound like it's something he does a lot. Check his credit cards, or maybe he has a membership somewhere. Please. It will get me out of here and give me time to think."

"It could put him in danger too, Cat," Badb cautioned. "If Ana is involved, you know who else is, and they won't stop until they are finished with whatever it is they have to do, no matter who gets in the way."

"I know," Cat answered solemnly. "But I need . . . I need to see him."

"Okay," Badb assured her. "Give me some time. I'll get back to you as fast as I can. Where are you going until then?"

"I have one stop I need to make. After that, I'm not sure. Just find Eddie."

Cat tapped out of the conversation and started her car again. She glanced at the clock, spotting that it was just after ten. She checked the interior of her vehicle, where she regularly hid knives for emergencies. Both were in their expected locations, providing her with peace of mind before she pulled out of the parking lot.

Light fog settled in over the top of Route 6 as Cat drove carefully, regularly checking her mirrors to ensure she wasn't being tailed. Her heightened senses made her ultra-aware of everyone and everything around her. Finally, she moved to the Monroe QuickChek, filling up with gas so she wouldn't have to stop anywhere else if she needed to go for a long stretch. Cat knew cameras abounded at the convenience store and kept her hood up while she pumped gas.

A steady drive through the town had her in front of Kelly's house in minutes. She parked the car in the driveway, got out, and closed the door quietly. Cat scanned the area for anything out of the ordinary, but the residential street sat quiet, with the occasional dog bark echoing in the night air.

Cat reached the front door and knocked firmly. She saw no lights inside and no reaction to her initial noise, causing her to rap louder on the wooden door.

"Come on, Kelly, answer," she mumbled.

"Who's out there?" she heard her sister's voice crackle over the doorbell speaker.

"Kelly, it's me, Cat," she rushed out, turning toward the doorbell and pulling her hood down. "I need to see you."

"Cat? Christ, you scared the shit out of me with the hood. So what are you doing here? Mickey and Teagan are both asleep, and I was getting ready for bed."

"Kelly, please," Cat begged. "It's important."

"Fine," Kelly huffed.

Cat heard footsteps plodding toward the front door before it swung open. Kelly stood, bewildered by Cat's appearance at the front door.

"What do you want?" Kelly asked, keeping her voice low.

"Can I come in? I need to talk to you."

Kelly moved aside so Cat could enter the house. Kelly walked downstairs, flipping the light in the family room/Teagan's playroom. Kelly picked up some stray toys, placing them in the toybox before sitting on the sofa. Cat sat next to her, staring into Kelly's face.

"What's going on, Cat? It's late, and we have a busy day tomorrow. I thought we had said everything we would tell each other."

Cat's hand stretched beneath her cloak, reaching over to take Kelly's. Kelly's instinct to pull away was thwarted when Cat held it.

"Kelly, I know I haven't done right by you in a very long time. I hoped this trip up here would give us a chance to smooth things over and . . . and maybe start over and learn to be sisters again, but I fecked that up too. I can't say I'm sorry enough to you, and now—well, I don't think I'll have the time to do it."

"You're leaving then?" Kelly said, sitting back and pulling away from Cat. "I expected as much. Why come here to tell me that? You could have just disappeared from my life again."

"Because I never wanted to vanish like that," Cat explained. "And I don't want to do it now, but circumstances make it necessary. There's a lot you don't know about me, Kelly, and I wish I had more time to explain it all to you, to let you know why I am this way."

"Are you in some kind of trouble, Cat?" Kelly asked. "If you are, maybe I can help. Mickey knows people with the troopers. I'm sure we can—"

"There's nothing he can do that will change any of this," Cat insisted. "You're better off not getting involved at all. In fact," Cat added, reaching inside her cloak and pulling out a manila envelope, "take this. I was going to leave it for when I left, but things have accelerated."

Kelly tentatively took the envelope and opened it. Three more envelopes lay inside. She pulled the first wide one out and peeled it open, revealing stacks of cash.

"Cat, what the—" Kelly spoke.

"It's $50,000," Cat answered. "Take it and take a trip somewhere—soon. Get away from Monroe for a while. It will be safer for you. Don't tell anyone where you are going. Use cash. No credit cards."

Kelly placed the wad of cash down on the sofa and opened the second, smaller white envelope. Inside was a slip of paper with numbers on it. Kelly looked at it, puzzled, before turning it back toward Cat.

"The first two numbers are bank accounts," Cat explained. "One is under your name, and the other is under Teagan's. They are offshore accounts I have been stashing money in for years. Use yours however you see fit. Teagan has more than enough to go to any college she wants, have a beautiful wedding, buy a house, and do whatever she wants to do with her life. A third number is the phone number of someone—someone special. If, for whatever reason, you need me, call that number. She can help you with whatever you require, anytime or anywhere."

"Cat, I don't understand any of this," Kelly said, putting the envelope aside. "You're scaring me."

"Open the last envelope," Cat told her.

Kelly ran her finger under the sealed portion to open the envelope. Two small velvet bags sat inside, along with a picture. Kelly picked up the photo to examine it.

"I found it at Mom and Dad's when I was there." Cat smiled. "Remember that barbecue?"

Kelly laughed at the image before her of Cat with her arm around a twelve-year-old Kelly, both in bright orange bathing suits, smiling by the pool.

"That was the summer Dad put the pool in after we begged him for years." Kelly smiled. "He made us wear those horrible matching suits."

"But he wore bright orange trunks too," Cat chuckled.

"That was just a few months before . . . before he left," Kelly lamented.

"I know," Cat added. Cat picked up one of the velvet bags, pulling the drawstring to open it and remove the necklace.

"Here," she said to Kelly as she placed it over Kelly's head. Kelly looked down at the gold necklace and the Celtic Sisters Knot pendant.

"What's this?" Kelly asked.

"Something I never want you to take off," Cat stated. "It's the Celtic Sisters Knot. Wearing this bonds you and me in a special way."

"Cat, we're already sisters," Kelly answered. "I don't need a necklace to remember that."

Kelly went to remove it, but Cat stopped her.

"No!" Cat insisted. "Don't take it off. Ever. Starting now. It's more than just a simple symbol." Cat reached inside her t-shirt and pulled out her matching necklace to display. "This will protect you in ways I hope you never have to face or understand. The other one is for Teagan. Make sure she wears it all the time."

Kelly nodded, holding the other velvet bag in her hand.

"Swear to me, Kelly. I mean it. Neither of you can remove them. When I leave here, you go upstairs and put it on her and tell her it's from me and has to stay on. Explain it to her however you have to so she listens."

"Cat, are you—are we ever seeing you again?"

"I hope so," Cat said, tears forming. "I hope more than you'll ever know. The next time we meet up, we'll have more time, and I will tell you everything, from start to finish. I promise."

Cat hugged Kelly tightly, placing her face next to her sister's.

"Is brea liom tú freisin," Cat whispered.

"I love you too, sister," Kelly added, sobbing.

"I'm glad you remembered that." Cat laughed, sitting back and wiping the tears away.

"The way Dad drilled Gaelic into us would be tough to forget." Kelly smiled.

"Teach it to Teagan," Cat said, standing up and taking her sister's hand. "Dad would love that. He'd be so proud of you, Kelly. I know I am."

Cat walked back to the front door, not wanting to release Kelly's hand. Instead, she leaned in, hugging Kelly once more before kissing her cheek.

"Slán leat," Kelly spoke, gripping the pendant in her left hand.

"I will," Cat added. She pulled her hood back up and paced down the front steps to her car. She backed out of the driveway with Kelly standing at the door, watching her as she pulled away.

Unsure of where to go next, Cat drove around aimlessly until Badb's voice entered her ear.

"You there?" Badb asked.

"Yeah," Cat answered. "Just so you know, I gave Kelly your number in case . . . Well, in case."

Badb gave no response.

"I didn't give her your name or anything," Cat explained. "Just the number, if she ever needs you or me."

"It's okay," Badb responded. "By the way, I found him."

"Who?" Cat answered, attempting to clear her head.

"Eddie Brennan, the guy you asked me to find, remember?"

"Oh, right," Cat said, snapping back to reality. "Where is he?"

"Waymart, Pennsylvania," Badb replied. "A place called Keen Lake. He owns a trailer there. I'm sending you a picture of the camper and the location."

"Where did you get a picture?"

"Social media is a blessing and a curse, Cat," Badb answered. "It's about an hour or so from where you are now. The directions should be popping onto your GPS now."

"You're too good, Bee," Cat acknowledged.

"Yes, I am. Are you all right?"

"Better now," Cat assured.

"Are you going to tell him?"

"Tell him what?" Cat questioned.

"Everything," Badb said pointedly. "Just know if you do, Cat, I'll support you, but there's no turning back from that. That information doesn't just fade away over time."

"I'm aware." Cat sighed, resigned. "I don't know what I will tell him or how much. I have an hour or so to think about that."

"Okay. You work on that. I'll keep my eyes and ears open to see if I hear anything about Lonergan, Ana, the Dullahan, or anything else."

"Thanks, Bee. You're the best."

"Don't forget that," Badb boasted before signing off.

Cat looked at the directions leading her on I-84 toward Port Jervis and the New York/Pennsylvania border. Other than trucks, the traffic proved light, allowing Cat to move quickly toward her destination. However, the dark, wooded roads encroached on her driving once she was off the highway. Even with her brights on, the winds and bends made driving difficult.

When the GPS indicated she was nearing her turn for Keen Lake, Cat drove past it, not noticing the small sign. Luckily, she was able to adjust and turn onto the property. She crept along a narrow gravel stretch, seeing nothing but blackness around her. No campsites appeared lit or even occupied as she moved. Finally, the reflection of a truck bumper caused her to slam on her brakes.

Cat recognized Eddie's truck bed and pulled in beside his, pulling her car up as far as she could so that it was nearly hidden behind his vehicle. She climbed out carefully, moving around the camper to the porch side, where just a tiny light illuminated the area outside. Peering through the blinds, Cat spotted a dim glow at the rear of the trailer.

Cat knocked lightly on the outer screen door when she saw it was locked. A shadow moved from the rear of the camper toward the door. When it swung open, she spotted the shock on Eddie's face as he stepped back, seeing her in her cloak, head covered. She pulled the coat back, peering in at him before he stepped to open the door so she could enter.

"What are you doing here? How did you even find me?" Eddie asked in shock.

Cat embraced him tightly, pressing her head to his chest before placing her hands on his face and pulling his lips to hers.

"Finding people is kind of my thing," Cat answered breathlessly after parting from Eddie.

"But why? You said—" Eddie began.

"I know what I said to you," Cat answered pointedly. "I'm not used to people caring about me like that, Eddie. I've taken care of myself for a long time now. Having someone say they are there for me like that, other than the people I fought with in my unit, it's foreign to me. I didn't believe it. I've been conditioned to expect people to want something from me without caring how it affects me. I'm learning that's not always the case. I'm hoping you'll give me another chance."

"Does that me you trust me?" Eddie asked.

"I do," Cat admitted.

"No more trying to hide or hold back?"

"I'll do my best, Eddie, but you have to know it's going to take some time. I need you to be patient with me. You may find out things about me—unpleasant, nasty things—that you might not be able to deal with, and I understand if you don't want to."

"You need to give me a chance, just like you're asking me to do with you, Cat," Eddie added, placing his hands on her waist.

Cat put her hands over his before leading him to the back of the camper where the bedroom was.

"Looks cozy," Cat commented as she looked around the small room that the bed took most of.

"It's not the Ritz, but it does the job when I want to get away," Eddie admitted.

Cat removed her cloak, tossing it aside, before laying on the bed and kicking off her sneakers. Her t-shirt rode up just enough to flash bare skin in Eddie's direction, luring him onto the bed with her. His right hand slid across her stomach, just above the waistband of her leggings.

Cat's left hand went behind Eddie's head, reeling him down to her lips. Once she had him there, her right hand made short work of the buttons on his flannel shirt, revealing the black t-shirt he had on underneath.

"You have too many layers on," Cat huffed, pulling the tucked-in shirt out of his jeans.

"It can get chilly here at night," Eddie replied, his left hand working its way under Cat's t-shirt to cup her breast.

"I promise, it won't be cold here at all." Cat groaned as she felt Eddie's fingers deftly unhook the front clasp of her bra.

Eddie moved, standing up to take off his flannel and his t-shirt. Cat eyed him lustfully as his strong hands went from touching her to undoing his belt buckle and pushing his jeans and briefs off.

Eddie wasted no time removing Cat's black leggings and hooking his thumbs into the delicate green panties to pull them off. His body hovered over hers before his lips went to work on her, burying himself between her thighs. Cat's hips instinctively thrust upward when she felt his tongue enter her. Her hands ruffled through his auburn hair, guiding him and then holding him in place once he found her clit.

Pressure built inside, and warmth flushed over Cat's body as she panted.

"I need you—Eamon, please," Cat gasped, working to pull him further to her.

Eddie followed her request, lifting his head from her body. He bent and picked up his jeans, rummaging in his pocket until he found the foil wrappers he sought.

"I'm prepared this time." Eddie grinned, tearing the condom wrapper open with his teeth before sliding it onto his erection.

Cat smiled back, sitting in front of him, before toying with the latex sheath on his shaft.

"I just want to make sure it's on right," she added coyly, her fingers surrounding his cock and stroking it.

"Cat, you're making me crazy," Eddie moaned as his knees buckled slightly.

"That's the idea," she replied before grabbing his hips and pulling him down.

When Eddie's cock entered her, Cat cried out, her body tingling. His thrusting steadily paced as he glided in and out, causing Cat to wrap her legs tightly on Eddie's lower back.

"Don't stop," she gasped, urging him on as her body grasped his.

Cat shut her eyes, pressing her fingers into Eddie's back as she moaned into his shoulder when she came. Wave after wave pulsed through her as Eddie tensed and had his orgasm shortly after hers. Cat moved her lips to his, kissing him repeatedly as she rode out the pleasure before collapsing into the mattress. Eddie rolled over next to her, his rapid breathing matching hers.

Eddie's arms enveloped Cat, pulling her body to his as she rested her head on his shoulder.

"Are you still chilly?" Cat asked, snuggling closer to Eddie to kiss his neck.

"Not in the least," Eddie professed.

"Mission accomplished." Cat grinned.

Eddie rolled to his side, looking directly at Cat's blue eyes.

"You know," Eddie began, taking hold of Cat's hands, "you know I'm in love with you," he rushed out. "I know you didn't want me to say it, but—"

Cat brought Eddie's hands up to her lips and kissed them.

"I know you are," she said softly, nodding.

Silence filled the air as Cat looked back at Eddie, smiling.

"You don't have to say it back," Eddie added, leaning over to kiss Cat. "I realize it's been only a week, and you have your baggage, but I needed to tell you. I'm glad I got the chance to say it face to face."

"So am I." Cat beamed before closing her eyes, succumbing to the physical and mental exhaustion of the day.

***

Cat stayed close to Eddie all night, keeping her body clinging to his. She worked not to physically react to every noise she heard outside, recalling where they were, but her eyes flew open at the slightest rustle of leaves or the sound of animals outdoors. Finally, when sunrise occurred, and the rays began to peek through the small window on the side of the trailer, Cat stretched and sat up. She resisted the temptation to get up and instead flung her arm over the bare-chested Eddie, running her hands across his torso and in his hair until he rolled her way.

Cat smiled broadly at him as his eyes peeked open.

"Hi," she said, placing her palm on his stubbled cheek.

"Good morning," he yawned back. "What time is it? I feel like I just went to sleep."

"You might have," she answered. "I know it's after sunrise."

Eddie glanced over at his watch on the shelf next to his head before placing his head back on the pillow.

"It's too early to get up on the weekend," Eddie groaned.

"Oh, is that so?" Cat added coyly.

Her right hand snaked its way under the down blanket, across Eddie's abs, and down to his thigh before taking hold of his growing erection.

"Part of you doesn't think it's too early at all." Cat chuckled.

"You're insatiable," Eddie said, leaning in to kiss her before rolling in the other direction.

"You're really not interested?"

"I'm always interested in you," Eddie mumbled. "I need a few minutes to wake up and get moving."

"Okay. Your loss," Cat announced.

She lay on her side, facing Eddie, before a smile crept across her face. Her right hand stayed on Eddie's hip while her left hand moved down to the waistband of her panties and slid inside. She teased herself with her fingers. Cat allowed one or two to dance inside, which caused her to moan. She used Eddie's hip to brace herself as she moved. A louder gasp had Eddie turn around to look at her.

"What are you—" Eddie began, before halting. Cat peeled her eyes open so they could barely see him as she continued to touch herself.

"You know what I'm doing," Cat groaned as her middle finger flicked across her clit.

Cat had Eddie mesmerized as he lay there, eyeing her every slow gyration. She flattened her palm against her damp pussy and rubbed. Then, suddenly, she felt Eddie's left hand on her hip, moving toward her.

"Sure, now you want to participate," Cat said softly. "Maybe I don't want your help now."

"Is that so?" Eddie reacted. The moment his left hand took hold of her right breast, squeezing it lightly and brushing around her nipple, Cat shut her eyes tightly and groaned.

"I can stop if you want me to, Cat," Eddie told her, bringing his face close to hers. Her breaths quickened as she rubbed herself faster. "Just tell me, and I will."

"Feck no," she groaned, grabbing his right hand and putting it over hers on the outside of her panties. But, once his hand met her rhythm, Cat didn't slow down any further. In moments her thighs clenched, holding her hand and his in place as she came.

Her breathing slowed, along with her heart rate, before she opened her eyes fully and looked at Eddie. He gaped at her in awe.

"That was amazing to watch," Eddie offered. "God, you're beautiful."

Cat removed her hand from her panties and brought it directly to Eddie's straining erection in his briefs. Her hand went in, gripping him as her wetness glided over his cock.

"Now I can watch your face," Cat said as she stroked him steadily, her thumb rubbing the base of the head of his cock.

Precum flowed from Eddie, making Cat's motions with her hand slicker. She slowed as she pushed him into her fist, tightening on him. Eddie grunted with every move until Cat stopped her fist just under the purple tip, drumming her fingertips on his shaft as Eddie's body shook.

"Did you want me to keep going, Eamon?" she whispered, watching Eddie struggle to hold on.

Eddie nodded rapidly, his hands rushing over to take Cat's face in his palms as he pressed his lips to hers.

With her grip firmly on Eddie with her right hand, she slid the palm of her left hand over the tip of his cock to push him over the edge. She closed her palm around him when he came, his cock pulsing as he let out a muffled roar.

Cat pulled her hands away from Eddie as the two kissed over and over until each collapsed back to their pillows.

Cat stared at the white ceiling, collecting herself and allowing the flush and blush to race over her body.

"I think I'm awake now," Eddie said as he placed a hand on his chest. "My heart is making sure of that."

"I don't think it's just your heart beating and throbbing," Cat laughed. "That was fun. We'll have to do that again."

"What? Right now?"

"If you're game, I'm ready," Cat grinned.

"I think I need a little recovery time," Eddie admitted.

"Fair enough," Cat told him. "I can get up and make us some coffee."

"Sorry, no coffee here right now," Eddie replied.

Cat rose from the bed, slipping her sweatshirt on.

"What?"

"It's the early season here, Cat," Eddie told her. "I'm not even sup-posed to be up here yet. The sisters let me come early because I help them with repairs around here. So there's no one around yet, and I didn't bring my coffee. Besides, there's a great coffee place just down the road."

"Okay," Cat added, grabbing her jeans. "I'll go get us some coffee, and that should give you enough time to recharge your batteries."

"I'll do my best," Eddie laughed, "but the shop is only five minutes away."

"That will be plenty of time for you," Cat insisted, giving Eddie a kiss. "Give yourself a pep talk, practice breathing, drink water, and then think about what we just did. That is all the help you need."

Cat stepped out of the trailer and into the cool morning air. The temperature surprised her, and she gasped, noticing a trail of her breath as she moved to her car. The thin ice and frost on her vehicle took a minute or two to dissipate before Cat backed out of her parking spot and headed down the road.

Finding her way out to the entrance proved more manageable with the daylight, but once Cat reached the end of the road, she realized she had no idea which direction to go. So she asked the AI of her Subaru where the nearest coffee place was, and it directed her less than a mile down the road to Black & Brass Coffee.

Cat pulled into the empty parking lot and walked inside the rustic building. The smell of fresh grounds permeated the air as Cat inhaled deeply. Alone in the shop, Cat ordered four cups of a medium roast just ground. She added a couple of apple turnovers and a pound of ground coffee to her order so they wouldn't need to rush out again.

Cat lingered in the shop, watching the young woman behind the counter as she worked to put everything together. Then, finally, Cat picked up the tray of coffee, the bag of pastries, and ground coffee and carefully made her way out the door and to her car. She gingerly placed the packages on the passenger seat before returning to the car to drive to Eddie's campsite.

Cat plucked the earpiece from her console and put it in, tapping it to connect to Badb.

"Are you around?" Cat asked mindlessly as she started the car and pressed the button for her seat warmer.

After a moment, Badb finally returned the message.

"I'm here. Where have you been?"

"I'm at Eddie's campsite in Waymart. Actually, I just picked up coffee, and I'm heading back."

"I tried to get you several times, but you never replied," Badb admonished.

"I'm sorry, Bee. I left the earpiece and my phone in the car when I got here last night. I was so focused on getting here that I—"

"Cat, they found him. Jack Lonergan's body. Late last night, after you left the compound. I don't think it has hit the media yet, but word is out, and they are looking for you."

"Shite. I was hoping for at least another day," Cat said solemnly, resting her hands on the steering wheel.

"Have you talked to Eddie yet about . . . about your life?"

"No, but I guess that conversation needs to happen."

"Sooner rather than later, Cat," Badb advised. "I don't know what will happen if the news gets a hold of the intel. If one of his henchmen talks, they'll give your name; I can't predict what will come down after that. It would be a shitty way for Eddie to find out everything."

"I know. I just have to decide what I will say and how much."

"Well, leave your feckin' earpiece in so we can stay connected," Badb warned. "We must coordinate and figure out where to go from here, especially if Ana is actually around."

"She is around," Cat said emphatically. "I did see her, Bee."

"I'm looking into it, Cat. I haven't found anything yet, but I'll dig. Love you."

"Love you too."

Cat clicked out and pulled the car out of the parking lot and toward Eddie's place. Her mind focused on what to say to Eddie and how much regarding her past and present. She breathed deeply as she reentered the Keen Lake property. A couple of wrong turns had her down closer to the lake, showing the bare skin of ice covering the water.

Cat made her way back in the correct direction, spotted the familiar rear of Eddie's truck, and parked next to it. She went to the passenger side, plucking the tray and bag, before shutting the door with her hip. Cat paced across the gravel toward the two steps leading to Eddie's porch.

"Here goes," she told herself, traversing the steps and standing on the patio.

The moment she heard the caw, she froze.

Her eyes shot to the large tree with limbs hanging near Eddie's trailer, and she spotted the crow.

Cat crouched, placing the tray on the wooden slats, before pulling the trailer door open and tumbling inside. The bedroom to her right and the small sitting area and kitchen were empty. She crept back toward the back bedroom, where the accordion door stretched across the doorway. Cat attempted to peer through but saw nothing. She quickly pulled the door open, slamming it on the track as she sped into the room.

The room was empty, with no sign of Eddie or even a struggle. Cat spun toward her cloak, reaching in to pull out her shillelagh before moving back toward the trailer entrance.

Nearing the doorway, cawing began again. Cat squatted and heard footsteps shuffling across the patio outside. The steps approached the entrance, and Cat sprang into action. She kicked open the trailer door, slamming it into the body just outside it and sending the large man tumbling to the floor.

Cat leaped out, somersaulting to the middle of the patio, to see one man on the ground and the other, standing nearby, caught off guard. She jumped toward him, wielding her cudgel and slamming it into his temple before he could do anything but crumple to the ground in a heap.

Cat stood over him and saw no movement, a trickle of blood oozing from his ear. Cat heard the first step of the other man before his body slammed into hers, sending her sprawling to the floor in his grip and knocking the club from her hand.

The first punch landed just below her ribcage on her left side, missing her ribs but with enough force for Cat to feel the pain. She winced as her arms pushed against the attacker, who likely outweighed her two to one. Her left hand got under his chin, and she moved, causing him to grunt as his neck stretched. He grabbed her wrist with his left hand while his right went to her throat and squeezed.

Adrenaline kicked in as Cat recognized the strangle move. She flailed underneath him and saw the grin on his face as she attempted to throttle him.

"I like your style," he huffed. "Seems a shame to kill someone like you."

Cat's breathing garbled as her body flared red. She brought her knees up, thumping against the back of her assailant to no avail. Finally, a glance to the right saw what she needed, and she stretched for the tray of coffee, grabbing a cup in her right hand and thrusting toward the attacker's face.

The scalding beverage hit its mark, dashing across his face as a few hot drops splattered back toward Cat. The man howled in agony, his hands instinctively rushing toward his head as he fell off Cat.

Cat used her elbows to push herself away and gasp, gulping the air rushing back to her body before standing up. She walked over to her attacker and kicked him, hitting him in his ribs with a hard strike.

"That's how you break a rib," she huffed, energy coursing through her enough to dull her pain.

The man rolled over to his back, screaming from the burns to his face as he pulled his left elbow in to protect his damaged ribcage. Cat looked over to the lifeless body near the door to ensure he had nothing left before turning her attention back to the prone thug on the ground. She grabbed the tray of coffee, pulling it to herself, before positioning herself on top of him, pinning his arms beneath her knees.

She grabbed an insulated cup from the tray, pulled the plastic lid off, and let the steam rise immediately. Cat brought the cup up to her lips, sipping it lightly.

"Damn, that is hot," Cat added. "What's your name?"

"Go to hell," the man spat, blisters forming under and around his eyes.

"Don't be like that," Cat sympathized. "I know it hurts, and getting taken down by a woman is soul-crushing to your ego, no doubt, but you don't have to worry. None of your friends will know. You know who I am and what I do?"

"I know you killed Jack, and that's why I'm here," he grumbled. "I don't give a fuck who you are or what you do."

Cat tipped her cup, so a hot coffee trickled on his chin, searing the flesh as he cried out.

"Now, I hate to waste coffee," Cat spoke. "So let's try this again. "What's your name?"

"Leon," he sputtered, his right eye swelling shut.

"What's your full name, Leon?" Cat asked, sipping the coffee calmly.

"You don't need that." He coughed, struggling under Cat's figure.

"I like to know who I'm dealing with, Leon. So I'll give you one more chance. What's your full name?"

Cat held the cup of coffee close to Leon's closing right eye. One drop seeped out, causing him to cry out.

"Leon—Leon Wayne Cunningham!" he shouted.

"There, that wasn't so bad, was it?" Cat comforted. "Are there any more of you around, Leon? Or was it just you and the corpse over there?"

Leon shook his head no.

"Where's Eddie?"

"Who?" Leon answered.

"My friend in the camper, Leon," Cat said, frustrated. "I'm starting to lose my patience, so think carefully about your next words."

"I don't know!" he shouted. "We were just here to take care of you, I swear. They probably took him in the other car—the black Suburban that the lady was in."

"What lady?"

Leon hesitated before answering.

"They'll kill me if I tell you," Leon fumbled.

"I hate to tell you this, Leon, but you're dead already," Cat said seriously. "What lady? Did you get a name?"

"No, I swear, no one ever said her name while I was around. She looks—she looks a lot like you. Red hair and fair. She's always in some kind of cape. That's all I know!"

"Well, Leon Wayne Cunningham, are you ready?"

Cat eyed Leon as he shut his left eye and began to mumble what Cat recognized as the Lord's Prayer.

"I'm not sure how much He can help right now," Cat answered. "On behalf of the Dullahan, give my best to Jack Lonergan."

"Wait!" Leon begged. "I'm—I'm with the Dullahan! We're on the same side!"

Cat paused before doing anything further.

"What did you say?"

"I'm Dullahan, I swear," Leon offered. "I can prove it. Look at my left shoulder."

Cat sat up, leaving her knees in place on Leon as she considered what he said.

"I have the tat! Just look."

"If you're lying to me, Leon, just to save your hide—"

"I'm not. It's there," Leon rushed out. "I've worked for them for three years."

"How come I've never seen you before at the compound?"

"I hardly go there, honest. I work in the field. I just go wherever I need to that day to collect money, drugs, girls, or do . . . other jobs. I live in an apartment in Roosevelt."

Cat rose, relinquishing her hold on Leon's arms as she stepped back, preparing herself for a fight.

Leon groaned as Cat moved from him, and he struggled to sit. Finally, he raised one hand to show Cat he wanted to remove his jacket.

Cat watched intently as he pulled the jacket off to reveal the short-sleeve shirt he wore. Leon tugged up the sleeve of the beige shirt, revealing the headless horseback rider swinging his spine whip over his head. Underneath the dark tattoo was the date, a little more than three years prior.

"Who sent you here?"

The cawing of the crow overhead caught Cat's attention. She looked to see it perched on the corner of the awning, staring at her and Leon. Then, black wings flapping, the bird swooped down, just over Cat and Leon's heads, causing both to duck down. Cat rose and looked at Leon as his eyes widened, and he lurched forward, falling at her feet. The steel handle positioned between his shoulder blades prominently displayed itself to her.

Cat dove behind one of the chairs on the patio for a semblance of protection before she heard the crow again. Peering around the back of the floral seat cushion, she spotted her.

The cloaked figure stood, left arm stretched out, so the crow had a landing perch before it lighted on her wrist. Peeling back the cloak hood, Cat saw Ana's stare. Cat rose from behind the chair, breathing heavily, before reaching down and grabbing her shillelagh.

"Where is he, Ana?" Cat shouted, her voice echoing in the stillness.

Ana stood silently, offering a morsel to the crow for a job well done, before the dark Suburban pulled up, squealing to a stop behind Ana. One of the back doors swung open as Ana moved, almost without a step, into the vehicle and out of sight. The car immediately pulled away as Cat took a few steps, catching nothing but the dust kicked up.

Chapter 18

C at ran back to the trailer, grabbing her cloak and purse before pausing in the bedroom. She scanned for any clues, but nothing revealed itself. Ana would have been careful in her movements not to leave a hint of what she did to keep Cat guessing. She stopped when she stepped back outside and saw the two prone bodies. She paused and tapped her ear, connecting to Badb right away.

"Bee, Ana took him," Cat rushed out.

"Are you okay?"

"I'm fine, but the two bodies on the porch aren't. I need some help."

"Okay, breathe, Cat," Badb advised. "Focus on the job, like we always do."

"This isn't like a regular job, Bee. It's all going to shite, and now Eddie is involved. I need to go after them before they get too far away."

"Cat, I know you don't want to hear this right now, but consider the facts here. If Ana is involved and they took Eddie, there's a good chance—"

"Don't feckin' say it, Bee!" Cat exploded. "We need to figure this out and get him back safely."

"Okay, I already sent a message to Nora. I'm waiting for her to confirm which will take care of the cleanup. Just give me a minute to hear back from her. Now, what do you know about Eddie?"

"Not much," Cat professed. "Other than Ana was here, and it was her. One of the thugs confirmed it for me before she killed him. Then I watched her disappear into a black Suburban and speed away."

"Did you get any plate numbers or anything?"

"No," Cat said, dejected. "Bee, I can't wait around here. I need to move."

"Nora confirmed with me. She'll be there in an hour. Are the bodies out in the open?"

"One is visible from the road. The other is by the front door. I'll cover Leon up and go."

"Do that, and I'll start working on finding Ana."

Cat scoured the area before spotting a green vinyl tarp covering the woodpile. She hauled it off the wood, dragging it to Leon's body.

Cat rolled Leon to his side, his mouth agape and eyes wide open in a death stare. She checked his pockets, finding his wallet. Looking at the contents, she found a few hundred dollars in cash inside, a driver's license bearing his name, and nothing else. His back pocket held a slip of paper with a phone number scrawled on it.

"Godspeed, Leon," Cat muttered, placing the tarp over his body.

Cat marched to her car, climbed in, and started it up before returning to her conversation with Badb.

"You got anything, Bee? I'm on the move."

"It's not like there are roadway cameras up that way, Cat," Badb said as her keyboard clacked. "And you know how many SUVs there are on the roads?"

"I might have something," Cat added as she sped down the road. "Leon had a phone number in his pocket."

"Let's hear it," Badb answered.

Cat read out the number as she drove, taking note of the 929 area code.

"It's a Queens number," Cat said after speaking. "By the way, I think the Dullahan is involved in all this."

"Of course they are, if Danny asked you to take out Jack," Badb told her. "Give me a minute."

"No, it's more than that, Bee. Leon was Dullahan, which means the other body was as well. I saw the tattoo. Someone sent them to get rid of me."

"Okay, one step at a time, Cat," Badb told her. "It's a cell phone number, likely a burner."

"Patch it in," Cat added stoically.

"Cat—"

"Just do it."

The phone's ring buzzed over the car speakers twice before it was picked up.

"Leon?" a husky voice growled. "Fuck, man. Ronny said you were dead, that the woman iced you with a knife throw. Where are you? Is it done?"

Cat let the silence hang for a moment as she worked to put a face with the voice.

"Are you in the car? How's Willie?"

"I'm afraid you missed both of them, Gene," Cat stated brusquely. "Ronny was right. Ana killed Leon before I had the chance. I assume Willie is the other guy lying dead on the ground."

Cat heard muffled voices as Gene barked orders out to someone.

"Oh, don't get shy on me now, Gene," Cat spoke. "First, where is she taking him? Second, who's behind this? I know you aren't smart enough to try to do this on your own. Then again, since it's all so fecked up now, maybe it was your dumb idea."

"You should have let them kill you," Gene hissed into the phone. "You would have been better off. Now you'll just be hunted. Do you think he doesn't know how to get to you?"

"And who might that be, Gene? Who's pulling your puppet strings?"

"Fuck you."

"Last chance, Gene. You can either tell me where Ana took him, or I'll come and torture it out of you. Do you think she is scary? You haven't seen me when I'm pissed off."

"Come find me, bitch," Gene muttered, and hung up.

Cat revved the engine up as she motored onto Route 84 and reconnected with Badb.

"Did you get anything from that?" Cat asked her. "I know who he is, but I don't know where or why."

"It's a burner phone, Cat. It will take me some time. It's not like finding someone who has a phone plan with Verizon. Let me try to put some pieces together."

"Any luck on the Suburban?"

"Nothing yet, but I'm working on it. I promise I'll ping you when I have anything on any of this. For now, just stay on in case something happens."

Cat drove along, struggling to maintain the speed limit and to focus as she considered what could be happening to Eddie. Why would they frame her for Jack Lonergan's murder? Who is the 'he' Gene referred to in the call? Is it someone in Lonergan's crew or with the Dullahan? For someone to go far enough to get Ana involved meant they knew Cat's past.

Crossing from Pennsylvania back to New York, Cat's patience wore thin. Her fingers reddened on the steering wheel as she wove in and out of traffic, the sun dancing off truck mirrors and windshields as she maneuvered along. Then, her cell phone finally began ringing, startling her from her stare.

"Don't answer that," Badb warned in her ear. "Let me block your phone first so no one can trace you."

Cat waited for several beats as the phone continued to buzz.

"What if it's Eddie, Bee? I need to get it," Cat rushed.

"Okay, go ahead," Badb assured. "You're good."

Cat pressed the answer button on her steering wheel, hesitating before speaking, but a male voice rushed across the line instead.

"Cat? What the hell is going on?" a garbled voice spoke. The man was clearly in a moving vehicle based on background noise.

"Eddie? Is that you? I can hardly hear you? Are you okay? Where are you?"

Static covered the line again as Cat thumped on her steering wheel, choking back panic in her stomach.

"Eddie? What's going on?" she yelled.

"Calm down."

A clear male voice came through, and Cat recognized that it wasn't Eddie.

"Danny?"

"What is happening, Cat? My phone has been blowing up all morning. Nice work on, Lonergan, but fuck, I didn't think people would ID you. You're supposed to be the best. So why would you walk in front of cameras?"

"Danny, I didn't kill Lonergan. Someone got to him before I did. This whole thing is a cluster. There are things you should know about what's going on. The people doing this are—"

"Cat, just come here," Danny told her. "You'll be safe at the compound, and we can go over everything then. I'll take care of you, I promise. Don't worry about where she's taking Eddie. You're my girl. I'll watch out for you."

"Who are you talking about, Danny?"

"I'm talking about you, Cat. You know you're always my girl, no matter what."

"No, when you told me not to worry about where she is taking Eddie. Who is she?"

The phone line went quiet as Cat pulled off the road to a texting area.

"You know, sometimes you're too smart for your own good, Cat," Danny huffed.

"Danny, what have you done?"

"This all could have been so easy, Cat, if you had just taken care of Lonergan the first time I asked you to do it. There wouldn't have been any big mess, no complications, and no Mr. Wonderful in the way. But you had to have your code and your way of doing things. My plans couldn't wait for you to come around, so I had to switch to plan B. I'm sorry it had to end up this way. Honestly, I'm impressed that I could pull it all together. Now Lonergan's gone, we can take his territory, and it all falls on you. Between the guys in Lonergan's crew and the cops, you probably were better off if they had killed you at the campsite. Feckin' Gene can't get out of his own way sometimes."

"Why? Why involve Eddie? Why go get Ana?"

"It's not personal," Danny said bluntly. "It's practical business, Cat. Da is never going to see things my way. I realize that now. If I'm going to take over everything, it's going to have to be on my terms. It had to start with Lonergan. Once I have that, anyone else small-time will fall into place. After that, I'll have enough manpower to move Da out, one way or another. You would never go for that—you and your feckin' loyalty to him. I'll never understand it. Anyway, you needed to be out of the way.

Once he's told you killed Lonergan, he'll either see things my way or . . . well, he won't, and that will be unfortunate if it comes down to that. Ana is my ace in the hole."

"And Eddie?" Cat asked soberly.

"A casualty of war, I'm afraid," Danny told her. "At first, it didn't bother me. But the more I thought about it, the more I realized he would get in the way. The thought of you choosing him over me just ate at me, Cat. I hate to lose."

"You have no idea how much you are going to hurt from this," Cat seethed.

"Now, why do you have to say things like that, Cat? This doesn't have to be difficult, you know. Just come back to me. I can protect you. Imagine what we can do together. It would be like it used to be, but so much better. We would be unstoppable."

Cat drummed her fingers on the steering wheel, attempting to figure out her next move.

"I've got it," Badb said into her ear. "I traced the call. He was calling from Monroe, Cat. I triangulated the cell towers to pinpoint where he is."

"And?" Cat said out loud, realizing she was still on with Danny.

"And what?"

"And then, what do we do about Ana?" Cat recovered.

"She's been paid handsomely for what she's done. I'm sure she doesn't need more than that."

"They were calling from your parents' house on School Road," Badb answered.

"So what's it going to be, Cat?"

Cat sighed deeply as she put the car in drive.

"I'm . . . I'm coming home," she said, fixing her gaze on the road before hanging up the phone with Danny.

***

Eddie groggily rolled his head from left to right before his eyes worked to open. He blinked rapidly as the blurry walls before him began to come into focus. His head lolled to the left, where a dark figure stood. Unable to make out the form, his heavy eyelids fluttered as best they could before the vision cleared some so he could make out the dark cloak.

"Cat?" Eddie slurred in a raspy voice.

The figure turned to face him and moved forward, pulling the hood down, so Eddie saw the outline of a face framed by red hair. A small smile moved across the lips before leaning in and kissing his cheek.

Eddie sighed as the lips moved from his cheek and the face positioned in front of him. His eyes settled on the vision before him when he realized it wasn't Cat.

The woman stepped back from him as he struggled with his arms and legs. He spotted the zip ties binding his wrists to the chair. He looked around frantically before recognizing where he was.

"Where's Cat? Who are you?" Eddie barked, coughing after he spoke.

Two men appeared from down the hallway, standing around Eddie as the woman leaned against the wall and observed.

"I thought you said he'd sleep for hours!" the shorter man yelled at the woman. She smiled and gave a simple shrug without saying a word.

The taller, brawnier man stared down at Eddie and laughed.

"It doesn't really matter, Bobby," he said, slapping the short man's shoulder.

"Fuck, Ronny!" Bobby yelled. "Watch the shoulder! It still hasn't healed since that bitch messed it up."

"Poor baby," Ronny mocked.

"Where is Cat?" Eddie asked again.

"Don't worry about her anymore," Bobby assured him.

"Gene said she's still alive," Ronny added, plucking a piece of gum from a foil wrapper before tossing it on the bare floor.

"No shit?" Bobby added. "Good. I'd love to get a piece of her."

"Yeah, you did such a bang-up job the first time you ran into her," Ronny scoffed.

"She caught me off guard," Bobby shot back. "Next time, she won't get the chance."

The woman let out a small laugh, getting the attention of all the men in the room.

"So you can make sounds," Bobby added, walking over to her. "You haven't said a God damn word since you got here."

"She didn't talk in the car either," Ronny added. "Kind of creepy."

"You have something you want to add to the conversation?" Bobby said as he walked over to her. "Let's see how you and the other one are when they have to face this."

Bobby pulled his gun from his shoulder holster and waved it in front of her. Eddie looked on as he saw the specter's eyes follow the pistol before her hand shot out from underneath the cloak, took the gun away, and placed the barrel next to Bobby's forehead, freezing him in place.

"Hold on there!" Ronny said, reaching for his gun.

The woman guided Bobby down to his knees as the pistol poked at him.

"Jesus, Ronny, do something," Bobby begged.

"He was just joking around, honest," Ronny said. "He's an asshole like that. Right, Bobby?"

"Yeah, what he said," Bobby pleaded. "I am an asshole."

Eddie watched, his eyes transfixed on the woman as her vision darted back and forth between the two thugs before she settled her view on Eddie. She smiled in his direction and pulled the gun up and away from Bobby, allowing him to stand. She turned and handed the weapon back into Bobby's shaking hands before pacing to the other side of the room, sitting in a dusty straight-back chair like the one Eddie was tied to.

The echo of a phone ringing bounced off the empty walls, drawing the attention of all in the room. It rang several times before Ronny walked over to the small table and plucked the cell phone off it, answering.

"Yeah?" he growled into the phone.

Eddie kept watching the woman. Finally, when his eyes caught hers, she gave a wry smile toward him.

"Okay, hold on," Ronny said before placing the phone on the table and pressing a button.

"The boss wants to talk to us," Ronny ordered. "Can you hear us?"

"Loud and clear," the voice answered. Eddie didn't recognize the man speaking, though he had a distinct Irish tilt to his voice.

"Hello, Mr. Brennan," the voice said politely. "We've never been formally introduced, though I have seen you at Millie Malone's in passing. My name is Daniel Darcy."

Eddie racked his catalog of names and recalled several with the surname Darcy, most notably in the New York City newspapers regarding the Irish mob. The light went in Eddie's head.

"You're the one who bought us drinks that night," Eddie realized.

"Correct!" Danny said, sounding elated and adding a clap. "You do have a good memory. I apologize for the unpleasantness of your current situation, but recent events have made it necessary. Unfortunately, you have been caught in the crossfire here, and I needed to take steps."

"Look, I don't know what you're talking about with any of this," Eddie spoke. "All I know is one minute I'm at my campsite, and the next I'm being sprayed in the face and dragged into a car to be taken to my sister-in-law's parents' house for some reason. And what happened with Cat? Where is she?"

The phone clicked silent, and Eddie heard the kitchen door behind him open and shut. Footsteps plodded across the floor as Eddie attempted to look over his shoulder, but he saw no one. Only the eyes of the others in the room let him know when someone was near.

"It's much better to do this in person," Danny spoke as he stood before Eddie. Eddie took note of the tall figure wearing a tan overcoat and dark brown leather gloves. "I hate talking on those speaker phones, and, at this point, it doesn't really matter if you see me or not, does it?"

"Where is Cat?" Eddie insisted.

"I heard you ask the first time," Danny replied coldly. "Whether you know it or not, Eddie, you have become quite a complication for me. Life moved along swimmingly until you came into the picture."

"You must be the one Cat talked to on the phone that night," Eddie surmised. "The night—"

"The first night you fucked her? Yes, that was me." Danny smirked. "You see, Cahira and I have always had something of an arrangement, shall we say. It's gone on for years. I'm quite fond of her."

"Funny that she hasn't mentioned you to me—not even once," Eddie shot back. "You mustn't be that important to her."

Danny laughed and stepped in front of Eddie, looking down at him. Danny drew his left fist back and punched Eddie squarely in the mouth. Eddie's teeth rattled as he shut his eyes. Silver bursts filled his eyelids, and the familiar taste of blood seeped into his mouth before he groaned in pain.

"I'm sorry about that," Danny added, shaking his hand lightly. "I don't often resort to violence myself."

"You just have other people do it for you, like these two?" Eddie asked as blood drooled from his mouth. "Or her?"

"Or Cat," Danny answered, facing Eddie.

"What?" Eddie added softly.

"Oh, I guess she hasn't given you all the gory details, has she?" Danny laughed. "You think Cat sits behind a desk all day crunching numbers over a security firm? Someone with her skills and knowledge, just like sweet little Ana here," Danny pointed to the woman watching the action, "would never be satisfied doing that. Cat's about as dirty as it gets, and I'm not just talking about sex."

"I don't know what you're talking about," Eddie answered, trying to piece things together while his head throbbed.

"She kills people for a living, Eamon!" Danny shouted. "And she's really good at it. The best."

The woman cleared her throat, getting everyone's attention.

"I mean one of the best," Danny corrected. "You see, Cat and Ana are cut from the same cloth. Celtic Sisters, if you will. However, no one is supposed to know about that, so let's keep it a secret, shall we? At least for as long as you have left, which, I hate to say, likely isn't very long."

"I don't . . . I don't believe you," Eddie answered.

"Well, believe what you want, Eamon," Danny added. "It makes no difference to me, but why would I lie? I have nothing to gain. You'll be gone, she's coming back to me, and everything will fall back into place."

"You sound pretty sure of yourself," Eddie responded.

"I always am. You seem like a pretty good guy, but you were never in Cat's league. Do you think she would be happy spending the rest of her life with some guy who wears a tool belt everywhere and barely gets by? She's gorgeous, has a ton of money, and has high standards. She's not going to some small town to spend her days with soccer moms and PTA meetings. She and I have differences, but I know one thing for certain—she always returns to me. You think I would drive up from the city myself if I wasn't sure she'd be leaving with me?"

"And if she doesn't want to leave with you? What then?" Eddie asked.

"That would be unfortunate," Danny lamented. "I would hate to see all that would happen to her if she went that way. There's a pile of shite waiting at the door if she chooses that path, and I don't think Cat would let that happen to herself or her family."

Chills ran over Eddie when he heard those words, knowing his brother and family were likely in danger. He struggled against the restraints once more but to no avail.

"You hurt anyone in my family, and I'll—" Eddie growled.

"You'll what?" Danny laughed. "You'll be gone before that ultimatum even comes to pass, Eamon. Right now, you're just the bait to lure her here. Once she shows up," Danny glanced at his watch, "and she likely will soon, that's it. I need her to see you and watch you die to let her know she's mine only."

"You're pretty fucking twisted," Eddie said as he spat blood in his mouth. "Why don't you let me out of these things, and we can settle it before she gets here? You want me dead so badly, do it with your hands! Or are you too much of a fucking coward to get that thousand-dollar coat messy?"

"I'm high up enough on the food chain where I don't get my hands dirty like that anymore, friend. But that's what these gentlemen and this fine lady are for. And, FYI, this is a $4,000 jacket, custom-made, so no, I don't want to mess it up with your blood and brains."

Eddie leaned his head back as the room fell silent once again.

"She's really coming here?" Bobby asked.

"Yeah, she is, Bobby," Danny answered calmly, pulling his vape out of his coat pocket. "Don't get your panties in a twist over it. You've got a fucking gun. She doesn't carry one. Maybe this time she won't make you look like a fool."

"It's pretty easy to do," Ronny jabbed, laughing.

"Fuck you, Ronny!" Bobby said, marching past Eddie to go face-to-face with Ronny. "You weren't there. She moves like a fucking ninja. I never heard her coming until she was on me. Let's see how funny it is if it happens to you."

"If the two of you quit bickering like an old couple and pay attention to your jobs, you won't have to worry about any of it," Danny yelled. "Now knock it off!"

Eddie's bare feet sat on the cold concrete floor, tied to the chair. He felt the vibrations beneath him and knew the furnace wasn't kicking on. Someone was in the basement. He played it cool, watching the argument unfold until his eyes fell on Ana. She stared back at him, a knowing look that let Eddie know she felt it too.

Ana clapped her hands together, the noise echoing over the cacophony of the argument the trio of mobsters seemed locked in. Danny spun in her direction.

"What?" Danny barked.

Ana held her index finger up to her lips to silence all and then pointed below their feet.

"Does all she do is play fucking charades?" Ronny spewed out.

"She's here," Danny said softly. "In the basement."

Ana nodded in agreement while Eddie's stomach clenched tight.

"Ronny, go," Danny muttered. "Don't kill her. I need her alive right now until we can finish this properly."

"Why me?" Ronny protested.

"Because your asshole friend over there can barely hold himself together right now," Danny hissed. We'll be waiting up here."

Eddie watched as Ronny crept toward the hallway where the basement door sat. He spied Ana moving as she floated next to Eddie, revealing the hunter's knife she had sheathed as she pulled her cloak back.

Don't let it be her, Eddie prayed.

Chapter 19

C at's mind raced over the floor plan of her parents' house. No one knew how to sneak in and out better than she did, giving her an advantage over anyone there. One issue to tackle, however, was that it was broad daylight. Whoever might be at the house would watch outside to see her coming. So devising a plan that included some element of surprise was more critical for her than usual.

As Cat's car moved up the hill of School Road, an idea dawned on her. She made a sharp left onto the old Rosmarin's Day Camp property, pulling her car as close to the dorm buildings as possible to keep her vehicle out of sight. She sat in the driver's seat, timing her breathing before Badb's voice resounded in her ear.

"You get there yet?"

"I just parked further from the house. I'm only a few hundred yards away. So it will be easier for me to find my way in. Do you have anything else I can go on?"

"Sorry, Cat, I don't," Badb added. "I'm not sure how many people are there or what. You could be walking into anything. But I'm sure they are expecting you at some point."

"I'm not worried about Dullahan men," Cat said confidently. "The problem becomes if Ana is there and what they ask her to do."

"I get it," Badb agreed. "Keep the line open. If you need me for any-thing . . . Well, for whatever I can do to help you—"

"Bee, if anything goes wrong—"

"Stop that right now, Cat," Badb shot back. "We don't talk like that. I'll be listening."

Cat said nothing else and pulled her cloak out of the car, donning it. She checked the pocket for her shillelagh and grabbed one of the knives hidden under the front seat, putting it at her hip. She trekked across the half-melted, brown grassy areas toward the row of houses across the street from where her parents lived.

Once Cat cleared some of the denser areas of leafless brush, she reached the backyard of the Murphy house. The backyard looked the same as it had when Cat was a child and they would play in the yard with all the neighborhood kids. The old metal playset still sat in its spot, showing more rust than Cat remembered. She walked by and gave one of the swings a light push, the chains squeaking as they moved.

Cat paced around the side of the house not visible from her parent's place, giving her a chance to scoot to the side door of the Murphy house that led to the downstairs family room. She recalled many days of making out with Evan Murphy, the oldest son, in the family room away from the prying eyes of his parents. She knocked louder than she had intended but was unsure if Mrs. Murphy ever left her perch by the front window these days.

It took a moment or two before Cat noticed light behind the dark curtains on the door. A pair of eyes appeared, peeking out at Cat.

"Who are you?" Mrs. Murphy called out, barely pulling the curtain aside.

"Mrs. Murphy? Hi. I'm Cahira O'Brien. My parents used to live across the street from you."

"Who?" Mrs. Murphy asked with a puzzled look.

"Cahira—Cat," she said. "I'm Kelly's sister."

A glint of recognition came across the old woman's eyes before she nodded.

"Right!" Mrs. Murphy exclaimed. "Kelly's sister. You're the one who disappeared years ago."

"Yes, that was me."

"I remember you hung with my boy, Evan," Mrs. Murphy spoke.

"I did," Cat answered. "Is he okay?"

"Oh, he's a fireman in the Bronx now," she said proudly. "Still single, though. Are you single? You two always hit it off."

"Give him my best," Cat added quickly. "I wondered if I could ask you a favor?"

"Sure, dear. What do you need? If your car broke down or something, I could call someone. I don't really drive much nowadays. But if it's something else, I can help you. There are people over at your parents' place who might be able to. I didn't notice any other car pull up across the way. Just those two big cars that are there already. Seem kind of fancy looking to be contractor's vehicles."

"Did you see how many people are over there?"

"Well, the one guy, someone just dropped him off. The other car had two men, but one was kind of helping the other. Seemed like two of the men were hurt. I don't know how helpful they will be in getting work done inside. And then there was the one dressed like you—was that you over there?"

"No, I haven't been over there yet," Cat rushed. "I'm going over to check on the work."

"Well, I think their boss must be over there too," Mrs. Murphy added. "A nice-looking man in a long coat went in not long ago. You probably want to talk to him. Are you and your sister finally selling the house? It will be nice to have people living there again. It was such a fun place when your father was still there, and your mother was healthy."

"It was a fun place," Cat agreed. "Those are the only people who you saw going in?"

"That's it? Were you expecting more workers? They never send enough people to do that work. I remember when Evan hired some people to fix the ceiling down here—"

"I don't mean to interrupt, Mrs. Murphy, but I need to get over there," Cat added. "That favor? I was wondering if you could watch the house for a bit while I go over there. I have to confront them about some of the work and the bills, and it might get a little testy over there."

"Are they trying to cheat you? You can't trust anyone these days! Good for you girls for standing up to them! What can I do?"

"No, you can't trust anyone. If you could watch and see if anyone comes out before me? If they do, I want you to call the police for me. It doesn't matter who it is."

"The police?" she said, aghast. "You think it will get that heated?"

"I think it could, and I want to ensure nothing happens. You would be doing Kelly and me a big favor."

"Of course, dear. I'll be happy to."

"Thank you, Mrs. Murphy." Cat smiled.

Cat walked off before Mrs. Murphy could pepper her with any more questions. Instead, she relied on Mrs. Murphy's inherent nosiness to help her if things went south. Armed with the information about who the older woman spotted, Cat determined it was two Dullahan men, Ana, and Eddie. It also sounded like Danny had arrived on his own, creating an issue she had not anticipated.

Cat walked down the driveway and scooted across the street, moving around behind the garage at the end of the driveway and away from any view from the house windows. She peered around the back wall of the garage toward the kitchen windows. Lights were on, but no one was visible, allowing Cat to race across the lawn to the far side of the house.

She positioned herself underneath the window to her bedroom, a familiar in-and-out escape route in her younger days. Peering over the outdoor sill, she looked in and saw the door to the bedroom shut. However, when she attempted to push the window open, she realized it was locked.

"Shit," she muttered, trying multiple times to open it before giving up.

Cat glanced down to her right and spotted her other option. She reached the small window to the basement, her failsafe option when her mother had started locking all the upstairs windows. The window cranked out from the inside, but it always had enough give for Cat to pry it open.

Cat squatted and pulled at the corner of the window. It budged slightly, but not enough for her to force it open. Instead, she pulled her knife from the sheath, using it to get the corner up enough so she could tug it open all the way. The trick then was to get through the opening.

Sliding through the frame would be no easy task now that Cat was older. She removed her cloak, stuffing it through the window before her, so it was on the floor first. Cat shimmied her way into the frame, legs first. The back of her shirt hooked onto the window crank, raising it to nearly her head and entangling her hair. Cat's left hand stretched back to release the shirt, and she struggled her chest over the sill before falling to the floor and landing on her cloak.

The coat tempered the noise, but it was still enough that someone paying attention upstairs might have heard it. Cat quickly donned the jacket to access her cudgel if needed. The basement was mostly empty, with some stray building supplies and tools in one far corner of the room, with various boxes of what Cat recognized as her mother's Christmas storage bins along with some of her boxes from her room.

Cat recognized the sound of the basement door handle turning. She shuffled over to the space beneath the stairs leading down.

"Just go!" she heard the familiar voice of Danny yell.

Footsteps tentatively worked onto the top step and then to the next. Cat reached for her knife, gripping it to ready herself. Whoever stood on the stairs made the mistake of closing the basement door, closing off their immediate exit path. The third and fourth wooden steps creaked under their weight. Cat moved when the right foot came into contact with step five.

Her left arm sprang forward, gripping the ankle and pulling it back toward her. The man fell over, tumbling down the remaining steps and inadvertently drawing the trigger on the gun he held, firing off one shot. While the man howled in pain, Cat swept into action. She spotted the gun on the floor and kicked it away with her right foot before her left thrust outward and caught the lumbering man on the jaw as he got to his knees.

He tumbled backward, striking his head on the cement. Cat spied as it bounced once, and he lay on the floor in agony. She jumped on top of him and used her palm to strike his nose, bloodying him immediately as he cried out.

"Help!" he screamed, blood flowing down his face as he gazed up into Cat's eyes.

Cat heard the turn of the doorknob again and looked back, catching a quick glimpse of the man pointing a gun at her. She rolled to her right, lifting the body of the man beneath her on top of herself so that her victim saw the weapon pointed at him.

"Bobby, don't!" the man screamed, but the telltale sound of the gunshot already echoed into the room. Cat felt the jolt of the bullet entering and exiting his body, skimming past her right hip and sending searing pain to her.

She sucked in air between her teeth but lay prone beneath the man as his body convulsed lightly before it stopped moving. Footsteps made their way down the stairs as Bobby shuffled nearer to her. The smell of blood and torn intestine filled Cat's nostrils as she bided her time, breathing lightly so neither her body nor his moved.

"I'm sorry, Ronny," Bobby mumbled as he reached the bottom of the steps. "I had to."

As the body was lifted off Cat's, she sprung up right behind Ronny, pushing an already-injured body back onto the steps and knocking the gun from Bobby's hand. Cat stumbled back, reaching for her side and seeing more blood than she expected. Then, realizing that most of it was Ronny's, she touched her hip and felt the long gash along the side of her tender flesh.

Bobby reacted faster than she anticipated, lunging back toward her to send both of them to the hard cement. Cat's head collided with the floor and bounced up, striking Bobby's forehead, so he rolled off her. Cat lay on the floor, working to recover quickly and get her vision on track. She saw the blurry outline of Bobby next to her as he got to his knees, shaking his head, before climbing on top of Cat.

"He doesn't want me to kill you," Bobby panted as he lay on top of Cat, his breath hot on her face.

"How nice of him," Cat grunted.

Cat squeezed her eyes closed before opening them again, feeling the weight of Bobby on her. Finally, her vision was more focused, allowing her to see the knot forming on his forehead was dark red and evident.

"I see I got you," Bobby said proudly as his hand touched Cat's bloodied hip, pressing a finger into it and causing her to wince.

"That means I owe you another one," Cat hissed back.

"It's not going to happen," Bobby answered, poking her wound again. "I'm still making up for what you did to me on your porch."

"I wasn't even trying back then, Bobby," Cat seethed. "But now you're starting to get on my nerves."

"What a waste," Bobby clucked. "A body like this, and you must be such a bitch."

Bobby's hand slid over Cat's bare skin as she wriggled beneath him.

"Is this the only way you can cop a feel, Bobby? It's probably as close as your micro dick can get to a woman, huh?"

Cat peered at Bobby as he gritted his teeth before punching her on her open wound. Cat cried out before regaining control of her threshold and emotions.

"Finally!" She laughed. "You do have some fight in you, after all. Let's get down to it now!"

Bobby looked down at her, baffled.

"You're fucking nuts, aren't you?"

"Bobby, you have no idea," Cat mocked. "Are we ready to start now?"

Bobby made the mistake of looking around for his gun, noticing it was a few feet away on the floor.

"You'll never reach it and be able to stay on top of me," Cat told him. "Even then, do you think you can get a shot off and get me before I get you? I'm wounded, Bobby, but how badly? You're worse off than me. Look at you. You're sweating and out of shape, gasping for breath already. What's it going to be?"

Cat read the confusion on Bobby's face as he looked back and forth, trying to decide his next move. Finally, he lunged off Cat's body and scrabbled for the gun. Before he had moved a foot, Cat stood over him, kicking the weapon further away before grasping his wrist and making his arm taut. She braced her foot on his rib cage as she twisted and pulled, forcing his shoulder upward and back to dislocate it.

Bobby howled loudly, frozen in pain as he rolled onto his back. Cat circled her victim slowly before spotting her knife near his feet. She plucked it off the floor before dabbing her fingers into the blood oozing from her hip.

"I have to give it to you, Bobby," Cat said as she straddled his body, leaning over his face. "You tried hard." Cat smeared the blood on her fingers across Bobby's forehead, doodling a small shamrock.

"Look, you don't have to do anything," he pled. "I didn't want to do any of this, but Danny—"

"Oh, don't worry. I'll deal with Danny next. But, first, I think I have something to settle with you. I told you the last time if I ever ran into you again, I was taking fingers."

"No, please," Bobby implored, balling his hands into fists.

"Don't beg, Bobby." Cat tsked. "You had no problem trying to kill me a few minutes ago. Funny how attitudes change like that. When you set your mind to something, you just do it. You'll never get anywhere in the organization acting like this. To be fair, though, I have to tell you, your chances of advancement after this are pretty slim."

Cat pulled the shillelagh out of her cloak, gripping it in her left hand before a short thrust crashed into Bobby's right side. Bobby's face went pale as he struggled to breathe.

"It's a liver shot, Bobby." Cat leaned in, whispering to him, "You're probably going into shock right now. I can't promise you it won't kill you. You're never quite sure how it will work out."

Bobby's hands relaxed as he gasped and struggled. Cat stood and placed her left foot on the palm of his right hand before crouching down and giving a quick swipe of her knife across three of his fingers. His eyes widened as he gurgled and attempted to raise the hand, seeing his pinky and thumb in place before his shaking hand went back to the floor.

"Now you stay here, Bobby, while I go and say hello to the other intruders in my parents' house," Cat admonished as she rose.

Cat picked up the two guns on the floor, putting one in her waistband and the other in her cloak before sheathing her knife and moving toward the stairs. She stepped over Ronny's body and hit the first step when she heard Danny's voice.

"Feckin' hell!" he shouted.

"You have no idea," Cat replied under her breath.

Cat traversed the steps, reaching the top silently before she peered around the edge of the doorway and down the hall toward the living room. She spotted the edge of Ana's cloak and steeled her nerves as she moved forward. Once she fully entered the hallway, the view of Ana became clearer. Ana stood poised behind Eddie, who sat motionless as Ana held a knife next to his head. Eddie turned his head slightly in Cat's direction to lock eyes with her.

When she entered the living room, all eyes were on Cat, including Danny's.

"You've looked better, Cat," Danny told her with a smile.

"It's been a rough couple of days," Cat added as she stopped short to keep everyone in her view. "I'll clean up when I'm done here. Are you all right, Eddie?"

"Yeah," Eddie nodded. "Cat, what—"

Ana placed her hand on Eddie's shoulder to silence him.

"I had to tell poor Eamon here about you—and us," Danny interjected. "I'm sure he has a lot of questions to ask."

"There is no us, Danny," Cat spat out.

"Now, don't be hasty in your decisions, darlin'," Danny said, turning on his familiar charm. "Hear me out and what I have to say first. You're not in any position to do anything unless you want Eamon here to have a few extra holes in him. By the way, toss out the weapons, please."

Cat looked over at Ana and watched her place the blade under Eddie's chin to force her hand. Cat pulled the gun out of her waistband and threw it on the floor, adding the second gun and her knife.

"The shillelagh too," Danny warned. "Just toss the whole cloak. I don't like not being able to see what you've got going on under there."

Cat unhooked the cloak, dropping it to the cement before placing her cudgel on top of the coat.

"Yikes," Danny spoke, getting a better view of Cat's blood-soaked shirt.

"Jesus, Cat," Eddie whispered. Cat looked over at him, raising her hands slightly.

"I'm fine," Cat lied. "Most of the blood is from your goons, Danny. I hope you'll cover their funeral costs."

"Now that's a shame to hear," Danny lamented. "Anyway, let's get down to business, shall we? I don't want to belabor this. So here's the deal, Cat. You come back to Forest Hills and work for me exclusively. You can help me oversee operations as I control more. You'll live a great life, and we'll always be together. You know how good we are as a team—during work and play. She's an animal in bed, isn't she, Eamon? I'm sure you're gonna miss that."

"And what happens to your father in all this?" Cat asked. "He's going to find out that you were involved in Lonergan's death, and he'll think I'm the one that did it."

"You won't have to worry about Da," Danny assured her. "I have a plan to take care of him that will work out for all of us."

"And Eddie?" Cat asked, looking at him tied to the chair.

"I'm afraid there's not much I can promise you about him, Cat. We both realize he knows too much at this point. I don't see any way he leaves this room other than in a body bag with the coroner."

Cat's eyes softened as she stared at Eddie. He swallowed hard before speaking up.

"I'm dead anyway, Cat. Do what's best for you," Eddie answered.

"How chivalrous of you," Danny said as he clapped his gloved hands. "A gentleman right to the end. It almost makes me want to leave you alive, Eddie. Almost. So what's it going to be, Cat?"

Cat turned and faced Danny, spotting the grin as he opened his arms to her.

"My girl. Come here," he invited.

"I don't think so, Danny." Cat smiled back. "I keep telling you I'm not your girl."

Danny put his arms at his sides and grimaced.

"Bad choice, Cat. See, now I have to get ugly with you. But first, you can watch Eddie get his throat slit. Then, Ana here is going to rough you up pretty badly—not enough to kill you, mind you, but get you close. Because I want you to be alive to watch when she goes to kill your sister and your niece before finishing you."

"You seem short on a few facts, Danny," Cat hissed. "As cold as Ana is, she won't kill me or my sister and niece."

Cat turned to Ana, looking at her.

"Ta siad cosanta," Cat spoke, taking hold of the Celtic knot pendant around her neck. "Deirfiuracha Ceilteach."

Ana nodded to Cat, holding the blade close to Eddie's neck.

"What the feck are you saying?" Danny bellowed.

"You should have kept up with your Gaelic, Danny," Cat advised. "We're protected, and so is my sister—all my Sisters."

"You women and your feckin' codes," Danny said, shaking his head. "Well, she can't do anything to you or your family, but that doesn't prevent me from doing something or her taking care of Eddie. You're still contracted to me, Ana. Just get rid of him."

Cat looked over and saw Eddie close his eyes as Ana readied her knife. She sprang into the air, kicking Ana, so she somersaulted, landing in a crouched position without her knife. Cat spotted the knife near her feet before plucking it off the floor. Then, with just a side glance, she fired it in Danny's direction, piercing his right hand and pinning it to the wall.

"Stay there," Cat told him. "I'll deal with you in a minute."

Cat and Ana circled one another, eyeing to see who would move first.

"Na bi ar mo bhealach," Ana spoke softly.

"You can speak English, Ana," Cat shot back, "And I won't get in your way of just leaving here now. So don't make this go further than it has to."

"Don't make me break the oath, Cahira," Ana warned.

"You've already broken it once, Ana. All three of you did, and you know what it cost. Trust me, he's not worth it. Danny is only looking out for himself. Don't let him own you like he did me."

"Just do something to her already so you can help me!" Danny yelled from across the room.

Cat looked in Danny's direction for a second when he spoke and quickly realized her mistake. Ana was on her immediately, peppering her midsection with punches to bring her to the ground. Cat's hip flamed before she fell, and the moment it landed on the floor, she yelled out in a combination of fury and pain. Her hand instinctively went to the wound as she spotted Ana marching toward her menacingly.

Cat rolled onto her back as Ana stalked her, pulling another knife out of her cloak. Before Ana could reach her, Eddie leaned back in his chair, crashing to the floor and tripping Ana, tangling her in her coat.

Cat lurched in Ana's direction, prying the knife from her fingers as she wrestled on the ground with Ana. She pulled the hood over Ana's eyes, allowing her to land a few punches to Ana's shoulders and torso before Ana gained enough leverage to roughly flip Cat over her shoulder and lock around her neck.

Cat struggled in Ana's grip, working to gain leverage to fight her way out. Every time Cat went to stand straight to attempt something, Ana forced her back to her knees. The vise on Cat's throat grew tighter by the moment as Cat's lungs burned.

"Just go limp, Cahira," Ana commanded. "It will be much easier if you don't fight me."

Cat, unable to form words, had her mind racing while it could, looking for a way out. Her vision took in Danny, still fighting to remove the knife from his hand, before she spotted Eddie on the floor. He thrashed furiously, attempting to get free to assist Cat, but to no avail.

On her knees and weakening, Cat worked to force her fingers inside Ana's ever-tightening hold on her. She struggled to focus and keep her eyes open as she carried a tenuous grip on consciousness.

"Yes!" Cat recognized Danny's voice echoing in her head. "Finish her!"

"I won't kill you, Cahira," Ana whispered stoically, "but I have to kill him. So sleep, and you won't have to watch it."

"It's okay, Cat," she heard Eddie's voice add solemnly. "You did all you could. Know that I love you."

Cat gasped and gurgled, her face blood red and purple, trying to force words out of her mouth to speak with him. Her vision narrowed in on Eddie and his face as he closed his eyes, not wanting to see what was happening.

"No," Cat pushed out, working her flailing hands behind Ana's head in an attempt to grab her hair.

It was then Cat felt it with her fingers. She concentrated, working her thumb and extending it as far as she could until it reached the side of the ring on her hand. Her hand shook with determination, stretching to hit the ring. She felt the ring give and quickly jabbed the back of Ana's neck, holding her ring finger firmly as the point pierced Ana's flesh, counting to five before pulling her hand back.

Ana's firm hold on Cat slipped away, letting Cat collapse to the floor. Cat gasped and gulped the air before looking up at Ana, whose hand went to the back of her neck where the pinprick hit her.

"What . . . what have you done, Cahira?" Ana asked, feeling slight swelling in her neck as she twitched slightly.

Cat worked as her breathing continued to labor a bit as she recovered.

"VX," she croaked out. "I had no choice."

Shock overcame Ana's face when she realized she had touched the injection site.

"You shouldn't have done that," Ana added coldly.

"What is going on?" Danny shouted. "Get up! Kill him, at least!"

Ana fell to her knees as she began to gasp for air. Cat scooted herself over toward Eddie, grabbing the knife Ana had dropped. She spun around on the floor to face Danny.

"She's done, Danny," Cat huffed, still recuperating. "You're next."

"Cat," Eddie rushed out, her attention turning back to him.

Cat pressed her forehead against his as he lay on the ground, shutting her eyes. Then, a thud as Ana toppled from her knees to prone on the floor caught her attention. One look at her graying face let Cat know it wouldn't be much longer.

"They will hunt you, Cahira," Ana warned, fighting to force words out. "They won't stop until you are caught."

"I know," Cat acknowledged.

A loud groan from across the room had Cat turning from Ana. She spotted Danny, having removed the knife from his hand and tossed it to the floor, bent at the knees as he grabbed his scarf and wrapped it around his wound.

"You're done for, Cat," Danny warned. "This isn't over."

"No. No, it's not," she hissed back, gripping the knife and standing up.

She spied Danny's eyes widen as he quickly made for the front door, dashing out before Cat could react. Cat collapsed back to the floor next to Eddie's head. When she looked over at Ana, she saw Ana's eyes wide, her mouth agape and frozen.

"Cat—Cat!" Eddie said firmly to grab her attention.

Cat shook her head, trying to erase the last few moments as she used the knife to cut the zip tie around Eddie's right wrist. The moment his hand was free, it went to Cat's face, pulling her toward him.

"Are you okay?" she whispered, caressing his cheek.

"I think so," Eddie hesitated. "What . . . what just happened? I don't understand—"

"Eddie, there's no time," Cat answered.

With Danny leaving the house, Cat knew it wouldn't be long before Mrs. Murphy was on the phone with the State Police.

"Mickey, Kelly, and Teagan," Eddie said, worried.

"They are okay," Cat assured. "I saw them before I came here. With any luck, they had a long head start somewhere. They'll be okay with the protection they have."

Cat stood up, pulling Eddie's chair back to the proper position but leaving his left hand and feet tied.

"Eddie, I have to go," Cat said as she knelt in front of Eddie.

"What? Cat, we need to call the police, the FBI, someone. And you need an ambulance."

"The police are already on their way," Cat said, resigned. "I can't be here when they arrive."

"Cat, you can't just walk away from this."

"I have to, Eddie," Cat replied. "People will be after me—the Dullahan, the Celtic Sisters, Lonergan's group, the police. I won't be safe, and that means you won't be either if you're around me."

"This can't all be real," Eddie said, astonished, pulling at the zip tie with his free hand to get it open.

"It is," Cat confessed. "I told you there were dark parts of me, parts I hoped you wouldn't see. Whatever Danny told you, it's probably true. You don't need to know more than that."

"I can help you, Cat," Eddie offered. "Get these ties off, and we can both leave."

"No one can help me now," Cat said. "I've lost my protection from the Sisters with all this. Ana was right. They will hunt me, and they won't stop until they get me. I can't let anyone else get hurt by this—especially not you."

"You can't just leave like this," Eddie pled.

"Tell the police whatever you have to tell them," Cat advised. "They'll find the bodies in the basement and connect them to the Dullahan. They won't find anything on her." Cat pointed to Ana's body. "She's no one, like me."

Cat cradled Eddie's face in her hands, gently pressing her lips to his.

"Thank you for loving me," Cat choked out.

Cat picked up her cloak, fastening it around her neck, before stowing the shillelagh and knife and walking toward the kitchen door.

"Cat! Wait!" Eddie yelled.

Cat refused to look back, moving steadily outside before pulling her hood up to conceal her face. She held her cloak tightly, pressing it to her hip to prevent blood from seeping out further as she moved into the woods toward her car.

The short distance proved arduous for her, and once she reached her car, she collapsed into the front seat. She positioned herself behind the steering wheel, glanced at her reflection in the rearview mirror, and backed out, leaving the Rosmarin property and steadily driving onto West Mombasha Road.

She touched her earpiece gently.

"Bee?" she croaked.

"Are you okay?" Badb replied. "The police should be there any second."

"I'm on the road. Ana . . . She's gone."

"She left?"

"No. I had—I had to . . . " Cat fumbled for words.

"Oh, Cahira," Badb said. "You know what that means."

"I do," Cat answered, resigned. "I had no choice. Too many people are in this now and in danger. Kelly and her family, Quinn, you—Eddie."

"He's alive?" Badb added with surprise.

"Yes. I left him at the house." Cat sniffed.

An awkward silence hung over Cat.

"What will he say?" Badb asked.

"I don't know," Cat answered. "Whatever it is, I can't be near here anymore."

Cat winced, her hand moving to her injured hip as she groaned.

"What's wrong?" Badb said anxiously.

"It hurts," Cat replied as tears trickled down her face.

Epilogue

The police entered the house moments after knocking and hearing Eddie's yells. More troopers and detectives arrived on the scene, closing off access to the surrounding roads as they investigated and gathered evidence. Ronny's body was removed from the basement, while Bobby, struggling to survive, was taken away via ambulance.

Troopers had a difficult time deciphering Eddie's story. He told a tale of being lured to the house he was working on for his brother's family, only to be confronted by a group of people. They insisted they wanted the property, tied him to the chair, and knocked him around until he was unconscious. When he came to, the body was on the floor next to him, and the house was silent.

Mickey's friend, Detective Luther Barnes, arrived on the scene and went straight to Eddie as he was getting attention from paramedics.

"Eddie, what the hell happened?" Luther asked before waving the paramedics out of earshot for a moment.

"I don't know—really, Lute," Eddie added, picking at some dried blood around his mouth. "I got ambushed when I got here. They told me they wanted my tools, money, the house, I don't know. They went on and on about stuff. I never saw them before. They roughed me up, and when I came to, no one was here except the body on the floor and, I guess, the guys in the basement."

"Do you know who she is?" Lute asked.

Eddie examined the space marked where Ana's body was found.

"I never saw her before today," Eddie told him.

"And the guys in the basement?"

"Them either," Eddie responded.

"Any idea about the blood stains on the wall there?"

Lute pointed to the far wall where Danny Darcy had been pinned by the knife.

"I don't know, Lute," Eddie spoke, shaking his head.

"Where are your shoes, Eddie? And how did you get here?"

Eddie looked up, staring at his friend.

"They must have taken my shoes when I was out. And I took a car here. Mickey borrowed my truck. Is he okay? I told the officers they were threatening to go to his place. Did you find him?"

"There was no one at Mickey's house. No answer on the Ring, so we went in. The door was unlocked, and no one was in the house. All their cars were there too. Any idea where they may have gone or might be?"

"No clue," Eddie replied, hoping Cat was correct and they had enough of a head start that no one would get to them.

"None of this adds up, Eddie," Lute told him. "Are you being straight with me? First, the weird stuff with the woman you're seeing, and now this. That's some odd shit for one guy in Monroe."

"I don't know what to tell you, Lute. I couldn't make this stuff up."

"Okay," Lute said skeptically. "Let's get you to the hospital to get checked out. I might have more questions for you once they finish with the scene here."

"Thanks, Lute."

The paramedics guided Eddie onto a gurney, not letting him walk himself out. As they moved him to the ambulance, he saw Mrs. Murphy watching from her bay window. He thought about what she may have seen and if the police had spoken with her.

Eddie lay on the gurney as the ambulance pulled away from the house, taking the trip toward Good Samaritan Hospital. Eddie draped his arm over his eyes, shutting them, and s visions of Cat immediately filled his mind. Questions darted through his head about her, but his heart had the gravest concerns.

I'll find you, Cat, Eddie thought. *Somehow, some way, I'll be there.*

***

Cat drove on, heading south on the New York State Thruway, pacing herself through traffic to keep a low profile. She placed her hand on her hip over her cloak and felt the dampness seeping through the heavy material and leaving stains on her hand. She fought through the pain and occasional haze before she connected with Badb.

"Bee, I can't make it back home."

"What's wrong?"

"The wound on my hip is worse than I thought. I need to get off the road."

"Do what you have to do," Badb advised. "Going home might be a bad idea anyway, Cat. Between Lonergan's group and the Dullahan, they will be watching your place. Even with the fortress you have there, it's a high risk."

Cat crossed the Mario Cuomo Bridge, got off at the first exit, and pulled into a gas station parking lot to rest. She walked from her car, staggering slightly before she went inside and grabbed a couple of bottles of water, some aspirin, a roll of duct tape, and a package of rags. Then, asking the clerk behind the counter for the bathroom, Cat managed to get inside and lock the door.

She removed the cloak and saw her blood-soaked shirt. She lifted the side slightly, revealing the larger wound. Cat washed it out gently, stomping her foot on the ground several times to work the pain and frustration out. She covered the damage quickly with a rag and used duct tape to hold it in place. The makeshift first aid gave her some sense of security to press on.

"You hanging in there, Cat?" Badb spoke with worry.

"Yeah," she groaned as she picked up her cloak and donned it, moving out of the bathroom and back to her vehicle. "I'm back at the car."

Cat opened one bottle of water, gulping much of it to rehydrate, before resting her head on the steering wheel and sighing.

"I don't know what to do, Bee," Cat groaned. "Everything is a mess. I fecked it all up, for all of us."

"Breathe, Cat," Badb reminded her. "We've been through worse. So sit tight for two minutes, okay? I'm working on something."

"Okay," Cat added. "I need some sleep."

"No sleeping!" Badb yelled. "Keep talking to me, Cat. You're going to be okay. Focus your thoughts."

Cat's mind drifted in and out, rolling back to days when she and Kelly were out in the woods with her father, hiking along as her father pointed out different trees and plants. Then her brain fast-forwarded to her teenage years, her mother yelling at her and peppering her with insults until she retired to her room or escaped outside. Cat trailed through the woods, running faster and faster. She moved on, past members of her unit, spying wounded on the ground, the image of Badb bleeding as she sat against a tree, until she reached a clearing and saw a trailer—Eddie's trailer—in the distance. She tore inside to the back bedroom where Eddie lay waiting for her, his arms open to cradle and comfort.

"You with me, Cat?" Eddie's mouth moved, but the voice was Badb's.

"I am," she said softly, her head resting on Eddie's shoulder as she closed her eyes.

"Wake up, Cat," Eddie said to her. "It's time to move."

"What?" she whispered.

"It's all arranged," he told her.

Cat lifted her head off his shoulder and looked up, sunlight tearing through the gray sky and across her windshield, causing her to shield her eyes. She turned to the right and saw the empty passenger seat next to her.

"Eamon?" she asked.

"I said it's all arranged, Cat," Bee spoke in her ear. "It's time to move. Can you drive a bit more?"

Clearing her head, Cat nodded before answering vocally.

"Yes, but I hope it isn't too far," Cat replied.

"Just a few miles. I sent the directions to your GPS. Head to the Westchester County Airport. Go to Fand Charters. Lucy is there to take care of you."

"Lucy," Cat spoke, barely audible.

"Yes, Lucy," Badb said again. "You remember her, right? She served with us, Cat. She knows what to do. You just have to follow the directions there. It's just a few miles. You can do it. You have to do it."

As quickly as the sunshine had appeared, it faded, and the dark, gray sky returned. Raindrops pelted the windshield as Cat restored her wits about her. She navigated her way back to 287, praying she could stay calm and focused enough to get through the storm ahead.

Acknowledgments

No book is ever completed without the assistance and encouragement of a big team of people. For me, that always begins with the folks at Scarlet Lantern Publishing. They provide me with the opportunity to do something I love, and I can never thank them enough for all the assistance, support, ideas, and encouragement they give me.

The magnificent artwork you see on the book's cover is thanks to Elizabeth Berry of Berry Graphics. The chance to work with her to craft something that fit the work perfectly was a joy, and I can't thank her enough for what she did. If you are interested in hiring her, go to and get a good look at how talented she is. Also, thank you to Kim Lyman for introducing me to Elizabeth—I certainly owe you one!

Hudson Valley Scribes are always there for me with ideas, encouragement, honesty, and guidance when I need it most. Place yourself in a room filled with other writers, and you will get the moral support you need to do the job. Thank you to the entire group for all you have done to help me.

Just like the previous book, much of this one was written at my secondary 'office' location—Meadow Blues Coffee in Chester, NY. Gina

Stafford plies me with coffee and pastries to keep me awake and nourished, and she is a constant source of friendship, support, and laughs.

To my Alpha and Beta readers—you know who you are—thank you for your contributions to this book and everything I write. You always manage to keep me on the straight and narrow when I need another pair of eyes to ensure I am making sense.

Finally, no books ever happen without the support of my family and friends. You are always there to cheer me on in person, through text messages, or on social media, and I can't thank you enough. My eternal rocks, Sean and Michelle, stand by me no matter what or how much I may want to give up at times, prodding me on, so I get the opportunity to do what I love. There are never enough thank yous and hugs for both of you.

Until Book 2—grá síochána agus sonas.

About the Author

Born in Queens, New York, Michael Geraghty moved to the small town of Monroe in 1978 and has called the area home ever since. He has been writing since childhood, earning a BA from SUNY New Paltz and an MA from Western Connecticut State University. He spent years working for the West Point Association of Graduates before some life-changing events occurred, changing his outlook on life forever.

Luckily, that included finding his way to Scarlet Lantern Publishing. He has since published eleven books, six under the pseudonym of Lacy Hart, before moving over to books bearing his name. All the books are contemporary, small-town romances that reflect his strong views of family, friendship, humor, faith, and relationships.

He lives happily with his wife, Michelle, and son, Sean, in Harriman, NY.

***

Books under Lacy Hart

Burnt

After Midnight

Sweet Nothings

Books under Michael Geraghty

Change-Up

Spring Fever

The Sweet Spot

Finn

Preacher

Liam

Demon

For What It's Worth

The Calm in the Storm

Visit his website at mikegeraghtyauthor.com and sign up for the newsletter, read blog posts, purchase other books and merchandise, and more!

www.ingramcontent.com/pod-product-compliance
Lightning Source LLC
Chambersburg PA
CBHW031216020726
47499CB00002B/605